Praise for

PHIL DUNLAP

"Phil Dunlap's . . . *Cotton's War* is a rip-roaring yarn that realizes the best traditions of the Western genre: strong, well-defined characters, the color of the West vivid and perfectly researched, and the writing entertaining and quick as a bronc set free to run wild. A surefire read for Western fiction fans."　　—Larry D. Sweazy, Spur Award–winning author

"*Cotton's War* is an old-fashioned, barn-burning, gut-wrenching Western story that moves at a gallop over dangerous territory. Phil Dunlap's sharp prose packs the punch of a Winchester rifle."

　　—Johnny D. Boggs, four-time Spur Award–winning author

"This is a well-crafted story with a good, clear writing style. It hits a good pace and keeps it up."

　　—John D. Nesbitt, Spur Award–winning author

"Dunlap uses his passion for history and the Old West to paint a realistic setting for his work. The prose is good without being heavy, and the story has a good pace that readers will enjoy. For those who share his love affair with gamblers, scalawags, and claim-jumpers with gold fever, this fun novel will keep you guessing."　　—*The Indianapolis Star*

"With a raft of well-drawn, even indelible, characters, the novel also offers a compellingly involved, quite plausible, and tightly woven plot."　　—*Booklist*

"[Dunlap] appears to be poised to become a new star in the Western writing firmament."　　—*Roundup Magazine*

Berkley titles by Phil Dunlap

COTTON'S WAR
COTTON'S LAW
COTTON'S DEVIL
COTTON'S INFERNO

COTTON'S INFERNO

A Sheriff Cotton Burke Western

Phil Dunlap

BERKLEY BOOKS, NEW YORK

THE BERKLEY PUBLISHING GROUP
Published by the Penguin Group
Penguin Group (USA) LLC
375 Hudson Street, New York, New York 10014

USA · Canada · UK · Ireland · Australia · New Zealand · India · South Africa · China

penguin.com

A Penguin Random House Company

COTTON'S INFERNO

A Berkley Book / published by arrangement with the author

For information, address: The Berkley Publishing Group,
a division of Penguin Group (USA) LLC,
375 Hudson Street, New York, New York 10014.

ISBN: 978-0-425-25077-8

PUBLISHING HISTORY
Berkley mass-market edition / February 2014

PRINTED IN THE UNITED STATES OF AMERICA

10 9 8 7 6 5 4 3 2 1

Cover illustration by Dennis Lyall.
Cover design by Diana Kolsky.
Interior text design by Tiffany Estreicher.

Chapter 1

———◆◆◆———

Dingo lay sprawled in the dirt with eyes wide and mouth askew in surprise, an expression he would retain in perpetuity. A man in a long black duster and stovepipe boots stood staring down at what he had just done. A thin trail of smoke curled skyward from the barrel of the .45-caliber Smith & Wesson Schofield revolver in his hand.

"You sure as hell shoulda listened better, Dingo. Now, look at what you've made me do. Nobody back-talks Carp Varner!" A wry smile crossed his lips. What he gazed upon wasn't a pretty sight. Not pretty at all. But then, blood never is.

The gunman angrily jammed his six-shooter back in its holster and stormed off to the nearest saloon, the *only* saloon in town. The body lying in the street only began to draw the attention of a couple of townsfolk after the gunslinger disappeared inside the swinging doors of the Whiskey Crossing Saloon, the one purveyor of whiskey, beer, and a single whore in the pitiful crossroads appropriately named Whiskey Crossing, Texas. The first person to approach the body was the town constable, and he did so cautiously, then merely clucked his tongue and drifted off to find someone to bury the poor soul. Two others gathered around with much the same response.

"Why would Dingo do something so foolish as to challenge Carp Varner, the vilest gun-toter in a hundred miles? Plain stupid, if you ask me," said a bearded man wearing a leather apron stained with smudges of ash and bearing small burns from the flying embers of a blacksmith's forge. He served not only as blacksmith but also as the liveryman.

"Good question, Emmett. Can't seem to conjure up no good answer, though," said the man who owned the only general store within twenty miles. "Maybe you should ask *him*." A cynical smile crossed his face as he looked down, pointing at the dead man's gun still in its holster.

A buckboard slowly came to a stop next to where the corpse lay. The driver reined his horse, hopped down, and began the task of hefting the body into the bed of the wagon. He looked around for anyone willing to help. The two gawkers finally offered a reluctant hand before wandering off to go back to their own responsibilities. None ventured to the Whiskey Crossing Saloon. And for good reason. A man took his life into his own hands just being in the presence of such a killer, especially when he was in one of his "moods." Chancing any remark that might set off the incendiary temper of the man in black was sheer foolishness.

The funeral was an informal affair and drew three people, one-third of the town's population. No one really mourned the loss, but then it wasn't such a loss anyway. Dingo had a number of shortcomings, any one of which was bound to get him killed sooner or later. His mouth was the most likely culprit. The fact that he carried a gun was of little consequence. Any ten-year-old girl could have beaten his best draw.

Since the dusty little spit of a town had no church, it likewise had no clergyman to bestow a eulogy over the departed soul. The mayor was forced to step in and say what he could. Unfortunately, he could find no words more fitting than "Ashes to ashes, dust to dust, uh, I can't remember the rest. Amen." He promptly turned on his heel and hurried back to his office, namely the table at the rear of the saloon that was held for his exclusive use. The top was covered with official-looking papers, although few contained anything more important than a handful of complaints over his general mishandling of town business, all of which he totally ignored. They'd been collecting dust for a whole year.

The constable didn't make an appearance for fear of more questions about his failure to show the notorious gunman the way out of town. In fact, he'd as soon the nasty-tempered gunslinger would leave of his own accord. That, however, wasn't the common thinking on the matter. The town actually had need of a man with Carp Varner's skills. At least one of them. He was the best gunsmith for fifty miles; he was also the only one. He could repair anything that fired a bullet, or even build one from scratch. When he'd blown into town about a month back, he found plenty of men willing to pay for repairs to beat-up, dirt-encrusted, or busted firearms. He found an abundance of business, at least until he'd repaired almost every gun in the county. Since the town itself was comprised of only four buildings and three tents, those needing his services began to trickle down to only one or two requests a week, not enough to keep a man like Varner in whiskey. That's when he tended to reveal his ugly side. His murderous side. He'd shot four men since coming to town, but none of his victims had held any standing in the community and talk of reprisals had been largely nonexistent. All four had been drifters, merely passing through for a drink or a poke.

While never incorporated because of a paucity of citizenry, Whiskey Crossing nevertheless voted itself a mayor and hired a constable—by way of a whiskey trade-out—to keep the peace. There had been some mention along the way that if a town was to have any chance of growing into a viable community it should offer an incentive for businesses to settle there. But a lack of initiative on the part of the mayor, who spent most of his days languishing over his pile of totally useless scribblings, a few back-East newspapers, and many empty whiskey glasses, had brought no interest from any potential businessmen. In fact, the only reason anyone ever stopped in Whiskey Crossing was that it was an unavoidable crossroads, situated at the apex of two intersecting valleys. That, and the town had a whore, a commodity of some worth to cowboys from surrounding ranches looking for company more pleasurable than a herd of longhorns.

The mayor looked up from his perusal of a month-old newspaper as a shadow draped itself across his table. It was the man in black, himself, Carp Varner.

"Mayor, this miserable town needs a mayor who'll do something to get folks to come, spend their money, and stay long enough to build the place up. My thinkin' is that four shabby, run-down buildings, three tents, and nine citizens, now that Dingo is gone, don't really constitute a town. Progress, that's what we need. I'm thinkin' I'd do pretty well in that capacity. Therefore, I'm plannin' on stayin' a bit longer and runnin' against you in the election next month."

"Uh-huh. I hope you've noticed that of the town's few citizens, most are my relatives. I wish you luck, though, I surely do." He went back to his reading.

The look on Carp's face turned from hopeful to dark.

"I'll figure some way around that dilemma, don't you worry none." Varner stormed off muttering to himself. The mayor watched him leave with a touch of trepidation.

The day of the election found Carp Varner casting a vote for himself with a smile of satisfaction. He had lobbied everyone he could for his or her vote. Feeling confident in the outcome and counting on a victory, Varner strutted around like a peacock to await the final verdict. As the time for an accounting drew near, the constable was called upon to ready the tally. Hearing the results, Varner was thunderstruck. He'd garnered but one vote, his own. He decided to spend the rest of the afternoon at the saloon pondering his next move. And getting well lathered in the process.

As Varner sat by himself with a newly opened bottle of whiskey, sitting beside its empty companion, his expression grew morose. Whenever such a dark cloud descended on the gunslinger, someone was about to rue the day they'd ever met him. And one of those someones was drawing near. Carp Varner had come to a conclusion, and he committed himself to its immediate execution. If there was a method to his madness, he had no notion of it. An aimless decision not formulated with logical parameters coursed through his slightly addled brain. The whiskey hadn't made his plan any clearer, and had, in fact, likely muddied the waters a bit more.

Unexpectedly, the mayor strode through the doors and into the barroom. He had both thumbs stuck in his suspenders and was flexing them in and out. His wide grin pretty much said it all. Gloating over his win at the polls was about to prove unwise. Carp Varner glared at the pompous mayor and slowly began to scoot his chair back. He stood, if somewhat unsteadily, to his full height. His eyes narrowed and his hand dropped to the Schofield on his hip. The mayor approached him, cackling like an expectant hen.

"You see, Carp, I told you there was no sense in wasting your time. I got this town locked up. Maybe next time—"

Those were his last words.

With a snarl, Carp Varner drew and fired two bullets into the unsuspecting and foolhardy mayor. Carp saw the bartender reach under the bar for something. Whatever it was, Varner wasn't taking any chances. He spun around, plugged the bartender, then turned to take down the two customers sitting at the only occupied table. Varner was already reloading by the time the men slumped to the floor. He raced toward the door as if he was heading for a Sunday picnic. But what was coming next for Whiskey Crossing, Texas, was anything but a picnic. Before he reached the door, Varner grabbed for an oil lamp that hung close-by. Because the day had been overcast and dark, the lantern was lit. He turned the wick up and threw it against the bar, and flames suddenly engulfed the floor, bar, and two tables. The dry wood allowed the fire to spread rapidly as Varner ran two doors down to the livery to get his horse, while everyone else was trying to either stop the fire from spreading to every building in town or make their escape from what was bound to become an inferno of the first order. As he led his horse from the stall, Varner tossed a blazing lucifer into one of the piles of straw. The barn fairly exploded as the flames rushed from stall to stall, quickly aided by grain dust and dry corn husks. With a strong, dry wind to fan the fire, bright tongues of death leapt from building to building like a mountain goat scurrying to escape a puma. Whenever a person burst out a door in a panic to escape the rapidly spreading inferno, Varner put a bullet in them. Two had done so, and it hadn't mattered to him whether they were men or women. They all fell to his murderous accuracy with the six-shooter. Licking flames blew tiny embers into the wind, dropping them all around, consuming outhouses, tents set up as temporary residences, and in short order, each of the four buildings. Without means to douse the flames, the town would soon become nothing more than a pile of embers. Not that it mattered all that much, because there were likely no citizens left alive to carry on.

Varner swung into the saddle and drove for the outskirts as fast as his mount could carry him. After about two miles, he reined his horse, turning in the saddle for a last look around before whipping the animal to a dead run for the

Texas border. He shouted back, "That'll teach you stupid bastards to mess with Carp Varner!"

By the time he reached the crest of nearby foothills, five miles to the west, he could look down and see the whole town—or what had been a town—now burned to the ground, leaving as its legacy nothing more than a few smoking embers and lingering shafts of smoke snaking their way skyward. He had no idea how many of the town's citizens had been caught up in the terrible and swift consumption of wooden buildings and tents. He also didn't care. Of its nine residents—including Varner, himself—he'd personally shot down five or six, and he figured those almighty consuming flames had taken care of whoever or whatever might be left. He squinted as he spied a lone, shadowy column of undulating smoke at the far edge of what had only a few minutes before been a town.

"Well, I'll be damned, that shaft of smoke makes it look as though someone *did* live through that inferno." Varner snickered at the thought as he spurred his horse on westward. *Not a chance in hell.*

Chapter 2

"Cotton, you been staring out that window for a half hour. What's eating at you?" Emily Wagner said. She placed a steaming cup of Arbuckles' coffee on the small table beside him. "Drink this. It's freshly brewed. Might help cure whatever's ailing you."

"It's nothin', Emily. Just got a head full of feathers this mornin'. Must be the election comin' up next month. Got a bad feelin'. I'm not sure just how the wind might blow this time, even though so far no one has decided to run against me. If some hotshot jumps in, I could end up comin' out here to work for you after all." The Apache Springs sheriff lifted the cup, careful not to spill a drop on Emily's just polished floor. He took a cautious sip, fully aware that Emily Wagner tended to serve her coffee almost at a boil.

"Oh, don't be silly, Cotton. If it hadn't been for you, this town would likely have dried up and blown away. Why, there've been enough gunslingers through here to start their own regiment. Shucks. There's not a chance of you losing even one vote."

"Most of those gunslingers were here because they were *lookin'* for me. They likely wouldn't have dropped by if I hadn't been here."

"Yeah, well you *were* here, weren't you? You can't tell me that Virgil Cruz and his gang wouldn't have still had their eyes on that gold shipment, whether you were here or not," she said, crossing her arms and looking disgusted.

"Maybe. Maybe not."

"Well, *Cotton Burke*, you can just stop moping around here and either get yourself off to that jail of yours or help some of my boys put up the rest of the fence back of the barn. Take your pick. I have too much work to do to sit around trying to cheer you up." Her faux outburst got Cotton so tickled he grabbed her by the shoulders and kissed her just to keep her quiet.

Still grinning from ear to ear, he picked up his hat and gun belt and marched out the door, whistling as he went. He could feel his quickened heartbeat as the door squeaked shut.

When he got to town, Memphis Jack Stump, Cotton's deputy, was sweeping dirt off the boardwalk in front of the jail. Jack stopped, leaned on the broom, and gave Cotton a cynical look as the sheriff stepped up the single step.

"Nice to see my deputy accepting some of the domestic duties hereabouts," Cotton said, with a sly grin.

"Don't get *too* used to it, Sheriff. It blew so hard last night that dirt was piled around the door, keepin' me from gettin' inside to make myself some coffee." Jack followed Cotton inside and leaned the broom against the back wall. He then stuck some paper and a few sticks of split wood inside the stove and lit a lucifer to the paper. "What made you decide to leave that comfy bed out at the Wagner place?

You know, I do understand why you don't like it that you got nothin' warm to snuggle up to in that squalid little dump of yours down the street," Jack said, sniping.

"Yeah, well it *is* startin' to get nippy at night. But I figured it'd be best if I'm close-by to give you a hand keepin' the town safe from all the riffraff. Couldn't take the chance we'd get a sudden blizzard come roarin' through that'd strand me with nothin' to do but watch cowboys makin' tracks in the snow."

"I reckon it *is* that time of year when you never know what you're gonna wake up to."

"Anything happenin' that I should be aware of?" Cotton asked.

"Not unless you figure old Pete Baker gettin' a snootful and fallin' off the porch at the saloon is newsworthy. Broke his arm. I'd have sent a rider out with the news if I'd thought you'd find the incident all that interesting," Jack said with a grunt.

"Reckon not. Although, if you happen to fall down and break somethin' *other* than your fool neck, better get word to me. I might just find *that* interestin'."

A scrawny young man stared forlornly at the scene before him, shaking his head. He stood at the edge of the still smoking ashes of what *had been* Whiskey Crossing. His state of mind was unmistakable. Tears ran down his sooty cheeks as he choked back sobs. Wisps of smoke from dying embers curled around him. He felt a pang of guilt for not being among the dead. *I should have been here to try my best to put a stop to what that bastard did.* Johnny had been just over the ridge after hauling a load of manure from the livery in the little pushcart designed for just that purpose. It was one of his daily chores that paid for his keep. When he'd heard the gunfire and the screams, he rushed to the top of the rise and peered over. That's when he saw Carp Varner whipping his horse to a run, firing his

gun in the air and laughing uproariously. Johnny raced down
the hill waving his fist, cursing as he watched helplessly
while Varner escaped the conflagration he'd created.

The young man shook his fist as he shouted, "The devil's comin' for you, you bastard! And I'll be the instrument
of retribution! So help me, I will."

Kicking aside smoking beams and pieces of tin siding,
clumps of adobe and blackened shards of glass, he searched
for whatever might be sufficiently salvageable to outfit him
as he set out to trail the man who'd killed every last one of
the town's citizens, the only family he had. He started his
search where he remembered the cash drawer had been
located beneath the bar at the saloon. He figured gold and
silver coins might have survived the fire. To his surprise,
the tin box had melted into a solid mass from the intense
heat and was unrecognizable as to its purpose. Try as he
might to salvage its contents—if anything remotely resem-
bling coins remained at the core of that molten mass—he
knew it would be useless as money. Barely into his manhood, eighteen-year-old Johnny Monk could only hang his
head and weep.

Johnny spent most of the remaining daylight trying to
gather anything he could find that might be of use. He was,
by his own count, the only thing that drew a breath left living in that godforsaken pile of debris. Not a horse, mule, or
donkey to use for transportation. Every man and woman
now nothing more than charred cinders. He couldn't even
bring himself to dig any graves, partly because the only
shovel he found had the handle burned to charcoal, and
also because he was too choked up to even look upon such
a grisly sight.

He did find two scorched whiskey bottles at the bottom
of a blackened heap. He poured out the contents and filled
both with water from the nearby stream. With no more
than the clothes on his back, his water, and the gun he had

thankfully strapped on before hauling the manure, *and* before all hell broke loose, Johnny started off in the direction Carp Varner had taken. A bright red bandana was the last thing he'd seen as Varner disappeared over the western hills. He knew little of the country hereabouts, but he wasn't reluctant to travel at night. Since the weather had yet to turn too cold, he figured to make good time for a boy on foot. With seemingly endless energy, his strides were long and purposeful. He had no illusions about catching Varner on foot, but he hoped to come across a ranch soon. Maybe he could work out a deal to trade a few days' labor for an old nag. It was a long shot, but regrettably the only choice he had.

When he reached the top of the rise over which he'd seen the last of Varner, he could make out only a faint trail in the distance, and was nearly overwhelmed by the enormity of the landscape, and the task, that lay before him. In the light of a full moon, the desert created surreal and frightening images; that strange, bright heavenly illumination cast jagged shadows from jutting rock formations, trees, and shrubs. His trek would take him farther away than he'd ever been from the town that adopted him when his father died soon after reaching it. The pain of that day was so firmly etched in his mind he shuddered at the remembrance.

Since there had been no real doctor within a two-day ride, Johnny's father had had little chance of survival after being bitten by a rattlesnake as he walked through the brush alongside his horse. Johnny—having barely reached fourteen at the time—was left to fend for himself among strangers; his mother had died of a fever soon after they began their journey west. Now here he was, a teenaged boy with the weight of the world bearing down on him and a grating hatred growing in his heart.

An easygoing lad, Johnny had found Whiskey Crossing an acceptable place to live until something better came along, which he figured to happen by the time he reached nineteen. But then, opportunities in that part of western

Texas were few and far between. And now, broke and unprepared for whatever the fates had in store for him, Johnny Monk would have to seek out his own salvation while dogging a vicious killer, and while bent on but one objective: revenge. It was an emotion with which he had experience, even at his tender age.

Chapter 3

———➤•◆•———

Carp Varner rode west at a good clip, reaching El Paso three days later. He'd pushed hard and his horse had been nearly ridden into the ground. He reined in in front of the corral at the livery, his mount heaving. Carp slid from the saddle as dust swirled around him. He watched a man come toward him. Taking note of the well-lathered horse, the man gave Carp a look that suggested he had little regard for anyone who'd treat a good piece of horseflesh that way. Varner ignored the man's snide look and draped the reins over a rail.

"You work here, old man?"

"Own the place."

"Good. Take care of my horse. Feed, water, and give 'er a rubdown. I'll be back in the morning," Carp said, tossing the man a greenback, which fluttered to the dirt. The man bent over with a groan, whisked the money into his pocket, and led the horse inside the barn, muttering something that sounded suspiciously like "Yessir, your lordship." Carp ignored the comment and made a hasty retreat to the nearest watering hole, a place called "El Paso Rose's."

He strode up to the bar, keeping a wary eye out for anyone who might recognize him from the last time he'd been through. Carp had made a habit of leaving evidence of his nasty temper all over Texas, most of it residing in cemeteries. The saloon was pretty crowded, but the only people he recognized were three men at a table already in their cups. All three weaved back and forth just trying to remain upright and not crash to the floor. He knew them to be nasty characters, although not all that fast with a gun. Certainly not in his league. The boys were brothers, the Callahan Brothers. One was a killer of sorts, the others just hangers-on. They were wanted in a couple of the smaller towns for robbery.

Carp eased up to the bar and ordered a whiskey, keeping his back to the Callahans to keep from being recognized. If they didn't see him, there'd be no trouble. Once, when they'd crossed paths in Amarillo, he'd had to club the older brother, Black Tom, over the head with his gun butt. Tom went down in the dirt, moaning and groaning, while Carp made off with his saddlebags, which contained the brothers' take from a recent stage robbery. Another brother spotted him and took a shot at him, but his aim was poor in the dimming light of evening and the bullet merely grazed his arm. Carp beat a quick retreat out of town in a cloud of dust, while the Callahans tried their best to follow. He lost them within a few miles and hadn't seen anything of them since. He wasn't looking forward to getting reacquainted, either, although he knew he could cut all three of them down before they could clear leather. Right now, he needed to rest up from his recent hasty retreat from the devastation he'd wrought in Whiskey Crossing. He figured there'd be no one alive to tie him into that burned out pile of debris. *But, lying low as best I can seems my best option, for the time being, at least.*

"Where's a good place to rest up for the night?" he asked the bartender.

"We got three rooms upstairs. Only one's occupied at the moment. Six bits for a bed and breakfast."

"I'll take it," Carp said, as he tossed the coins on the bar. The bartender handed him a key and pointed upstairs.

"Second room on the right."

Carp wound his way through the room full of cowboys, made his way up the stairway unseen by the Callahans, opened the door to his room, and tossed his saddlebags on the floor next to the narrow, iron bed. The mattress, such as it was, had rips and tears at one end where cowboys had failed to take off their spurs, chewing up the linen covering and spilling wads of cotton batting like confetti. He was too tired to care. He dropped onto the squeaky bed and drifted off in no time.

The next morning, he went downstairs for the breakfast he'd paid for. When he got to the bar, all that was left was some pickled eggs and three pieces of dry bread. The only piece of thinly sliced beef was lying on a plate already covered with flies. He pounded the bar to get someone's attention. No one came, and the saloon was devoid of other customers. He reached into the jar and scooped up a couple eggs and went outside. He plopped down in a chair. The town was just waking up, with freight wagons and buckboards rolling slowly up and down the street. Two men on horseback paid him no mind as they drifted by, both wearing badges.

Still hungry, Carp got up and followed the wooden walkway to find a restaurant. Half a block was all it took before he came upon a hole-in-the-wall Mexican place that advertised tortillas with frijoles and rice for ten cents. He went inside. A short, hefty lady came to his table and asked if he'd like coffee. He said yes and decided to order his frijoles with jalapeños, which, it turned out, were plentiful, spicy, and hot enough to take the skin off a man's lips. He ate them anyway, washing them down with generous gulps of coffee to quell the possibility of a blistered throat. After breakfast, he wandered down the street, looking in a few shop windows, before going after his horse. He had no intention of lingering too long *anyplace* in Texas, especially anyplace that endured the likes of the brothers Callahan.

As he was about to cross the street to the livery and corral, he failed to notice a large man stepping out of the bank. They collided, with the result being that the other man lost his balance, dropping a leather bag and spilling several gold coins onto the boardwalk. The man was furious as he caught himself before falling into the street. He got up, red-faced and sputtering. He took one look at Varner and spewed out a string of curses at the same time he was reaching for his revolver. Varner didn't flinch, drawing and firing in an instant. The man flopped off the boardwalk and groaned. Lying in the dirt, the man twitched once more before lapsing into unconsciousness and dying as the dust settled.

Seeing the scattered coins and the leather bag the man had dropped, Carp hastily grabbed the bag and what coins he could and made a run for the livery. He tossed some coins at the owner, quickly saddled his mount and sped off north across the border into New Mexico Territory, his intended destination before he'd decided to stop overnight in El Paso.

Coming to a tiny trickle of a stream about five miles out of town, Varner found refuge in a tangle of shrubs and scrub trees. He needed to let his horse rest before proceeding on. He also needed to see if he could spot any posse that might be following him. He climbed to the top of a rugged escarpment and cupped his hand over his eyes to shade them. He wiped his brow free of dirty perspiration with his shirtsleeve. The day was clear and bright, making it easy to see any dust that might be rising from anyone hot on his trail. To his amazement, he saw nothing. Not a hint of pursuers.

He slipped and slid back down to where his horse was nibbling at mounds of short grasses gathered around the bases of some scraggly cottonwoods. He would need water before he started off across the wasteland that lay ahead. The measly stream was too dirty and too shallow to even reach the lip of his canteen. He'd been lucky that no posse was on his trail, but he began to wonder if it was because they knew something he didn't. Maybe the direction he was headed, straight into a blazing desert, could turn out to be what cost him his life, especially if he didn't locate water soon. Scanning the horizon, he looked down on what looked like a thin ribbon of trees wandering through the desert.

If there are trees growing in a row, they must be following a stream or river. I think I'd better do the same.

Mounting up, he decided a change of course would be to his advantage. Heading down out of the mountains, he rode for about an hour before coming upon a wide but shallow river where the water was plentiful and cool. But that joyful revelation wasn't the only surprise that greeted him as he walked his horse into the rushing waters. Four riders sat watching him from the far bank. All well armed and all grinning. They wore sombreros with bandoliers across their chests, loaded with cartridges.

Damn! I was sure as hell right about a posse! But why aren't they coming after me?

That's when it hit him. The riders were Mexicans guarding their own turf from northern intrusion, probably because of all the cross-border cattle rustling that had been going on. Carp tossed the riders a salute and rode off to the north, following what he now figured to be the Rio Grande. He looked back several times to make certain his assumption had been correct. It had.

If I follow this river far enough, it ought to lead me straight to Las Cruces. A good place to rest up, especially since no one there knows me.

Chapter 4

———◆◆◆———

Carp Varner's hopes of laying low for a spell in Las Cruces were short-lived. He'd wasted no time making himself persona non grata by clubbing a hapless Mexican, with his usual aplomb. A conscience was something with which he'd never felt the need to saddle himself. He rode out in a hurry, certain he would have a posse on his tail in no time. But history seemed to repeat itself. He fairly flew across the desert and over the mountains, with nary a hint of anyone on his trail. So he headed northwest to find some other place where he wasn't known. Perhaps a place where his talents would fit well. And the smaller the town, the better.

After what seemed to him a year in the saddle, Varner slipped into Apache Springs in the early evening and left his horse inside the livery when he couldn't find the hostler and figured he'd gone for dinner. He removed his saddle, attached a note with instructions, and tossed it over a wooden horse next to the stall. He then hung the bridle and blanket on a peg, gave his gelding a bucket of grain, and wandered down the street to find a room at the hotel along with a bite to eat. He had no idea whether the law in New Mexico had any reward posters on him yet, or even if any existed. There was not a living soul left back in Whiskey Crossing, Texas, to give chase. He'd made damned sure of that. There were no witnesses to his crime except some smoldering ruins which he'd left behind in a hurry. And he made certain he'd already ridden far enough away to avoid recognition from any cowboys who might have met up with him sometime as they passed through the miserable crossroads. He had no doubt that no one could have escaped the conflagration, and he had no interest in going back to make double sure. He'd never spotted anyone on his trail, so he figured he'd just hole up in this little out-of-the-way town to consider his future. That column of smoke had looked somewhat like a lone figure, but it could only have been his imagination, an apparition of departed souls formed in the rising columns of smoke. Although, in the back of his mind, *something* was eating away at him. He just couldn't come to grips with what it was.

After finally remembering the leather bag he'd taken from the man he'd shot in El Paso, he opened it and found it contained nothing more than receipts from a business and a few coins. *Wasn't worth the trouble or the risk.* He'd need a way to make some money, something honest for a change, not that it mattered all that much to a man who'd shown no compunction burning a whole town to the ground and killing its citizens. But it did make sense to keep from attracting attention to the fact that he had no visible means of support, which might, at some time in the future, bring his crimes down on his head. The one talent he had for making a living was the thing he did *second* best: the repair and care of firearms. His most notable gift was, however, his quickness with a handgun. As he walked toward the hotel, and in need of money to even pay for a room, he noticed a small shop with a shingle saying it was the gunsmith shop. He figured to just drop by and see about getting hired. Temporarily, of course.

When he cupped his hand over his eyes to peer through the shop's dusty window, he saw an old man hunched over his workbench, holding a stripped-down Colt frame in his hand. A paper sign in the window said the shop was closed, but he tapped on the door to get the man's attention anyway. When the door opened, Varner knew in an instant there would be trouble. The old man recognized him as soon as he got inside far enough for light from the three oil lamps to illuminate his face. Carp had no choice but to act, and act quickly.

"Cotton, we got a problem," Jack shouted as he approached the jail. Cotton looked up from doing some paperwork when his deputy, Memphis Jack Stump, came bursting in the door.

"Slow down, Jack. What's happened to get you in such a lather?"

"It's Carl Burnside. One of the other storeowners found him lyin' on the floor of his gunsmith shop this morning. They took him down to Doc Winters, but it don't look good, not good at all."

"What happened to him?"

"Don't know. Thought I ought to come tell you first before hoofing it on down to the doc's to see what I can find out. If that's okay with you, of course."

"I'll go with you," Sheriff Burke said. He snagged his hat off a peg and followed Jack into the street. A chilly breeze whipped up dust and sent it swirling through town in miniature dirt devils. The fall season was but days away, and already a few of the deciduous trees had begun to turn red and gold, a sure sign that winter wasn't far off.

When they got to Doc Winters's porch, the grim-faced

doctor greeted them. He came out wiping his hands on a towel. He slumped into the only chair on the porch, staring off into the distance. He barely acknowledged their presence. Cotton waited in silence to see if the doctor was going to volunteer information as to the gunsmith's condition. Jack wasn't that patient.

"What's the story with Burnside, Doc? He goin' to make it? Any idea what happened to him?"

Winters gave Jack an impatient scowl, scrunching up his mouth before the words began to trickle out.

"Even if he does live, he's going to need lots of care. I doubt he'll be working on anyone's shooting iron anytime soon, if ever."

"What happened?" Cotton asked.

"It appears to be a condition I haven't seen much out here. It's when a blood vessel in the brain bursts. It's called apoplexy."

"How's a thing like that happen?"

"Can't say. He could have fallen and hit his head. He's got a nasty bump as evidence of that happening. Or it could have been something that got him all excited suddenly, and he could have fallen after it happened. There could be any number of possible reasons. Maybe just his advanced years. I don't have any answers yet, Cotton. Sorry."

"Has his wife been informed?"

"I can't say. Haven't seen her for, oh, maybe four months. Someone should let her know."

"Then I reckon it's up to me. Is she going to be able to care for him while he gets better?" Cotton asked.

"There's no guarantee he's ever going to get back to the way he was. Wish I could tell you more, but I can't. He's mostly crippled and unable to speak. If he could only say something, it would make treating him easier. Only saw this kinda thing once before, and that time it didn't turn out well, even though the man lived, he was never himself."

"Keep me informed, Doc. A town like Apache Springs

can't go long without a gunsmith." With that, Cotton left
the doctor's office, with Jack close behind.

"That ain't good news," Jack said, as they crossed the
street. "You think if we went down to his shop we might
find some reason for him collapsing like that?"

"That's not a bad idea, Jack. Tell you what: you go look
around and I'll call on Mrs. Burnside, let her know what's
happened."

Jack nodded and headed off for the gunsmith's storefront.
Cotton went to collect his horse, since the Burnsides lived
about a mile outside of town. When he arrived at the Burnside place, he was surprised at the sad state of things that
he saw. He'd known the old gunsmith ever since coming to
Apache Springs, and he'd been impressed with how both
the man and his wife kept everything neat and organized.
The Burnsides' plot of ground was small, no more than
enough to have a few chickens and a milk cow, but then the
man had never claimed to be a farmer, he just liked pri-
vacy. A small structure sat at the back of the property to
house what few tools Mr. Burnside needed. It was a three-
sided building, little more than an elaborate lean-to. It,
however, seemed to serve the purpose.

Cotton dismounted and walked across a yard surrounded
by a short picket fence. Walking onto the porch, he noticed
how a deadly silence seemed to gather all around. Knocking on the door resulted in no response. He attempted to
peer through one of the windows, but couldn't see through
the dust, plastered on by fierce rainstorms that drove the
soil ahead of them in horizontal waves. It looked like the
windows hadn't been cleaned for a year or more. That kind
of housekeeping didn't follow with the fastidious home-
maker he'd known Mrs. Burnside to be. He knocked again
and, again, was greeted by an eerie, dead silence. He tried
the door but found it locked. He walked around to the back

thinking the lady of the house might be out there doing her weekly wash or feeding the chickens. What he found, however, was quite unexpected.

Off to the side of the house under a cottonwood tree was a freshly mounded grave with a simple cross protruding from one end. Scratched into the wooden marker were the words ELIZA BURNSIDE. BELOVED WIFE 1830–1880. That was all. But that was enough. It surprised Cotton that Burnside had never said a word about his wife being ill or in failing health. The man had ridden in every day and tended to his business just as if nothing were wrong. Cotton realized how devastating the loss of his wife must have been. That incident alone could easily have brought on that "apoplexy," that Doc Winters said it was.

On his slow ride back to town, Cotton began to have thoughts about who besides Emily would give a hoot if *he* suddenly dropped over? His living alone, having no real commitment to anyone or anything except the town, sent a shiver up his spine. *It may be time to rethink my relationship with Emily.*

When he reined his mare up in front of the jail and dismounted, he saw Jack trotting along the street toward him.

"What'd she say, Cotton? Pretty upset, huh?"

"I'd have to say I found her beyond caring, unfortunately."

"What do you mean? Why, Mr. and Mrs. Burnside were closer'n two peas in a pod."

"What I mean is: Mrs. Burnside has passed away. And I'll bet that's what brought her husband to his knees. Poor soul. I'd say he was completely lost without her. What'd you find at his store?"

"I'm not sure I know what to make of it. You'd best come along with me and see for yourself," Jack said, turning about with the obvious expectation that the sheriff would hurry along right behind him. That turned out not to be the case.

"Hey, Cotton, you comin' or not?" Jack said, with a hint of disapproval in his voice.

"Yeah, I'll be there in a few minutes. I'm goin' to see Doc Winters first. I'll catch up. You go ahead."

That morning, after arriving in town, Carp Varner stepped into the only saloon in Apache Springs and immediately caught sight of Melody. *Looks like I might finally be at the end of a long and dusty trail. This could be where I'm goin' to have to stop my wandering and settle for a spell. I can see myself all wrapped up in the sheets with that pretty filly. I surely can.*

A cunning, hungry smile crossed his lips as he stepped up to the bar and was quickly greeted by the bartender, Arlo, who wiped a wet spot from in front of his new customer.

"Howdy, stranger, what can I get you?"

"Well, that pretty little lady over there for starters. Give me a whiskey to seal the deal."

"The lady to which you're referrin' is the owner and she's not available anymore, leastways not since hookin' up with Memphis Jack, the deputy sheriff. Still want the whiskey?"

"Certainly. I don't intend to let a little thing like a whore's stupid commitment come between me and my desires. And you can count on it, I *do intend on havin' her.*"

Arlo set a glass in front of the stranger, poured it full with whiskey, then leaned over to speak without others hearing. "Whatever you say, mister, but don't say I didn't warn you. Memphis Jack isn't a man to trifle with."

"Well, my good man, I'd have to say he isn't alone on that count."

Chapter 5

————◆————

Pick Wheeler was whistling to himself as he slowly rode a flea-bitten mule out of the hills and down into Apache Springs. His grizzled face bore a well-lined smile for the first time in months, maybe years. He rocked from side to side on the back of one mule, letting the lead rope to his second mule slacken at the unhurried pace. The pack was piled high with clothing, a straight-back wooden chair, a copper tub, a near worn-out feather mattress, and a ten-gauge shotgun. When he turned the corner at the town's entrance, he straightened as his thoughts turned to his prospects for that day. Old Pick Wheeler had been prospecting in the hills outside Apache Springs for almost two years. His silver claim had never brought him the riches he'd sought, and he was never able to buy more than a few supplies, just enough to keep body and soul together. He'd claimed to have built up a small nest egg at Darnell Givins's Apache Springs Bank, but no one ever saw him make any deposits, and never any withdrawals.

Pick reined in his mule in front of the livery and dismounted. The hostler shielded his eyes as he stepped out into the sun with a warm greeting for the old man.

"Good to see you, Pick. What can I do for you?"

"Like to leave my animals with you while I do some business. That be all right?"

"Sure, Pick. Happy to help out."

"Much obliged." Pick gave a nod as he strode off in the direction of the saloon. The liveryman called after him.

"Hey, Pick. Don't you think you ought to go to the assayer's first, so you don't spend all your silver on foolishness?" The liveryman snickered.

Pick grunted and called back, "Don't you worry none, Mother, I plan to behave."

The liveryman shook his head with a grin. He turned and coaxed the two mules inside the barn doors, kicking up sawdust that covered the floor.

Pick continued on undaunted by his friend's admonition concerning his well-being, until he reached the steps to Melody's Golden Palace of Pleasure. He stopped before entering to slap the dust from his clothes, take off his battered bowler hat, and lick his fingers to slick down what little hair he had; then he pushed through the swinging doors. He walked straight up to the bar, where Arlo, the bartender, was wiping the surface with a badly stained rag. Arlo looked up as the man approached.

"Well, well, Pick Wheeler. Haven't seen you in here for a month of Sundays. Where you been keepin' yourself?"

"I been diggin' so much silver my bags are about to burst. But I'm tired. I'm an old man, Arlo, and I can't keep up with such backbreaking work day after day. I'm about to drop in my tracks."

"I'll draw you a beer while you sit yourself over there at one of them empty tables. Maybe a little rest will help settle your mind before you start back to your diggin's."

Pick dragged himself over to the nearest table and plopped into a chair. Arlo removed a glass off the stack behind the bar, pulled the handle on the beer tap, and drew off a full pint of the golden ale. He carried it over to the old miner and set it before him. Pick thanked him as he slurped the foam off the top, grinning a nearly toothless grin. While he drank slowly, Pick looked up at the balcony, as Melody Wakefield came out of her room and leaned on the railing a moment before gliding down the stairs. Smoothing the wrinkles out of her satin dress, she glanced about, seeming to take notice of each and every one of the saloon's patrons before walking over to talk to Arlo. Pick watched her every move. When her eyes fell on him, his head bent and his shoulders slumped, the sure sign of a nearly worn out prospector.

"Did the whiskey I ordered arrive, Arlo?" Melody put her hands on her hips in a display of the authority of ownership.

"Yes, Miss Melody. I had them stack the boxes in the back room."

"Good. I got a very good price on this shipment. Ordered it all the way direct from Kentucky. Some little upstart brewery near a town called, uh, hmm, oh yeah, Bardstown. But I figure it has to be premium quality because the salesman swore to it. I told him if it wasn't, he'd be walkin' the territory without his manhood intact."

"I reckon he likely took you seriously, Miss Melody. Most men do." Arlo gave her a snort as he pulled a bottle off the back bar. "Want a drink, ma'am?"

"Not right now, Arlo. I'll wait for Jack to get his lazy ass out of bed. Say, isn't that Pick Wheeler over there? Crazy old coot probably already blew his poke on that one beer sittin' in front of him."

"That's Pick, all right, but I allow he's crazy like a fox. Why, I've overheard him braggin' he has over two thousand in the bank. Of course no one's ever seen a penny of it. When he comes in, he orders one beer. That's all. Just keeps on crowin' that his bags are burstin' at the seams."

"What's your opinion, Arlo? He doesn't strike me as bein' wealthy. He just looks like a beaten old goat."

"I'll admit he doesn't strike me as havin' been all that successful at minin' silver, either. I think he is too tired to go on. Leastways that's what he said."

"That's interesting. I'll go talk to him. Maybe I can cheer him up," Melody said. She walked seductively to the table where Pick was still taking small sips from his one beer.

"Mr. Wheeler, I'm the owner of this fine establishment. Name's Melody Wakefield. Are we treating you well?"

Pick looked up with tired, sad eyes. His voice trembled as he spoke. "Wh-why, yes, miss, I'm always treated well here. The bartender is a fine fellow."

"May I sit with you?" Not waiting for an answer, she promptly squeezed into the nearest captain's chair with a rustle of several layers of silk and satin. Pick nodded after she was already seated.

"Pleased for the company, ma'am."

"Would you like a drink? Something more rewarding than that beer?"

Melody signaled Arlo to bring a bottle. He hurried over with a new bottle and two glasses, setting one in front of each of them.

"None for me, ma'am. That stuff's too rich for my pocketbook."

"It's on me, Pick. Why, a gentleman like yourself should have nothing but the best. After all, you're a man with lots of money and a successful silver mine."

"Yes, well to tell you the truth, Miss Melody, I'm a very tired old man, as you can probably tell by all the wrinkles in my face. I'm thinking of retiring, giving it all up and headin' back East, maybe St. Louis or Kansas City. I got enough to keep me in style. Don't need no more. I'll just advertise for someone with a hankerin' to dig in the ground."

"And what about your men?"

"I been workin' the mine all by myself for a spell. Didn't

care for sharin' the wealth with a bunch of lazy fools that I had to stand over to get 'em to work."

"Oh. Well, I certainly do understand. Probably would never succeed with the likes of any of the worthless miners I see come through these doors running things. Your mine deserves the best. Someone who will take up where you leave off, build it into the best silver producer in the county."

"Uh, well, yes, ma'am, I reckon you got a point there. But where would I find someone like that?"

"Look no further, Mr. Wheeler. You and I are about to get down to the business of *ensuring your retirement*." Melody gave him a wink and poured his glass full of some of her newly acquired Kentucky bourbon. "Let's drink to your settling down in someplace like, say, Chicago, right on the lake."

Pick Wheeler was delighted by this beautiful woman's desire to help him with his plans for retirement. If he played his cards right, his future would be as solid as a hunk of iron, and a whole lot more profitable.

Chapter 6

—————◆—————

Cotton stood on the porch staring down at the weathered plank floor. Doc Winters was leaning on one of the porch posts, trying to light a pipe. Neither looked like things were going well.

"I'm real sorry, Cotton. There wasn't a thing I could do. He just slipped away like he was taking a nap. And now you say his wife is dead, also? Terrible, just terrible."

"Could his wife's death bring on an apoplexy like you said happened to him?"

"At his age, it most certainly could have. It also could have been that bump on his head. I just don't know for sure."

"Burnside was a damned good gunsmith and a fine fellow. A lot of folks around here are goin' to miss him," Cotton said.

"You suppose he's got family nearby that we should get ahold of?"

"Never heard him speak of any. I suppose I could go look through his papers. I think I remember him havin' a desk at the back of the store. Although, I'll admit, I'd feel strange searchin' through a man's personal and private documents."

"I don't envy you. But someone has to and I can't think of anyone better qualified."

"Thanks, Doc. Maybe I'll get lucky and find somethin' useful. Oh, and when you get the arrangements made for the burial, we'll need to get the word out. Burnside had a lot of friends in these parts," Cotton said, tipping his hat and stepping off the porch. He headed straight for the gun shop.

When he got there, Jack was standing behind the counter with one hand cupping his chin, deep in thought. He looked up as the bell over the door signaled Cotton's entrance.

"Find anything of interest, Jack?"

"Can't say for certain, but it sure is a puzzle. How's Burnside doin?"

"He isn't."

"You mean . . ."

"Yep. He slipped away without ever regainin' his senses."

"That's a damned shame. Good man, Burnside."

"So show me what's got you lookin' so thoughtful."

"It's right there, on the floor by his chair. What d'ya see?"

"Looks like a piece of barrel stock. From the length, I'd say it's likely for a rifle. So . . . ?"

"Look close. Don't that dark smudge on it remind you of blood?"

Cotton turned the section of gun barrel over and perused it more carefully. He held it up to the light.

"Does at that. Take it down to Doc Winters and see what he says. Ask him if he's thinks Burnside could have been hit with it."

Jack scooted out the door as Cotton gave the handles of the rolltop desk a good yank. *If Burnside kept any personal papers anywhere, they should be in here.* He wasn't surprised at the pile that lay before him. He rolled the chair over, sat down, and began his search for anything that might suggest a family member somewhere that he could contact. Mostly he found stacks of schematics for every which kind of firearm: revolvers, rifles, shotguns, even one that showed how to disassemble a Gatling gun. There were papers in every drawer, every cubbyhole, even stacked on top. *This is going to take a while,* Cotton thought. He leaned back with a handful of sheets from one stack and started leafing through them, mesmerized by the complexity of the various schematics.

"Well, yes, there was some blood on the back of his head. Not much, though. I figured he'd hit his head on the floor when he collapsed. Why are you asking, Jack?"

"Any chance it could have come from a blow with a piece of a gun barrel? Maybe something like this?" Jack held up the piece of steel.

Doc Winters frowned as he stroked his chin.

"It . . . is . . . possible, I suppose, and that for sure is a bit of blood. But you'd think there'd be much more blood if Burnside was struck by anything as heavy as this. Of course, he was rather frail, and with the death of his wife weighing heavy on his mind, hmm, well, it might not have taken much to bring him down. Is that what you're thinking happened?"

"I can't say for sure. Cotton just wanted me to see if it was possible. That's all. Thanks for your time, Doc."

As Jack strolled back down the street toward the gunsmith's shop, he decided to make a quick side trip to the saloon for a spot of brandy. *Cotton won't care if I don't come back immediately; he's likely up to his ass in Burnside's pile of papers, anyway.*

Pushing through the doors, he spotted Melody in deep conversation with Pick Wheeler. He decided against breaking into their exchange, since Melody would probably try to entice him to go upstairs with her. *That* Cotton for sure wouldn't like. Arlo could sense what Jack was there for and was ready with a glass and his personal bottle of French brandy.

"What's that all about, Arlo?" Jack asked, hooking a thumb in Melody's direction.

"Dunno for sure, but it appears to me the boss lady may be working out some sort of deal with Pick."

"Deal? Deal about what? That old goat doesn't have anything Melody could possibly want."

"I agree, but you know Melody, she'd bet on an ant race if the odds were right." Arlo chuckled.

Jack gulped his drink and hurried outside before Melody had a chance to grab him. When he opened the door to the gun shop, he saw Cotton sitting in Burnside's favorite swivel chair surrounded by what looked like hundreds of papers strewn all about. The look on his face suggested he hadn't found what he had hoped for. Jack tried his best to enter unobtrusively, but Cotton's keen hearing betrayed him.

"'Bout time you got back."

"Sorry about that. Had to, uh, answer the call of nature. Find anything useful, Cotton?"

"No, not yet. How about you go through the bottom two desk drawers while I gather up all the mess I've made. I've already been through all the cubicles. What did Doc say?"

"Said it was possible, but he couldn't say for sure."

Jack crossed his legs and sat with a grunt on the hard floor. He pulled one of the lower drawers out and began flipping through the disorganized jumble he found there. After leafing through page after page, he stopped and held up a document rolled up and tied with a string. He thrust the rolled bundle at Cotton, who took it with a puzzled look.

"What's this?"

Jack just shrugged as Cotton took a couple minutes to read through each page. "Looks like you found what we were lookin' for."

Chapter 7

———◆·◆———

I expect you'll be wantin' to look the mine over before investing that kind of money, Miss Melody. Be more'n happy to ride out with you to have a look-see," Pick said, all smiles.

"I'd be a fool not to, Pick. I've been a businesswoman for a long time, and I don't intend to begin making bad investments out of a clear blue sky."

"When would you be wantin' to make the trek?"

"First thing in the morning. I'll have my riding clothes and boots and my buggy and horse all ready. I'll meet you at the livery. That suit you?"

"You *do* know the mine is far up in the hills, totally inaccessible by buggy, don't you? And walkin' a narrow, rugged trail filled with sharp stones wouldn't do much for a lady's fancy boots. I think you better ride an animal better suited to the rough terrain, like maybe a *mule*."

"A mule! Me, on a mule? Not on your life."

"It's the only way to get there, Missy. Sorry."

"You do know I'm offering you a lot of money for a hole in the ground, don't you? Two thousand dollars is nothing to sneeze at."

"Oh, yes, ma'am. And grateful I am, too. But that still don't get us up there any easier."

"Oh, all right. Be here at seven, sharp. Got it?" Melody pursed her lips and pushed up from her chair. Pick followed suit. He left as quickly as he could get out the doors. Melody stared after him for a moment, then called over to the bartender, "Arlo, I'm going to the bank. I'll be back after a while. That's just in case Jack comes in."

"Oh, he's already been here, ma'am. He dropped in while you and Pick were in deep conversation."

"I wonder why he didn't say anything."

"Said he didn't want to disturb you. Thoughtful fellow, that Memphis Jack."

"Uh-huh," she said, her voice filled with sarcasm. She lifted her skirts and hurried out, swinging her bustle hard enough to knock a man down, should one dare come in close proximity.

"That's correct, Mr. Givins. Are you hard of hearing? *Two thousand dollars* in hard cash. And a receipt for every penny of it saying Pick Wheeler's deeding me the mine."

"Are you sure about this, Miss Melody?" Judging by his tone of voice, Givins obviously wasn't.

"I'm not accustomed to explaining myself, sir. If you'll kindly have the paper ready by the close of business tomorrow." Melody shot out of her chair and scurried out of the bank before he could object further. She was decidedly grumpy. First Pick Wheeler wants her to ride a mule for God knows how many tortuous miles into the foothills, then the bank manager questions her judgment in making a business deal. *Men! All I need now is for Jack to disapprove of the dress I'm wearing. Well, I'll fix him. When he gets back, I won't be wearing anything at all.* Finally, a glint of satisfaction crossed her face. Teasing Memphis Jack had become one of the great pleasures in her life. When she arrived back at the saloon, she stormed straight up the curving staircase, letting slim fingers glide along the polished bannister. Arlo heard her door slam shut.

"This puts a different slant on things, doesn't it?" Cotton said. He leaned back and stared up at the patterned tin ceiling. He tented his fingers and seemed to wander off in thought. His narrowed eyes suggested serious contemplation. Several minutes went by before Jack finally figured he'd waited long enough. He was bone tired, growing hungry, and had lost patience with Cotton for not sharing his thoughts as to Burnside's bundle of surprises.

"Cotton, dammit! You're drivin' me crazy with your silence. What's in them papers, anyway?"

"Oh, sorry, Jack. Didn't mean to disquiet you. This bundle has some interestin' things about Mr. Burnside. It says his only livin' relative is a young man named Turner Burnside, who, it appears, is also a gunsmith. It seems Burnside lost contact about four years ago when some sort of business troubles cropped up. Up to that time he'd been corresponding with his sister, who is Turner's mother."

"So how the devil are we goin' to find this fellow?"

"That's a good question. One for which I have no answer. Burnside does say the last he heard of him was right after his mother died of cholera, and he'd lost contact when the last entry was made."

"We could send out a few telegrams to various sheriffs in Texas. I doubt it would do any good, but it's worth a try, don't you think?"

"Could be. Or it could eat up our whole operatin' budget for the year. We don't even know if he lived in Texas or . . . We'll sit tight for a spell and see what happens after we get the newspaper to publish the story of Burnside's death. Maybe some other papers will pick it up and save us the money."

"Good idea. Now, if you have no serious objection, I think I'll get somethin' to eat. Melody probably thinks I'm tryin' to starve her to death."

"Uh-huh. *That's* goin' to happen. I read somewhere it takes three days of not eatin' to take off one pound. Don't know if that's true or not, but if it is, Melody can manage to survive for quite a spell."

Melody was still upstairs when Jack entered the saloon, shaking his head again over Cotton's remark about her. Arlo nodded to him on his way through, and he wasted no time hiking up the stairs. When he opened the door, there she was sitting in front of her mirror applying some bright red rouge to her lips. She looked around at his entrance. She was stark naked. Jack's empty stomach could wait.

She rose slowly from her satin-covered stool, lowering her eyes seductively and holding out her hand to him. He smiled as he took it, and they fell onto the feather bed. Her eagerness suggested to him that there might be more to her overtly amorous moves than met the eye. But he wasn't going to question her motives. Enjoy the moment; that was Jack's motto. And he did.

Thirty minutes later, Melody rose up on one elbow and, tracing squiggly lines on an exhausted Jack's chest with her long fingernails, said, "Jack, I have something to tell you."

"Uh-huh."

"I think you're going to be very happy about it."

"Uh-huh."

"Well, don't you want to know what it is? Aren't you the least bit curious?"

"Uh-huh."

"Hmm, well, I'm going to tell you, anyway, whether you're interested or not.

"Uh-huh."

"I'm going to buy Pick Wheeler's silver mine."

Jack's eyes popped open. He was wide awake now. He sat up in a shot.

"Wh-what did you say? Pick Wheeler's silver mine? You?"

"Yes. Isn't it exciting? He wants to retire from working so hard so he can go back East to live off all the money he's made. The old fool was just going to walk away and put an ad in the paper to sell it. I talked him into selling it to me. Isn't that grand?"

Jack was having trouble containing his emotions. His words seemed to be coming to him in a jumble of nonsense and curses. He swallowed hard in an attempt to get control of himself before he spoke.

"Just what in the hell makes you think you can run a silver mine, Melody? Damn! And how could you make a deal before having an expert look it over? How do you know there's any silver left in it?"

"Oh, I'm going to ride out there with him in the morning to see for myself. He wouldn't dare try putting something over on me. He knows I'd cut off his manhood and shove it down his throat."

"Melody! This, this is insane! You'll end—"

"Jack, calm down. You know I'm a very good businesswoman. There's not a chance of my making a mistake here."

"But . . . but . . . ," he sputtered, completely out of anything logical to say. He had long been aware that when Melody got something in her mind, a stick of dynamite couldn't dislodge it. All he could do was fall back on the damp tangle of sheets and groan.

Chapter 8

———•◦•———

Johnny Monk was in a state of near collapse. He'd been stumbling, almost to a fall, for the last several miles, trudging across the rocky desert for two days now, and he was near tuckered out. His water bottles were empty. He'd all but given up hope of finding another soul, when a trickle of smoke rose in the distance. Campfire? Chimney? It didn't make a darned bit of difference. It signaled another human being, and that spelled hope, something of which he was sorely in need. So that's the direction he headed.

Dehydrated and exhausted, Johnny Monk stumbled to grasp the fence post twenty yards from the front of the run-down ranch cabin. There were no signs of life—no horses, no cattle, no voices. But he didn't dare approach without a warning. That kind of thing could get a man shot.

"Hello, the house. Is anyone home?" he shouted. Wiping perspiration from his brow, he made no attempt to move closer without an invitation or at least an acknowledgment of his presence. He hollered again, then waited a few moments. He heard not a sound. Staying outside what he figured to be reasonably safe and proper distance, he moved slowly off several feet to see if there might be someone out back. Then he spotted a well at the rear of the house, and his thirst was getting the best of his common sense. He started through the gate toward what he hoped was cool, clean water. But he hadn't gone ten steps before a smoky shot erupted from an open window and a bullet slammed into the dirt no more than three feet in front of him. He stopped and held up his hands, not certain what to do next. He called out, once more. "I'm not here to steal anything, mister. I'm just real thirsty. I just need a drink, that's all. I been in the desert for several days and my water bottles are dry as a bone. Please, just a drink . . . and I'll be on my way . . ."

The front door slowly squeaked open, and a frail young woman appeared. She was holding a Smith & Wesson .32-caliber, spur-trigger revolver, although shakily. She looked too weak to even lift the thing, small though it was. She motioned with the barrel of it to let Johnny know it would be okay for him to go to the well and pull up a bucket of water. He acknowledged that he understood with a mumbled "thanks" and began making his stumbling, halting way toward the back of the house. The lady kept the gun pointed at him until he was past her line of sight. *That's a relief*, he thought. It made him less uncomfortable now that the revolver was no longer pointed at him. That soon changed, though, as he heard the opening of the rear door and there she was, weapon in hand.

Johnny pulled the rope and drew up a bucket of water. He used a tin scoop to dip out a cool drink. After several minutes attending to satisfying his immediate needs, he filled the two bottles and hung them around his neck as before. Ready to move on, he glanced up to thank the lady, but she was nowhere to be seen.

"Ma'am, I sure do appreciate your generosity. You likely

saved my life. I'll be on my way now." He had just started
to walk around the side yard when he noticed something
strange in the doorway. He was reluctant to head straight
for the house, but it looked very much like the little shooter
was lying on the floor of the porch and a shoeless foot was
sticking out from a prone position.

"Ma'am, are you all right?"

He got no response. He moved a few steps closer to
enable a better look-see.

"Don't know if you heard me, but I said thank you for
the . . ." He was now close enough to recognize that the
woman was lying flat on her back, the weapon no longer
being held. He eased closer.

"Are you sick or somethin'? Maybe I could help if you
thought it would be okay if I come some closer."

Still no answer. Emboldened by her lack of movement,
Johnny put his water bottles on the porch and commenced to
step to within four feet of the woman. She was unconscious.
*Well, whether she wants it or not, I reckon I better see what
can be done here.* He took a step forward and stooped to get
a better look at her face. This was no full-grown woman. Up
close he could tell she probably wasn't even as old as he was.
She was pale, and her eyes fluttered like they were trying to
stay open, but to no avail. Her breathing was shallow, and
she made little groaning sounds. Johnny didn't know much
about women, in fact he knew nothing at all, but it was clear
this lady needed help. And right away.

He bent over to get a grip on her arms to help her sit up.
She was limp, as lifeless as a rag doll. *I'm going to have to
pick her up and carry her over to that bed.* He could only
pray she didn't wake up, panic at being carried to her bed by
a strange man, and do something foolish that might imperil
them both. Although, he couldn't imagine what that might
be, particularly in her present state. He placed her gently on
the bed. He stuffed a thin pillow beneath her head and
started looking around for something to bring her a drink of
water in. *The cup at the well. Of course, how could I have*

forgotten that? On his way back out, he glanced around to see if there was any food in the house. He could find no root cellar, no smokehouse for storing meats, no barrel of salt pork, and no firewood beyond the few spindly sticks making the wispy trail of smoke that had attracted his attention in the first place. That fire had all but gone out. *It looks like she hasn't eaten for days, maybe more. I'm going to have to see what I can scare up in the way of a rabbit or two.* Knowing he'd never get close enough to shoot a rabbit with his six-shooter, he looked around to see if she might have a rifle somewhere. That's when he spotted it: a single-shot sharpshooter's rifle mounted above the fireplace, stock-mounted peep sight and all. He stared in awe at that rifle, barely able to take his eyes off it. He recognized it as a Springfield Trapdoor model of about 1873 or maybe '75. He remembered that a fellow had come through Whiskey Crossing toting one. It got lots of attention, especially after the shooting exhibition he put on. Johnny took it down very carefully. When he opened the breech, he found it empty. He groaned in disappointment. *Now I'll have to find something to shoot with.* It was one of the newer models, chambered for .45-70 cartridges. He began pulling out drawers and looking into cabinets. *Has to be some bullets around here somewhere*, he figured.

As he mulled over where the best place to look would be, his attention was drawn to the lady. *Damn! If I don't do something, and quick, she could die.* First, he brought her a cool drink, lifting her up enough so she wouldn't choke on the water; then he set about finding some ammunition for the rifle. As he continued to move about, shuffling through her personal belongings, he thought he could feel her eyes following his every movement. But when he turned in her direction, she appeared to be sleeping. He'd been unable to find bullets to go hunting with, food for their immediate needs, and something to tide them over until he could figure how to get her to safety. He'd checked her little revolver and was shocked to find she'd fired off her last bullet at him.

And there was nothing to indicate another soul inhabited the cabin. No men's shirts, boots, long handles, or socks. So how had this poor young lady managed to survive all by herself without even sufficient ammunition to defend herself? He was puzzling over that very question when he was startled by a weak voice.

"What might you be looking for? I'm too poor to have anything of value if thievery is your intent . . ." The lady had struggled up on one arm and was blinking as she tried to focus her eyes on him. "The last animal who came through here could find nothing but the food he took, either."

"Oh, no, ma'am. You have me all wrong. I got no intention of robbin' or hurtin' you in any way. I was just lookin' for some bullets for that rifle so I can go shoot us a rabbit or two for dinner."

"Oh. I-I'm sorry."

"It's just that I figure in your weakened condition and all, you likely ain't up to fixin' a meal. Besides, I didn't see hide nor hair of anything edible hereabouts anyway."

"Would you mind bringing me another drink of water?"

"Yes, ma'am." Johnny filled the cup with more water and put it to her lips. She drank nearly the whole cup.

"Thank you," she said, barely above a whisper. "I know what you're thinking. I can see it in your eyes. You want to know what a woman is doing out here on this hardscrabble piece of land."

"I admit that thought had crossed my mind. Especially since I don't see any sign of a man. And I ain't quite got it figured out how you survive here."

She turned her head, trying to avoid his gaze, as she sank back onto the pillow. Her attempt at avoidance hadn't succeeded, and he could see tears forming in her eyes. He winced at the whimpering sounds she uttered. He'd never liked hearing a woman cry. It reminded him of his mother, whose cries of pain from the fever had sent chills up his back. He really didn't have any idea what to do. After a few minutes, she stopped, turned to him, and whispered, "There are a few bullets in a box under my bed. Take what you need and Godspeed."

Johnny gave her a smile. "Don't you worry, ma'am, I'll get us something we can eat sooner'n you can say 'lickety-split.'" He slid a cartridge into the chamber of the rifle and tore out of the cabin. He was out of sight in less than a minute.

Chapter 9

A foggy seven o'clock sharp found Melody impatiently pacing outside the saloon, waiting for Pick Wheeler. She was dressed as he'd instructed, ready for a ride into the wilderness, in a very unflattering outfit cobbled together from one of Jack's flannel shirts, a deerskin jacket, and a pair of men's pants rolled up so they didn't trip her. She wore brogans she'd borrowed from Arlo and only had to put three pair of heavy wool socks on to keep them from falling off. When she saw Pick coming down the street leading two of the scraggliest mules she'd ever seen, she nearly called the whole thing off. But she didn't. An opportunity to strike it rich outweighed her reluctance to suffer the indignity of being seen astride some flea-bitten mule.

"Mornin', Miss Melody," Pick said cheerily. "Nice day for a ride, don't you think?"

"Knock it off, you jackass. I'm here for only one reason, and a ride in the hills on one of these mangy critters isn't it. Now, help me onto the back of this beast and let's be off."

Pick was amused by her belligerence at being forced to appear in public as anything but feminine. He bent over and held his hands cupped for her to step into. She did, and he grunted as she put all her weight on him. He gave a mighty heave and she settled atop the mule. She growled at his veiled suggestion that she was heavier than he'd expected. The mule didn't appear all that amused, either.

It took nearly three hours to reach Pick's mine property. The mine itself lay at the bottom of a cliff. The mules had no intention of negotiating the steep, rocky incline.

"Well, Missy, this here's where we get down and get to goin' by shank's mare."

"Excuse me, Pick, but I don't walk down steep inclines. Now, you just get this mule moving or I'm turning around and heading back to town. Understand?"

"Suit yerself, lady, but I guaran-damn-tee you that mule isn't goin' to take one step further."

Melody sat staring angrily, first at the mule then at Pick Wheeler. She couldn't decide which one was the more stubborn. After running all her prospects through her exhausted brain, she wiped a film of perspiration from her brow, swung one leg over the saddle horn, and, holding on for dear life, slid down the mule's side until she felt solid ground beneath her feet with a jolt. Solid though it may have been, the hill was littered with small pebbles, sandy soil, and clumps of things she dared not try to identify.

"All right, you moron, I'm here. Now let's get to it."

Pick turned away from her before she could glimpse his sardonic smile, eminently pleased at his victory. He didn't offer her his hand, but instead took off in a direct line for what appeared from above to be a timbered entrance to his diggings. His experience with the landscape got him down to the entrance quickly and easily. Melody's lack of anything remotely akin to experience with hiking this rugged landscape or any other sent her slipping and sliding almost the entire way, all except for the last twenty feet, which she traveled as if her posterior were a sled, after losing her balance on loose gravel.

She got up in a huff, grumbling and brushing herself off as she managed to stand straight as a ramrod, to let the old miner know she wouldn't be cowed by anything or anyone that put obstacles in her path to success.

"Well, you old goat, show me the way in there."

Pick opened a door that appeared to be a castoff from another mine, probably one of the many failed ones in the vicinity. He had to ease it open carefully.

"Can't hurry things around here. Anything made outta wood sooner or later falls prey to those damned termites." When the door was open, he slipped inside and lifted a coaloil lantern from a peg on the interior of the door frame.

He pulled a lucifer from his pocket, struck it with his thumb, and touched the flame to the wick. Suddenly, the sides of a tunnel were revealed, dark and narrow. Melody looked around. She'd never been in a mine before and hadn't had any idea of what to expect. Judging from her expression, this dank hole in the ground wasn't what she'd envisioned. Pick took another lantern from where it sat on a stack of timbers and lit it, handing it to Melody.

"Here you are, Missy. You're gonna need some light to keep yourself out of trouble. Mighty easy to stumble in here if it's too dark. Your eyes will get used to it in a few minutes, though."

Melody was obviously not too certain of the safety of the wooden beams keeping the ceiling from crashing down on them, pinning them to the wet floor for eternity. Pick seemed perfectly confident, but then he'd been digging holes in the ground for years. And she had no intention of letting on just how scared she was. She took measured steps to keep up the pace as he sloshed along, going deeper and deeper into the hillside.

Melody was just about to speak up and ask a question,

when she stopped, her eyes wide as saucers. Pick looked back at her, stopped, and offered a subtle grin, fully aware of what was puzzling her.

"Uh, Pick, what is making all those little sparkles in the walls? They seem to be catching the light from my lantern. What the hell is it?"

"Melody, that's what you're paying me all that money for. That's silver!"

"Oh, my . . . it's everywhere. I never imagined you could see it so easily. Why, I can just walk up and pick a piece of silver, real silver, right off the wall."

"Yep. Real purty, ain't it?"

"I'm not sure pretty is the right word for it. But it does do my heart good to know I've made a fine investment. How much silver do you figure there is?"

"Dunno. Reckon you'll have to find that out for yourself. But I'll be thinkin' of you whilst I'm in Chicago, winin' and dinin' them fine ladies."

"Then let's get back on those confounded imitation horses of yours and make for home. I can't wait to seal this deal before you change your mind."

"Hmm, well to tell the truth, I do feel a tad wistful about leavin' it all behind. But, a deal is a deal, and I ain't one to go back on my word."

They exited the mine to find the late morning sun making its trek for the noon hour. The birds had ceased their singing because of the clatter of humans rattling up the hill. Melody hastened to begin her climb to where the mules had been picketed at the top. Pick followed far enough behind and off to one side to make sure that if Melody should lose her balance and take a tumble, he didn't end up on the bottom of the heap. Lying with a whore was one thing, but being crushed by one in a landslide of rocks, cactus, and sand was something entirely different.

Strangely, whether it was from enthusiasm about returning to Apache Springs as quickly as possible or because she was getting more used to traversing the uneven ground, Melody sprinted to the top like a mountain goat. Pick was surprised by her sudden agility. He didn't even have to give her a leg up to mount her mule.

Chapter 10

———◦———

By the time Johnny Monk returned to the little cabin, the young lady was sitting in a rocking chair. Her face seemed to have gotten back some of its color and she looked more at ease.

He held up the two rabbits he'd managed to shoot with the Springfield. She gave him a smile for the first time since he'd come upon her lying in the doorway to the cabin. He told her he'd skin the rabbits and make a fire. But first he'd have to chop a few more pieces of wood. Fortunately, right behind the house, he found some wood and an ax, although the blade was rather dull from accumulated rust. He didn't have time to try sharpening it; he'd have to make do with what he had.

As soon as he had a fire built up in the stove and the two rabbits ready for the frying pan, the lady had regained enough strength to pitch in. She found a small amount of lard in a can and some flour in a paper sack hidden behind a skillet. This puzzled Johnny, but he decided he'd keep that and all the other questions he'd saved up for after she had eaten and he could tell she was feeling better. He did take notice, however, that she had changed into a flowery gingham dress while he was out chopping wood or, more accurately, beating it into kindling. She took charge when it came time to actually frying the meat, for which he was more than glad. He could kill a dinner, but he wasn't that adept at making it edible.

"Why don't you go sit down and rest for a spell? You've been fussing over me all day. Heavens, what could have come over me to cause me to just faint dead away? Lucky you came along when you did. The coyotes could have dragged me out and had a meal of me. I don't know how to thank you."

Johnny said nothing as he watched her take two hands to heft the iron skillet onto the stove. She wasn't much more than a slip of a thing, and while he had no idea how old she was, he could tell she'd been through some pretty tough times. Her hair was a mousy brown and appeared not to have been brushed or combed for weeks, but she had the makings of a pretty young lady. He smiled as he watched her stand over the frying pan with a look of anticipation. *Bet she hasn't eaten in a month of Sundays*, he thought. The girl forked the pieces of fried rabbit from the skillet onto a platter and brought it over to the table. She sat and folded her hands to pray. Johnny didn't know exactly what to do, but he kept his mouth shut and followed her lead. He listened, slightly embarrassed, when she thanked the Lord for sending *this fine young man* to her in her time of need. *Amen*.

They both ate like ravenous wolves. Johnny had eaten little except a rabbit he'd trapped and a javelina he'd shot since leaving the ashes of Whiskey Crossing, and now he found himself in an awkward situation. He harbored a deep need to continue his quest to find Carp Varner and kill the bastard. But now, faced with leaving a young woman alone to face any number of possible evils, he was torn by what his proper course of action should be. He was shaken from his woolgathering by a voice, her voice, seemingly much stronger. Sweet and melodic.

"What is your name? I don't believe you told me. Or did you? I can't seem to remember those hours just after you came along."

"My name's Johnny, Johnny Monk. What's yours?"

"Rachael."

"I don't mean to pry, Rachael, but what's a lady doin' out here all alone? I can tell you from experience it ain't safe."

"I didn't start out alone. My mother died from a fever soon after we began building the cabin. Then my father went to find work somewhere, another ranch maybe. Said to wait right here. He promised he'd come back for me. He didn't."

"How long ago did he leave?" Johnny asked, scratching his head in wonderment that a father would leave his daughter alone to fend for herself.

"In the spring. Early May, I reckon it was."

"Lordy, Rachael, it's the first week of September. Where do you figure he got off to?"

"I . . . I . . ." Her eyes could no longer meet his. She looked away as if ashamed of some terrible act.

"You don't figure he's comin' back, do you, Rachael?"

She hung her head and sniffled a little. Johnny felt bad for her. She seemed to want to cry but couldn't. He figured she'd already cried herself near to death. He wasn't quite sure what he should do next. When he started to say something, Rachael broke in.

"Could you stay for a while, Johnny? Just until my pa comes back, that's all. I won't be no trouble, I promise."

He found himself torn between what he felt was his mission and doing the honorable thing for this young woman. Honor was important to Johnny Monk. His mother and father had both stressed time and time again how important it was for a man to stand straight and always do the honorable thing. That meant helping folks the best he could, at least that's what he thought it meant. He began to stroke his chin.

"Course, if you don't want to, I'd understand. I reckon you got things of your own to do. A young man don't need no scrawny, homely girl to look after. Why, I'll just bet you was on your way to seek your fortune when you come across me."

"Uh, I don't think you're . . . uh . . . homely *or* scrawny. I think you look just fine. And I don't reckon there's no fortune waitin' for me to drop by and pick it up. But . . . I . . . uh . . . do sorta have a, er, mission, I reckon you could say."

"What kind of mission, Johnny?"

"I'm goin' to kill me a monster, that's what. A murderin' monster that burnt up a whole town and killed lots of people. There weren't nothin' left but a smokin' pile of sticks and stuff. Why, I was lucky to get out of there with my hide intact."

Rachael's hand flew to her mouth. "Mercy sakes alive! I never heard tell of such a man. What'd he look like?"

"Well, he was kinda tall and he always wore a long black duster and a red neck scarf. Carries a Smith & Wesson Schofield revolver, all shiny, with ivory grips. And he's a dead shot, too."

Rachael recoiled at Johnny's description of Carp Varner. She covered her eyes as tears burst forth like a spring shower. Her whole body began shaking as if the angel of death was at her doorstep.

"What is it, Rachael?"

"That's him! He came by several days ago. He stole all my food, took everything of value my pa left me, and then he . . . tried to . . . have his way w-w- . . ." Her tears were now an agonizing testament to what she'd been through. Johnny didn't need a further description of Carp Varner's capabilities. He'd seen what the despicable snake was capable of. He wanted to put out of his mind the vision he got of Rachael falling victim to such demonic acts.

"Did, uh, did he . . . ?"

"No. I was able to evade all his advances. He'd probably have caught me sooner or later, but he seemed in an awful hurry to get shed of the place. When he tore outta here, he lit a lantern and threw it on the porch. Flames erupted all over. He just shouted something I couldn't make out. I reckon he figured to pay me back for the rejection by burning the place. It had rained for two days and the wood was pretty soaked. I was able to get a bucket from the well and douse what fire there was."

Johnny's hatred for Varner was growing by the minute. He moved to Rachael and took her in his arms, hoping that if he gave her comfort, her sobs would soon subside. He didn't really have any idea about what to do with a woman in tears, but he had a very good idea of what needed to be done with Carp Varner, and he fully intended to be the instrument of retribution for her and for all those lost at Whiskey Crossing. But first, he had to figure out what to do with Rachael. Pretty soon, she pushed back and turned to sit in the rocker. Her eyes were red from crying. It didn't take a worldly man to see what all the trauma of losing her father and mother had done to her, and now this vicious attack by a murderous gunslinger had all but brought her world to an end. That's when he surprised himself by the next words out of his mouth.

"I'll stay with you, Rachael. Together, we'll set things right. Count on me. I won't abandon you."

She looked up at him with the first ray of hope he'd seen on her pretty face since he arrived.

Chapter 11

When Melody and Pick rode slowly back into Apache Springs, it was late afternoon, and except for the few lanterns popping up in the windows of a couple shops on the dark side of the street and in the restaurant, folks seemed to have called it a day. Melody was so tired she nearly fell off the mule's back trying to dismount. She was muttering something about never going into a hole in the ground again, so help her. As she started for the steps to the saloon, she turned and said, "Pick, you be at the bank at nine A.M. sharp. We'll get this deal settled and you can be on your way."

Pick had already started toward the livery with the mules as Melody stomped up the steps. Inside the saloon sat five or six men drinking and laughing. It was too late for any serious card games to be in progress. One of those men was Carp Varner, although he had chosen to avoid company and sit off to himself. He had an open bottle of whiskey sitting in front of him, but it looked as though not a drop had been poured or spilled. As Melody stormed by in her rush to get upstairs, Carp spoke up with what he figured would be an irresistible enticement.

"Say there, pretty lady, how about I join you in your 'boudoir'?" He sat back and pushed his hat off his forehead.

"Get lost!" she shot back with a snarl, then motioned for Arlo to follow her. On her way up the curving staircase, she whispered to the bartender to heat some water so she could take a bath. He ran down again and headed for the back room to get a fire started under a bucket of water. On his way, he was again accosted by the rude man in the black duster.

"Hey, bartender, what's it gonna take to get the lady to pay attention to a paying customer?"

"Like I told you before, mister, she's not available. Pick another. It's for your own sake."

"I take what I want! Guard my words well, friend, you'll see what I mean. It'd be a good idea if you passed that on to the lady," Carp said sharply, before Arlo could disappear into the back room. Carp poured a glassful and gulped it down. It would be his first drink of the day.

Melody had soaked in the sudsy warm water for about a half hour before stepping out of her imported copper tub and drying off. She slipped into a robe and eased into the room she shared with Memphis Jack Stump, who had gone to bed quite early. She bent over his still form, kissed his cheek, then shook his shoulder.

"Jack. Jack! Wake up. I have marvelous news. We're going to be rich," she said, getting into bed alongside him.

"Huh? What's that? What the hell time is it anyway?" He was muttering in such a confused way, Melody wasn't certain he'd understood what she said. She figured a more blatant approach might be necessary, thus she applied one. She snuggled closer and began kissing him all over. He started to fight her off, but as deep sleep faded and wakefulness increased, he regained sufficient consciousness to participate in whatever game she had in mind. He rolled over on his back, blinking in the darkness.

Melody didn't give up on her intention to bring him fully awake by whatever means necessary. "*J-a-a-a-ck, h-o-o-o-ney*," she whispered, in a voice dripping with honey. "Are you ready to hear my *great* news? *H-m-m-m*?"

As Jack suddenly grabbed her by the shoulders and pulled her so close she could hardly get her breath, he muttered, "Uh-huh. I *will* be in a few minutes."

"I guess it can wait that long," she gasped.

Carp Varner stumbled several times, nearly losing balance each time, as he made his way to the hotel. The now nearly empty bottle dangled from his hand, then slipped from his grip and crashed to the ground. As he went, he whistled a tune he'd made up. He'd no more than reached the bottom of the stairs when he began muttering, at first almost inaudibly, but slowly growing louder and louder as he climbed the steps to his third-floor room.

"Ain't no damned floozy gonna make a fool of Carp Varner, no siree. She'll wish she'd done her d-damnedest to satisfy my every want and need, or I ain't the spawn of ol' B-Bloody Bob Varner, the meanest, killin'est son of a bitch the frontier ever heard of."

He struggled to find the keyhole, punching at the presumed location of it over and over until finally succeeding. He kicked the door open so hard it hit the wall and bounced back in his face. He slapped at it, then crossed the tiny room and fell facedown onto the iron bed. He was soundly snoring in seconds. The door remained wide open the rest of the night.

* * *

Jack awoke early to see Melody sitting at her mirror running a brush through her thick blond hair. She was dressed like she was going out. "Good morning, sweety," she cooed.

"G'mornin', Melody. Say, what was all that you were mutterin' about last night when you came in? I don't think I got much of it."

"You wouldn't wake up, so I had to help you, and then when we were done, you went right back out again. I knew it could wait until morning. And here it is, all sunny and bright. Another beautiful day."

"Uh-huh. Melody, when you're this cheerful this early in the day, there's somethin' a-brewin', and I figure it's gonna be somethin' I won't take kindly to. Am I close?"

"Jack, you're the most suspicious man I've ever known. In fact, you're going to be as excited as I am when you see the deal I've put together."

"Uh, deal?"

"Yep. Remember I told you I was going to buy Pick Wheeler out? Well, by ten o'clock this morning, I'll be the sole owner of one of the richest silver mines in the territory. Why, there's silver just pouring out of the walls." She sighed with pleasure at the remembrance of the sparkling traces of silver she'd seen reflected in Pick's lamplight.

"You have to be joking. I can't believe Pick Wheeler's mine is worth two cents. Why, that old goat is nothing but an insufferable braggart. You'd do well to steer clear of him."

Melody ignored his comment, continuing to run the boar's-hair brush through her luscious locks. She rubbed some rouge on her cheeks, then dabbed perfume on her throat. She stood a look at herself in the mirror, turning left then right, just to make sure she was radiant from every angle. Jack fell back on the pillows.

"Please, Melody, give this some more thought. Let an

expert go into the mine and confirm Pick's claim. He's a crafty ol' goat, and I don't trust him one bit."

"No need to. I've seen the silver for myself. And you can trust that I know silver when I see it. That mine is absolutely full of the real thing, all right." She closed the door behind her, leaving Jack fuming. She could be heard humming all the way down the stairs.

Chapter 12

———⟶•⟨•⟶———

Cotton was cleaning a rifle at his desk when Jack stormed in and slammed his hat on the floor. He dropped into a straight-back chair and crossed his arms. He looked like he'd either bitten into a persimmon or was ready to go out and kill someone. Cotton didn't look up when he noted Jack's foul mood.

"Melody stomp on your foot, Jack? Maybe she dropped somethin' foul in your porridge. Which is it?" Cotton said nonchalantly.

"It's not funny, Cotton. She's gone completely out of her mind."

"You say it as if I didn't already know that."

"I doubt you knew about this latest dumb move."

"Try me."

"She woke me up to tell me she's goin' to buy Pick Wheeler's silver mine. There, now tell me you knew she'd do something *that* stupid."

Cotton frowned and worked his mouth.

"She tell you why she decided to do such a thing?"

"Said we'll be rich, by damn. Rich! Do you believe it?"

"Pick has been pullin' little bits of silver out of there for quite a spell, maybe he's just tired and wants to quit."

"Uh-huh, and he's found himself a willin' sucker to make his getaway complete."

"What'd you say when she told you?"

"What could I say? I told her she was crazy, but it *is* her money and I don't have any say in how she spends it."

"You askin' me to do somethin'?"

"No. I know you can't do anything unless it was illegal or he held her at gunpoint."

"When's the deal goin' down?"

"Aww, hell, she's over at the bank as we speak signin' the papers. I just hope she doesn't plan on *me* diggin' in the ground for her. That isn't about to happen."

"The assayer probably would be willin' to go out and take a look if she asked him real purty-like. Better yet, why don't *you* ask him?"

"She says Pick took her out and showed her through the mine hisself. Held the lantern up so she could see all the sparkly pieces of pay dirt just drippin' off the walls."

"That's interestin'."

"Why do you say that, Cotton?"

"That isn't the way silver shows itself. Might not hurt for you to go out and take a peek in that mine yourself."

"Any chance you'd be interested in ridin' out with me?"

"On the possibility that Melody has gotten in over her head, once again? Not a chance."

"I know you got no love for Melody, but you'd be doin' a friend a favor. Look at it that way. I mean if Melody loses everything she's built here, she'll be forced to go back to Gonzales. Then I'd have to make a choice whether to go with her or stay on as your deputy."

"Sounds like your decision might come from below your waist."

"It's not funny, Cotton. At least think on it. I need help here."

Cotton rubbed his chin. "All right, I'll think on it. But right now, I got to find someone to finish up workin' on some of the guns that Burnside left. Since we don't know how to locate the nephew, the store is kinda up for grabs. And folks need their guns."

"Well, don't cogitate on it too long. I'd like to make sure the deal is honest before Pick folds up his tent and heads for parts unknown."

"Right now, I'm goin' to Burnside's store and try to take some sort of inventory. Then I'll have to notify folks with guns in there bein' worked on. They can either pick them up or wait till we get another gunsmith. Why don't you come along? It'd make my job go a tad bit faster with two of us on it."

Jack nodded and followed Cotton out the door.

As Cotton and Jack were passing by the bank, Melody, Pick Wheeler, and bank manager Darnell Givins were just stepping out. They stopped to chat among themselves on the boardwalk in front of the double glass doors. On a bench under the bank's large front window sat a man in a long black duster smoking a long, thin cigar, hat pulled low. The three paid him no mind. Melody was so excited about what she'd done, she kept reminding Pick that with all that money she'd just paid him, she hoped he wouldn't go out and squander it foolishly. He assured her he wouldn't, as he patted a large bulge in his pocket.

"Mighty nice doin' business with you, Miss Melody," Pick said with a wide grin.

He tipped his hat to the others and started off down the street. Melody and Darnell continued their conversation, although a little less enthusiastically.

"I hope you know what you're doing, Melody. Pick makes

a *very small amount* of money from the mine, and he sure
hasn't gotten filthy rich off it."

"Likely because he's such a lazy oaf. Why, I saw that
silver for myself, sparkling in the light, coming from everywhere. Instead of being a tightwad, wanting to keep it all
for himself, he could have hired some men to help him. If
he'd been more industrious, he most certainly would have
made it big. And that's exactly what I'm intending to do."
She turned on her heel and strutted down the boardwalk
back to the saloon. She held her head high just to make sure
all the ladies in town noticed her.

When Darnell went back inside the bank, the man on the
bench got up and strolled off, crossing the street and heading for where the sheriff and his deputy had gone in—the
gunsmith shop. The man waited for a few minutes, then
pushed inside. Cotton looked up at the sound of the bell over
the door.

"Sorry, mister, but the gunsmith shop is closed. The
owner died and we're takin' inventory to determine what to
do with all guns in here," Cotton said.

"I heard about the unfortunate accident. When I asked
about where to buy ammunition, the bartender at the saloon
told me all about how the poor man fell and hit his head.
It's a rotten shame; it surely is."

"Yeah, well come back after we've straightened this out.
Uh, I didn't catch the name, mister."

"Name's Carp Varner, Sheriff, and I may be able to lend
a hand."

"Well, Mr. Varner, I'm not certain how you can help,
but I *do* appreciate the offer."

"The way is simple. Let the town allow me to work the
business until other arrangements can be made, and it can
rake off a percentage of the profits. You see, I *am* a gunsmith."

"Hey, Cotton, that sounds like a solution, doesn't it?"
Jack said, looking pleased at an outcome that would prevent him sitting on a stool writing down all the guns and
pieces of guns in column after column.

Cotton seemed to be thinking it over when Carp spoke up again. "Tell you what. Let me fix a couple of the firearms that need it the most, and you can judge my work. I wouldn't expect a man to take me on my word alone."

"All right, Mr. Varner. I'm pretty sure Mr. Burnside was working on that Sharps rifle he had laid out on the counter there, and the Colt lyin' next to it. See what you can do with them. Then we'll talk."

"You have a deal, Sheriff. I'll bring 'em down to you when I'm finished."

"Fair enough. I'll be at the jail." Cotton gave Jack a jerk of the head, and the two of them left the shop.

"That was a stroke of luck, wouldn't you say, Cotton?"

Cotton didn't say anything, as he was obviously too lost in thought at that moment.

Chapter 13

———◆———

Johnny Monk had found the sharpening stone in the lean-to. One leg of the three-legged stand was broken, and he had to jury-rig it by balancing part of the base on a rock. The grinding pedal seemed free enough, and it moved with ease. He had the grinding wheel sitting up near a pile of wood he'd gathered from deadfall in a thinly wooded area nearby. He was raking the ax back and forth across the wheel as he pushed the pedal to put an edge on it. He was almost finished when Rachael came out looking like someone altogether different.

He took in a breath at the transformation. She was no longer an ashen-faced child with dark circles under her eyes and frizzy, matted hair. She'd put on a different gingham dress, washed her face, and put some rouge on her cheeks. She'd also washed and brushed her hair, and tied it up with a yellow ribbon. And the result made Johnny blink several times to assure himself he was looking at the same girl he'd found lying on the floor in a dirty dress and barefoot.

He stopped the grinding wheel to stare at her. She blushed and looked at the ground, clearly embarrassed by the surprise on his face. She began making circles in the dirt with her foot.

"Rachael, you . . . are . . . beautiful," he said. He couldn't stop looking at her.

"And . . . and you are the hardest worker I've ever seen."

Johnny stopped for a moment, looked down at the pile of chopped wood, and chuckled.

"Uh, maybe I have gotten a little carried away. Come to think on it, I'm not quite certain why I'm doin' it. We can't stay here much longer. Pretty soon the rabbits will get the idea I'm after 'em and they'll skedaddle. Then what'll we eat?"

Rachael's pretty smile turned to sadness. She sighed and looked longingly over her shoulder at the cabin, as simple as it was.

"I reckon I've known all along I couldn't stay here, what with my pa gone and all."

"Yeah, and we need to figure a plan for our travels, too. First off, you can't walk in bare feet for long. You'll cut yourself to pieces. We'll have to find something for you to wear."

"We still got one rabbit, the one you got this mornin'. I'll get to lookin' around for travel duds if you'll get the rabbit ready for the skillet. Fair enough?"

"You bet, Rachael. I'll get right to it. You go ahead."

He watched her go back inside the dark one-room cabin. He thought to himself as she disappeared inside, *I could sure get used to spendin' all my time with her. We got along like the best of friends from practically the moment I laid eyes on her. And she's darned purty, too. I am one lucky fellow.*

After they'd eaten every last morsel of rabbit, Rachael began dragging out the various items she thought might be helpful for their inevitable trip to find help, or a more permanent place to stay. She piled what few clothing items she could find in one pile, along with things like leather straps that might suffice as belts and a couple of old bonnets her mother had brought when they started out for the frontier. She'd also found several more bullets for the Springfield rifle, which she handed to Johnny, items he was mighty happy to see. She'd dragged out a pair of old shoes that she'd used mainly for working in the garden. They were pretty badly worn, but she proudly tossed them on the pile, too.

"Gosh, Rachael, looks like you've found enough stuff to get us on our way in style."

She gave him a sad smile. He could see it in her eyes: she really didn't want to leave her home, the only one she'd known for quite some time. Probably not all her memories were good ones, but they were *her* memories. Johnny was wise enough to see her struggling with abandoning the crude cabin. His history on the frontier wasn't much different. In fact, he'd still be in Whiskey Crossing if that damnable Carp Varner hadn't burned the place to the ground. He, too, had some sadness about leaving wherever you call home, but in his case, catching up to Varner was more than an impulse, it was a mission. And he planned to track down the hateful snake and blow him into the next century if it was the last thing he ever did.

As the two of them went through the pile of odds and ends, Rachael separated those items she figured she'd need, with Johnny's help in deciding, especially since he likely knew more about the terrain to the west. He didn't dare tell her he hadn't been any farther west than she had. This was his first time, and he was a little uncertain about traveling with a young lady to defend. But he dared not let on to her that he had any doubts whatsoever. He watched her try on one of the bonnets. She was giggling at the very thought of being seen outside in such a ratty thing. But Johnny had convinced her that fashion couldn't come into play when they might be out in the blazing sun for days on end. He had no idea how far they'd have to go to find another ranch or if borrowing a horse was even possible. He also had no idea of whether there'd been any Indian sightings recently, and if so, were they hostile?

After about an hour of picking and choosing what they should take with them, keeping only those things that would prove invaluable to their safety and well-being, Rachael had been able to find a canteen in addition to Johnny's two whiskey bottles. He had his revolver and the Springfield rifle, now with about seven bullets. Rachael had stuffed rags in the shoes so they'd fit better, and she was going to wear a long denim skirt, the only other piece of apparel she owned, to help protect her legs from burrs and smaller cacti.

They stood outside for some time, wondering if they'd forgotten anything. As far as he could conjure, they were about as ready for such a trip as anybody could have been given the circumstances. He tried not to show his anxiousness to get on the road, because he knew Rachael was having a hard time letting go. But if he didn't push her, he was certain she'd soon get it settled in her mind that she had to move on.

That's exactly what she did.

"Okay, Johnny, I'm ready to follow you wherever the path leads."

His heart jumped at her words. To him, anyway, they seemed to hold an even larger meaning. He reached over and took her hand, and they started down the road side by side like two kids.

As evening drew near, he began to think about making camp for the night. Just as he was about to suggest the desirability of finding a place to sleep that would bring shelter and a modicum of safety, she spotted a light, maybe a campfire, she couldn't tell. He strained to see what she was pointing out, then it popped into view like a star from behind a cloud.

"You have good eyesight, Rachael. But there it is, either a lamp or a campfire. I can't tell which, but I suggest we head in that direction. We best be as quiet as possible in case whoever made the fire isn't friendly."

"Okay, Johnny. I understand. You can count on me not to get all giggly and silly like *other* girls."

Johnny got the point. He was being subtly chastised for not giving her credit for using good common sense. "I apologize. That was rude of me. It's not like you're some schoolgirl."

"No, I'm not. And I hope you won't forget *that*, either." She gave him a look he couldn't really decipher, but he knew instinctively that he'd better pay closer attention to whatever she said from now on.

Within about a half hour they were inside of a hundred yards of the light they'd been following. It was an oil lamp hanging from the roof of a porch on a ranch house. The two looked at each other with relief that their fears had been for naught. When they got to the fence gate, Johnny stopped and called out to anyone in the house. The door opened and a man stepped out with a rifle in his hands.

"Who is it and what do you want?" the man asked.

"We're just two weary folks who've been walkin' since early this mornin, hopin' to find a friendly face and a warm place to rest. A little food wouldn't be bad, neither."

A woman's voice could be heard coming from inside.

"Seth, sound's like young folks. They couldn't mean us harm. Ask them in."

"Thank you, ma'am," Johnny said as he stepped inside behind Rachael.

The woman took one look at her and said, "Land sakes, Seth, it's Rachael Winslow from down the road. Mercy, child, whatever are you doin' out here?"

"My pa left some time back, and I'd like to find him. Johnny here is trailin' a man for killin' a passel of folks in Whiskey Crossing. So we'd be beholden to you if you was to let us sleep in your barn for the night, and if it ain't too much trouble, we sure could use a bite to eat."

"You two come right in here and set yourselves down at the table. I'll cook up some grits and a steak and drop a couple biscuits on the griddle. Got some fresh eggs for your breakfast in the mornin', too. And I'll bet you won't turn down a drink of milk, neither."

That brought a grin from both of them.

After they'd eaten their fill, the lady's expression turned dour. She was wringing her hands, and Johnny got the feeling he was about to hear some bad news. It came within seconds.

"Rachael, honey, I don't know how to tell you this, so I'll just blurt it out. Seth was goin' to set out for your place to tell you, but he fell off a fence and broke his leg. He's just now gettin' fit to work again. I had to stay here and tend to the animals. But now that you're here, I can't hold off any longer, now's as good a time as any."

"What is it, ma'am? Is it my pa? Have you seen him?"

"About a month ago, Seth was goin' to the barn to feed the cow when he noticed a horse trottin' up the lane. There weren't no rider. He recognized it as your pa's. He followed the trail left by the horse, and he come upon your pa lyin' in the ditch about two miles south of here. Looked like the poor man had been shot, although it was hard to tell for sure. Shot and robbed is what Seth says. Been there for a spell from what I gather, too. I'm so sorry, honey."

Johnny could see how hard Rachael was trying to hold back the tears. He wanted to grab her and hold her so tight she couldn't talk. But he wasn't sure how the lady would take to such a display of affection, so he put his hand on her arm and gave it a pat. She didn't shed one tear, though, much to Johnny's amazement. His feelings for her soared at that moment more than ever before. This was no girl-child. This was a woman, full-blown, and a pretty tough one at that.

Chapter 14

———◆———

The next morning, at breakfast, the lady must have figured it was all right once again to speak of Rachael's father. She brought up the subject as she placed two plates in front of the visitors.

"We buried your father, child. Gave him a good Christian burial, too. And the horse, which is yours by all rights, is in the corral. You can take him whenever you've a mind to."

Johnny and Rachael looked at each other. This was the break they had been hoping for; a horse would aid their travels mightily. Johnny didn't say a word, but he was thinking that finally good fortune was beginning to smile on them. He felt a twinge of guilt over thinking that Rachael's father lying dead in the ground had in some way provided them with a good omen, but the thought was there and he couldn't deny it. What he *could* do was keep his thoughts to himself, which he did with difficulty.

"Ma'am, would it be possible to go see the grave?" Rachael asked.

"Of course, child. Seth laid him to rest under a tree on the far side of yonder hill," the lady said, walking to the window and pointing to a sloping stretch of grass that rose from the edge of a creek. "I'll ask Seth to take you over there, so he can show you himself."

"Oh, that's all right, ma'am, Johnny and I'll just mosey on over. I'm sure we can find it. No offense, but I think it would be fitting and proper to pay my last respects more private-like. That is, if you don't mind."

The lady gave an understanding smile, nodded, and opened the door for her. Rachael turned to see if Johnny was coming, and noticing him fixing to get up from his chair, she walked out the door and across the yard, confident he'd follow.

When they got to the fresh mound of dirt covered with stones large enough to assure that wild animals wouldn't be digging up the corpse for a meal, Rachael stopped short as if she wasn't certain she really wanted to do this. Johnny gave her a questioning look.

"There's somethin' I didn't tell you before, Johnny. I hope you won't think badly of me, but I have a terrible secret."

"You? How could someone as sweet as you have a terrible secret? I don't believe it." Johnny frowned to fully show his doubt of her statement. But as soon as he did, Rachael turned away from him and began wringing her hands. She wasn't looking at the grave of her father but, instead, was staring off into the distance.

"That . . . that monster a-lyin' under yonder mound of dirt wasn't my pa. I hope you'll forgive me, but I lied to you. My real ma and pa are still livin' in Illinois on their farm. Things weren't goin' so well, and they were all but busted, about to lose everything they'd worked so hard for. One day, this man came along and offered to buy me. My folks aren't bad; they were just in dire straits. So I was sold into slavery, even if it ain't legal. The man wanted a young girl to do his cookin', cleanin', and tend his garden. He was hopin', I suspect, that after I got used to him, I'd want to get married even though he was a lot older than me. I never did get to thinkin' that way. So, on occasion, he'd take a willow stick to me, maybe bloody my face, too, whenever he got a snootful of hard liquor." She hung her head after spilling her story. She shuddered and hugged her arms.

Johnny was stunned. He'd never imagined a person could do such a thing to a lovely young girl. Then his thoughts turned to Carp Varner and what he'd done, and the reality of a harsh existence no longer escaped him. To his great satisfaction, he realized that he only cared more for Rachael, not less. After all, it wasn't her fault her parents were callous and uncaring.

He took two steps toward her and put his arm around her shoulder. They would stand there for another hour, silently gazing across hills that looked like an unmade bed. He hoped she understood that he found no fault in her.

Cotton was leaning on the bar at Melody's saloon talking to Arlo, when Carp Varner strolled in and, spotting the sheriff, came over carrying the Sharps. He ordered a whiskey and asked Cotton if he'd like one, too. The sheriff declined, saying it was too early in the day for him.

"I dropped by and the deputy said you'd be here. I finished the work on this rifle. You can tell the owner to come by and pick it up." Varner held the rifle up for Cotton to see. The sheriff took it, looked it over good, and handed it back.

"That's good work," Cotton said. "I'll ride out and tell the owner to pick it up and pay you. By the way, did you get a chance to look over any of the others that seemed like they were also needin' some sort of attention?"

"I did indeed. I'd say there's another dozen or so that need major fixin', and another three or four that just need a good cleanin' and oilin'."

"That somethin' you think you'd be interestin' in takin' on?"

"Well, yes, if you think folks around here would take to

a stranger workin' on their hardware. I would even be interested in takin' over the old man's business if you had a hankerin' to discuss such an arrangement. I might could even pay a little somethin' for the business."

Cotton thought about that for a second. "I'll talk it over with the mayor. As far as I'm concerned, it sounds like an answer to a need, at least temporarily. The legal aspects about the whole thing would have to be worked out, however, once I've had a chance to try trackin' down any living relatives of Mr. Burnside, since I have no right to sell someone else's business. You go ahead with some of the others that need attendin' to, and I'll get back to you on the particulars of a deal. I'll be sure you get paid for whatever work you do. That all right with you, Mr. Varner?"

"Sounds fine. Mighty fine." Varner drank his whiskey in one gulp and strolled out the door as nonchalantly as he'd walked in.

Arlo had a suspicious frown as Cotton rejoined the conversation they had been engaged in when Varner came in.

"Looks like you got somethin' on your mind, Arlo. Care to share it with me?"

"I can't put my finger on it, but to be honest, I don't completely trust that feller."

"You've always been a pretty good judge of character, so I'd appreciate anything you've got to say on the matter."

"I got no evidence of wrongdoing, or anything like that. It's just that his attitude since he first hit town has been overconfident. Claimed he's bound to be beddin' Melody afore long, and he made it sound like a sure thing."

"First of all, Arlo, you *do* know that Melody is a whore. That's what whores do. Secondly, Varner's goin' to have to tangle with Jack first. And that won't be easy."

"That's what I told him. He didn't seem impressed. In fact he snickered at the thought, kinda like he fancied himself as somewhat of a shootist."

"He wouldn't be the first one."

Cotton gave Arlo a wink and left the saloon, smiling to himself and thinking, *I wonder how Melody is gonna handle two fellows vying for her affections. She'll be damned tough to live with. This I gotta see.*

When Johnny and Rachael returned to the ranch house, Seth was sitting on the edge of the porch whittling on a piece of wood. He looked up, carefully placing the wood—which resembled a crude rendition of a horse—on the step and gave them a nod.

"I see you're back from visitin' your pa's grave, young lady. Hope you liked where I laid him. I figured any man would appreciate the view from that knoll."

"I, uh . . ." She paused before continuing, obviously feeling awkward about her response. Johnny saw her hesitation and jumped in.

"Your location was perfect, sir. He'd be pleased, I'm sure. We were impressed with what a beautiful piece of land you got here." He quickly looked over to see what Rachael's reaction would be. She was still noncommittal, choosing to offer a weak smile instead.

"You were gone a spell. I wasn't sure a pack of wolves didn't choose you for their lunch," Seth said with a cackle. "Well, it's about time for some vittles. Better wash up out back."

"Thank you, sir," Johnny said, as he took Rachael by the hand and led her around the side of the house.

"I, uh, couldn't speak. I'm sorry, Johnny, but the thought of saying anything nice about that awful creature turns my stomach."

"I understand. We won't speak any more of it. If questions come up, let me handle them. That way you don't have to lie or make up stories about what a fine man he was."

"Thank you," she said, giving his hand a squeeze. "I figured I could count on you from the moment we met, even if I wasn't in my right mind just then. Still, in my heart I knew."

As they washed their hands, the lady of the house stepped outside. "You two best hurry up afore Seth gobbles up everything on the table." She chuckled as she went back inside.

Chapter 15

Melody was sitting on the edge of the bed when Jack came into their room in the early afternoon. He removed his gun belt and dropped it on the chair. He walked over and sat next to her, bending down to tug his boots off. He tossed each in turn on the floor, then fell back onto the thick feather bed with a groan; all the air seemed to go out of him.

"What's the matter with *you*?" she asked, reaching over to stroke his cheek.

"I'm tuckered, that's what. Plumb tuckered. Been up since five."

"Tuckered? From doing *nothing*?"

"Nothing! You think I do nothing? Let me tell you, woman, I work plenty h—"

"Yeah, I know," she said, covering his mouth with her hand. "Listen, I want you to ride out to my new mine with me. I need to see if there are any miners nearby that are interested in coming to work for me. I'd rather not go alone.

Besides, you need to see what a grand investment I've made."

"Aww, can't it wait till tomorrow? I told you I'm too—"

"Uh-huh. You told me. But this can't wait. So let's get a move on before it gets too late."

Jack sat up, groaning as he bent to snag a boot from the floor. He knew he would get nowhere arguing with Melody. There wasn't a chance in hell he was going to get his way, no matter which way the wind blew. He strapped on the Remington and opened the door, giving her a sweeping bow, suggesting she lead the way, as any servant would. She gave him a sour look as if she didn't appreciate the innuendo.

"At least you didn't make me ride a mule like that jackass Pick Wheeler did. He said only mules could reach his mine. I think he lied to me. This mare seems to have a sweet disposition," Melody opined. "You're sure she can make it?"

"Uh-huh. Just don't kick her in the ribs to get her to do your bidding, or you might find she can turn real temperamental. They don't call her *Volcano* for nothing," Jack said and gave her a wink.

At first Melody looked frightened by the name, then after a moment of thought, she narrowed her eyes and became the old Melody. "You wouldn't dare! If this horse even *thinks* of unseating me, you damned well better catch me before I hit the ground, or so help me, Jack, I'll castrate you."

Jack began to chuckle, then he broke out in a gale of laughter. Melody just glared at him with all the venom she could muster.

After riding deeper and deeper into the foothills, following much the same path Pick had taken, or at least that's the way she remembered it, she saw something she thought looked familiar.

"Up there, Jack, isn't that a couple of mules?"

"Congratulations, Melody, your little jaunt with Pick has made you able to identify some of the wildlife."

"Don't be a smart-ass, Jack. I know a mule when I see one. And that one on the left looks real familiar."

When they got closer, Jack dismounted and slowly approached one of the mules. The animal acted skittish and out of sorts. Its coat was full of cockleburs and cactus scrapes. The saddle and bridle were still on, with the reins dangling and being dragged along. He looked over at the other animal, which had wandered off another hundred feet. Both were grazing on the bleak, nearly grassless downslope of a hill. The pack animal was still burdened with a fully loaded wooden pannier. The mule moved away from him with every attempt to get hold of the reins. Melody kept a close eye on the mule as she threw one leg over the saddle horn in an effort to get off her horse, but Jack held up his hand, looking around to see where the owner of the mules might have gone, or at least to pick up some sort of trail.

"Stay there, Melody. There's something not right about this. These animals look as if they've been abandoned in the middle of the desert. And there doesn't appear to be any sensible reason for doing such a foolish thing." Jack continued his surveillance of the area. "Do either of these animals look familiar?"

"The one with the saddle does. I already told you it looked familiar. Don't you ever listen to me?"

Jack continued to very slowly approach the mule, talking gently and working his way around to a better place to grab the reins. As the mule got to a dip in the ground where enough water collected during the monsoons to help the grass grow abundantly, the animal seemed to lose interest in him and munched on a thick patch of the verdant green. Jack reached out very carefully and snagged one rein, still talking in a low voice. He was finally able to corral the animal so he could get a better look at him. He didn't like what he saw.

"What are you looking at, Jack? Did you find something to tell you who they belong to?"

"Uh-huh."

"Well, don't make a mystery out of it. Whose mule is it?"

"It's Pick's. I figure they both are. It's for sure his old scarred-up saddle. And I'd know those hand-made panniers anywhere."

"Then we must be close to the mine. If that old fool is trying to gather up a little traveling money, I'll kill him," Melody shouted.

"I don't think that's what he's doin'."

"How the hell do you know what he's doing? He could be up there right this minute pulling *my* silver out of *my* mine and filling *his* pockets. That bastard!"

"I reckon I don't really know what he's up to, but I do know there's a lot of blood on this saddle, and it doesn't belong to the mule."

"Blood! You suggesting something happened to Pick?"

"Kinda looks that way. C'mon. We'll get closer to the mine. He might be injured."

Melody looked down the hill, trying to identify anything that might remind her of the exact location of her mine. Jack led the one mule over to where the other stood, figuring that if he had one in tow, the other wouldn't sense any danger and would come along quietly. Just as he gathered up the rope to lead the second animal, Melody called out.

"There it is, Jack. That's the entrance. Down there! See that dark place near those rocks?"

Jack looked to where she was pointing. He led the two animals back to his horse and swung into the saddle. He'd tied the pack lead onto the other mule's saddle horn and led them both toward the place Melody had pointed out. When they reached an area devoid of anything but dirt, rocks, and old hunks of timber, he saw the entrance to what must have been the mine all the fuss was about. It was a pitiful excuse for a working mine, at least in his mind. He shuddered to think what they might find in the massive hole he was staring into. He could only sigh at the secrets held by that chasm.

"That's it! That's the silver mine. Come on, let's get inside so I can show you how rich we're going to be." Melody fairly jumped from her horse's back, nearly twisting her ankle and falling when she hit a rock.

"Damn, Melody, you got to be careful where you step in a place like this. You could break a leg and there sure isn't anyone around to care for you."

"Don't worry, I'm being careful. And, as far as going inside that old hole, I'm not worried. What do you think I brought you for?"

Jack started for the entrance but was shoved aside by an overeager Melody. She was at the entrance before he could locate his tin full of lucifers. She was already inside when he approached. She thrust a lantern out to him.

"Here, light this and let's get started," she said, with the eagerness of a child on her first adventure. She shoved the lantern into his hand, staring at him with a "What's keeping you?" look.

After lighting two oil lanterns, Jack stood in the yellow glow they threw off. He looked around as Melody began shouting.

"See! Do you see all those sparkles, Jack? They're everywhere! What did I tell you? This mine is *full* of silver!"

Jack was picking at something in the side of the tunnel. He had a disgusted look on his face. He was shaking his head when Melody grabbed his shirtsleeve and began shaking him.

"What's wrong with you? Aren't you happy about all this money just leaking out of the walls?"

"No, Melody. I'm not happy. You've been *taken*. This mine has been salted!"

Chapter 16

"I . . . uh . . . don't know what that means. What're you saying, Jack?" The look of panic on her face was unmistakable. She may not have known what "salted" meant, but she knew instinctively by the way Jack spit out his words that it wasn't going to be good. She balled up her fist in anticipation of Jack's answer.

"It means, my dear, that Pick Wheeler saw you comin' a mile away. He likely loaded up that old shotgun of his with silver shavings from coins and fired them into the walls. There's no mistaking it. Silver doesn't show up this way."

Stunned, Melody stood in silence. Her breathing became unsteady, and she looked like she was about to faint. In fact that's what she did, at the same time Jack reached out to catch her. He carried her outside and sat her against a boulder. She was pale and dazed.

"D-does that . . . mean . . . there's no silver? He just stole all my money?"

"I don't know. There may still be some back further in the tunnel. No way to tell until an expert comes out to survey the mine. If you'll recall, that's what I warned you to do in the first place before you handed over all your cash to that old highbinder."

Jack left her sitting alone, breathing heavily and looking scared. He went back into the mine to have a look around. After several minutes deep inside, he figured he'd seen all he needed to. He blew out the lantern and placed it on a stack of unused beams near the entrance. When he stepped into the sunlight, he saw Melody in a huff, on her way back to the horses. She was understandably anxious to get to town. Jack removed the saddle and bridle from the one mule and the lead rope and pack from the other, then set the two animals to wander freely. He followed after Melody. When they reached the horses, he helped her up. He climbed into his own saddle and eased his horse around.

"Let's go, Melody. There's nothing more to see. You only have to go about ten feet further into the tunnel to see where the silver petered out," he said, turning to her. He could see the pain in her eyes. Her face was drained of color. But he also saw a flash of something beginning to build. He'd have bet his last dollar she would explode any minute. He didn't have to wait long. When Melody Wakefield got royally pissed off, she could be hell on wheels. It looked like this was going to be one of those times.

Carp Varner was hunched over the workbench at the gunsmith shop when he heard footsteps behind him. He spun around while at the same time snagging a Smith & Wesson Schofield .45, fully loaded and ready for action. It was his, not one from the pile of well-used firearms set aside for repair. He always kept his at the ready. A gunslinger can never be too careful. This, however, was one of those times when being hasty could have cost him. He came face-to-face with the sheriff, who held both hands in the air.

"Whoa, pardner, no need to be gettin' edgy. A fella could get hurt makin' a false assumption."

Carp placed the revolver back on the bench and gave the sheriff a guilty grin.

"Yeah, sorry. I've been told before that I sometimes act a tad impulsively when someone sneaks up behind me. I reckon I got a thing about folks comin' up too quiet-like. Didn't mean nothin' by it."

"Yeah, sure. I probably should have knocked or somethin', although I'm surprised the bell didn't ring."

"Yeah, I took it down. All that jinglin' set my teeth on edge. You lookin' for somethin' in particular, Sheriff?"

"Just curious. How're you comin' with that bunch of derelicts?"

"I'm getting' on top of it. Most of the problems are from folks not keepin' their firearms clean. Some of 'em were so dirty you could grow corn in the barrels."

"I'm not surprised. These people are mostly ranchers and farmers. Don't get a chance to use a gun very often."

"You get a chance to talk to the mayor?" Carp said.

"Not yet. He's been out of town for a few days, a sick sister or something. I'll talk to him as soon as he returns. You keep on with what you're doin'; I figure we'll be able to work somethin' out to your satisfaction. It's no secret, we *need* a gunsmith."

"Sounds like the town has seen its share of gun toters. That why you're anxious to keep folks armed and ready?"

"Could be, Mr. Varner, could be. But then, I notice you weren't far away from that forty-five you wear. You must feel the need to be ready, too, huh?"

Cotton turned and left the shop before Varner could cobble together an answer.

When Jack and Melody rode into town, she didn't wait for him to help her down. At that moment being ladylike was the farthest thing from her mind. She stormed up the steps to the saloon and shoved the batwings aside like they were only there to be a nuisance for her. Arlo gave her a greeting, which, as it turned out, was just the catalyst she needed to let the world know she was on the warpath and someone was going to lose his life.

By the time Jack got there, Arlo was standing behind the bar, hands spread apart, with a look of shock on his face. "Uh, hi, Jack. Everything, er, all right?"

"I see Melody let you know she was havin' a bad day, huh?"

"Y-yes, yes, I reckon you could call it that. I . . . d-don't ever recall hearing some of those words come out of a lady's mouth before."

"Melody just pretends to be a lady, Arlo, you should know that by now. She can be as tough as any hard-bitten range rider on his worst day. Don't worry, she'll get over it." Jack strolled up the stairs as casually as if he was just dropping by for a visit. He pulled the door to Melody's boudoir closed behind him, whistling softly all the way.

Jack knew he was in for a rough time until Melody figured out it was as much her fault as Pick Wheeler's that she'd been taken. It was she who insisted that he shouldn't just walk away from such a valuable asset. Jack wasn't even sure just where she was in the process of revelation, but one thing he was sure of was that there had been no sign of anyone other than Pick Wheeler, alone, working that gaping hole in the ground. There had *never* been any other miners. In fact, he figured it might be a good idea to talk to Darnell Givins, the bank president, and get his opinion on how much Pick had taken out of his mine and whether he'd ever paid anyone else. But before he could put that plan into action, Melody came out from her curtained powder room and lit into him like a banshee.

"Jack! I need to know where the hell you were when that bastard was stripping me of all my hard-earned cash. Where? What good is a deputy sheriff that doesn't keep law-abiding citizens safe from the likes of a varmint like Wheeler?"

Jack just shook his head in disbelief. It was clear to him that Melody would never accept responsibility for her own predicament. *Greed is a powerful thing.*

Chapter 17

———◦◦◦———

Cotton was pensive after his chat with Carp Varner. His misgivings about the stranger came not from any specific knowledge, but from a feeling of mistrust deep down. Although it certainly came partly from the eagerness the man had shown to go for his gun. Cotton tried unsuccessfully to shake his doubts.

Returning to the jail after his ride to the mine, Jack was trying unsuccessfully to hide his anger at Melody's foolishness. No words passed between him and the sheriff before Cotton had a fire going in the stove and a pot of coffee beginning to brew. It took the aroma of boiling Arbuckles' to prod a few words out of either of them.

"Saw you ride in with Melody, Jack."

"Uh-huh."

"Pleasurable ride?"

"Huh uh."

"Wanta talk about it?"

"Hell no!"

"Sounds like the romance has hit a snag."

"More'n a snag."

"Hmm. You didn't by any chance take a little trip out to Melody's newest bold venture, did you?"

"Yep," Jack said, lifting the pot and filling two cups with steaming coffee.

"And you found it to be the bonanza she claimed it was?"

"You know damned well I didn't. In fact, what I found was a mine that had been salted with silver shavings, probably from coins. There's no silver in that godforsaken hole. Nothin' more'n a few rotten timbers and a handful of mice."

"Ol' Pick played her, huh?"

"And stole a pile of greenbacks from her."

"What do you figure on doin' about it?"

"What can I do? It's done. He's probably halfway to Chicago by now."

"Well, in case you hadn't noticed, saltin' a mine is illegal. I'll draft up a wanted poster, if you can get Melody to offer a reward. We'll catch him. Hopefully he won't have spent all her money by the time someone with a need for the reward lays eyes on him."

"Considerin' all she lost, I'd say a reward is the least she can do. I'll suggest it to her."

Cotton walked over to the open door, sipping his coffee as he went. He stood in the doorway silently. Jack's temper had cooled somewhat after he'd heard Cotton's common-sense approach to his problem.

"I got a feelin' I'm not the only one around here that should spill what's eatin' 'em."

"Very perceptive, Jack."

"Well, lay it out. I'm listenin'."

"I can't put my finger on it exactly, but there's somethin' not quite right about our new gunsmith, Carp Varner."

"You figure he's wanted somewhere?"

"I looked through all the dodgers we've collected for over a year now. Can't find anything. Of course, that doesn't mean he hasn't done *somethin'*."

"Just nothin' you can pin on him."

"Uh-huh."

"What're you figurin' on doin'?"

"It's what we're both goin' to be doin': keepin' a close eye on him."

Carp Varner stood up from his workbench, stretched, and went to the window at the front of the gunsmith shop. He watched the comings and goings of the few people on the street at that time of morning. He then went to the door and turned the key to lock it. He pulled down the shade on the door and turned to begin a task he'd been eager to start since taking over the gunsmith's duties. He went first to the rolltop desk and opened it. Inside he found the many cubicles and small drawers crammed full of papers and small envelopes. He opened each carefully and without haste, so as not to let others, in particular the sheriff, discover his intention to find any hidden money he might secure.

Mostly he found nothing more than a few receipts for work done, a couple of bills unpaid, and five promissory notes. The only stash of money amounted to twenty-five cents in coins. *The old fool wasn't going to get rich fixin' these beat-up shooters. Good thing I've been able to latch onto my own resources.*

Looking around for a suitable safe place to keep his own stash, he came across a metal box that could, if needed, be padlocked. Should the need arise, of course. Ironically, it just had. He figured he'd drop in to the hardware store and pick up one of the newest locks available. He pulled out a wad from the saddlebags he'd brought in when he arrived and transferred the contents to the box. He put the box in a desk drawer, covered it with papers, and pushed the drawer closed. Seeing that his search-and-find adventure had left no evidence of his poking around, he raised the blind on the door and unlocked it, turning the OPEN sign around for all to see, in particular those who wished to avail themselves of his services. He could hardly contain a wide grin.

"There was one thing that puzzled me about our goin' to see Pick's mine," Jack said, settling into a ladder-back chair and leaning against the wall.

"And what was that?"

"Pick's two mules. They were just standin' around, one saddled and the other with its pack rack piled high."

"Pick wouldn't leave his animals to fend for themselves like that. Why didn't you tell me about this first, before whinin' about poor Melody's circumstances?"

"Well, I didn't remember until just now. Besides, I looked around and didn't see any sign that Pick had even come back after takin' possession of Melody's money."

"I assume you thought to lead the poor animals back to town and deposit them at the livery. You did do that, didn't you?"

"I unsaddled them and set 'em free. I couldn't leave 'em tryin' to fend for themselves with saddles and tack to contend with."

"All right, you go down to the stage office and see if the old fool bought a ticket for some place, while I go try to round up a posse."

"Uh, yeah, sure. You think somethin's happened to ol' Pick?"

"I don't figure we'll know unless we go look. Now, get out of here. I'm goin' to the saloon. I hope there's at least a few fellers that'll still be sober and would be willin' to search for a card-playin' pal."

"Good luck with that. Way I hear it, Pick Wheeler didn't have many friends."

Cotton frowned and pointed to the door. His message was clear.

"I'm goin', I'm goin', but don't blame me if you come back empty-handed," Jack said, shrugging his shoulders.

Cotton followed him out and headed straight for Melody's Golden Palace of Pleasure. He had no sooner arrived than Arlo motioned him over.

"What's going on? I've heard rumors that Pick Wheeler took Melody for a pile of money. That couldn't be right, could it, Sheriff?"

"Where'd you hear these rumors, Arlo?"

"No one in particular. Mostly cowboys jawin' about this and that. Hardly anything useful ever comes along, though. So, is it true?"

"My best advice is to not spread the rumor any farther."

"So, you aren't saying one way or t'other?"

"I'm just followin' my own advice."

"Would you like a drink?"

"Nope. I'm lookin' for some volunteers to ride out and see if we can scare up ol' Pick. Know anyone who's got some time on his hands and don't know what to do with it?"

"Pick's missing?"

"Looks that way."

"Well, them boys at the back table are mostly talking about the woes of the world. I haven't seen a card fall yet. Might ask them."

"Obliged." Cotton sauntered back to the table with four cowboys, each leaning back in his chair, more interested in sharing his thoughts on the state of affairs in New Mexico Territory than in a card game. "Howdy, boys. How'd you fellas like to take a ride into the countryside? I could use some help locatin' one of your friends, now apparently missin'."

"You lookin' to deputize us, Sheriff?"

"It isn't necessary, but if you'd feel better about goin', I'd be willin' to swear you in."

All four scooted their chairs back and stood, ready to follow the sheriff's lead. One of the cowboys spoke up.

"Who did you say we was lookin' for, Sheriff?"

"Pick Wheeler. Does it matter?"

"Does to me," said one of the men. He turned around

and went back to sit at the table. Another followed him. Cotton was down to two volunteers, and he hadn't even left the saloon.

By the time they reached the door, Jack was on his way over.

"Did he take the stage, Jack?"

"'Fraid not. No one at the stage office has seen hide nor hair of him in a month of Sundays."

"Then how do you figure he left town?"

"He rode his mule and took his pack with him, too. He didn't sell them to Melody. They weren't part of the deal."

"So the animals found their way back to the mine without Pick?"

"Looks like. I wonder if he stopped the stage on his way, decidin' he didn't want to get to Albuquerque with two mules he no longer needed, and released the critters to forage on their own," Jack said.

"Lettin' mules wander off on their own without takin' the saddle and pack off, well, that don't seem like somethin' Pick Wheeler would do, even as nasty a character as he is," Cotton said, rubbing his stubbly chin.

"Then, we'd better get these fellows sworn in and saddle up," Jack said, clearly getting anxious to solve Melody's problem so she'd get off his back. "Maybe we can figure out where all that blood came from, too."

"What! You found blood! Why the hell didn't you tell me?" Cotton sucked in a lungful of air and let it out in disgust. He slammed through the door.

Chapter 18

———◆◆◆———

Johnny and Rachael were perched on the back of the horse that had belonged to the man everyone had assumed was Rachael's father. Johnny rode in front, with Rachael's arms wrapped tightly around his waist. He liked the way she felt; her small yet firm breasts pushing against his back sent a thrill coursing through him. It introduced him to an excitement he'd not experienced before, and he hated the thought of having, at some point, to dismount and move on. He also liked the smell of her when she laid her head on his shoulder, especially when the wind blew her hair, tickling his cheek. Although he was well into his eighteenth year, his knowledge of girls had been severely stunted. There were no young girls in Whiskey Crossing. In fact, the only woman who remotely attracted him was a thirty-year-old whore who went by the name Gold-tooth Sally, for an obvious facial attribute. He never sampled her sought-after charms, mainly because he'd never had enough money to meet her price. Swamping out a saloon after closing hours and cleaning the stables, while honest, steady work, had proven only sufficient for three meals and a bed each day.

And now, good fortune had come upon him in the form of a lovely young lady who seemed to appreciate his company. His days had brightened despite the hardships they'd endured together. Coming across the very place where Rachael's "master" was buried, and where his horse had wandered to, had also been a stroke of good fortune. They could, if they didn't push their mount too hard, make it to a town of sufficient size for them to possibly obtain some type of short-term employment. Any money they might cobble together, they'd agreed, would be put toward stagecoach passage farther west. That was the direction Johnny figured Carp Varner was headed, at least from the few signs he'd seen up to now. Even though Rachael had only a passing and unpleasant knowledge of Varner, she sensed from Johnny's telling of his evil exploits that he was a man who should be caught and made to pay in the harshest way possible for his crimes.

The riding had been easy thus far, and the air smelled fresh from a recent rain. Wildflowers dotted the landscape from here to there to everywhere—striking shades of purple lupine, yellow brittlebush, and cactus flowers, each attracting bees and birds, and unseen things as well. Cottonwoods, birch, and willows lined the several small creeks they'd crossed. Sufficient grass dotted the land that there arose no danger that the horse might starve. In discussing with Rachael their trip across western Texas, Johnny made certain he left out the part about dangers they might face, like scorpions and rattlesnakes and pumas, and all the other creatures that take full advantage of the dark of night to come out of hiding and feed on the unsuspecting. He figured she'd heard about all these things, but he wasn't all that certain she'd spent many nights outside, under the stars, with only a blanket and a rock for a pillow.

It was a certainty they would not reach any sort of settlement before nightfall, so Johnny began scouring the horizon for someplace to make camp. Rachael, too, must have
known they'd need to stop soon. If she was getting hungry,
she'd know Johnny was also. He'd need sufficient light to
bag something to eat, since the only food they'd brought
with them was wrapped in a checkered cloth and rolled up
in the saddlebags, and though Johnny hadn't examined their
stash, he suspected it mostly consisted of biscuits or bread,
with maybe with some jerky thrown in. Whatever it was, he
was certain the intent had been to supply them with items
that would sustain them without turning bad during the long
ride to civilization. Seth and his wife wouldn't hear of their
departing without something to fill their bellies the farther
away they got. Rachael made a suggestion that a copse of
trees off to their right might be a good place to settle for the
night. It wouldn't have taken a lot to talk the boy into getting
off the horse he'd been astride for more than nine hours.

Having guided the mare between the trees to a place
that looked safe and reasonably comfortable, although a
little too rocky for his pleasure, Johnny dismounted, helped
Rachael down, and quickly began searching the landscape
for signs of wildlife. He lifted the trapdoor on the Springfield and slid in a cartridge, then snapped it shut, ready for
whatever might happen by. One rabbit would do just fine,
he thought. However, though he tried as hard as he could,
the place they'd chosen didn't seem to be teeming with critters eager to become someone's dinner. He heard not one
bird, and found no tracks in the sand. A thin ribbon of a
spring, little more than a seep, wandered down the side of
a rocky hill and through the trees, certainly not deep
enough for any fish. He was puzzled by the lack of larger
tracks, though. No sign of deer, horses, or cattle were to be
seen along the stream's edge. He had a sudden sense of
something off-kilter. Could there be some unseen danger
lurking just beyond his usually acute awareness of his sur-
roundings?

He was now faced with a problem: Did he dare tell Rachael of his premonition or hold off and wait for whatever was going to happen, then react accordingly? *No, that's foolish, simple-minded thinking. I can't put her in danger just waiting for an imagined threat to show itself. It would be best for us to move on, find another spot. This can't be the only desirable place for a camp.* Rachael had wandered down to the stream and was squatting at the edge, cupping her hands and splashing water on her face to rid her eyes and mouth of trail dust. She was directly beneath a substantial rock outcropping. A large ledge hung over where she drank. Whatever it was that had Johnny's skin crawling remained elusive. But the more he scanned the landscape, the more he felt discomfited. Rachael seemed quite content, oblivious to any danger, real or otherwise. Was he simply imagining some ghostly presence? If so, why was it so pervasive and growing in intensity? He stared at the ground as he pondered the situation.

In an instant his fears came screaming into reality in the form of a tawny puma perched on the ledge jutting out immediately above where Rachael played in the gurgling stream. The large cat was poised to jump. Johnny let out a warning yell as he raised the Springfield, cocked it, and pulled the trigger. He managed to hit the animal, but not fatally. *Damn!* he thought. *Now Rachael's in more danger than before. Few things are more dangerous than a wounded mountain lion.* He had no time to reload the rifle, so he drew his revolver and, racing toward her, began firing as quickly as he could at the animal that was now on her. The cat screamed at each hit, but in its frantic need for food, it refused to roll over and die. Finally, all six shots expended, Johnny grabbed up the rifle once more and began violently clubbing the puma in the head with it until, with blood splattered everywhere, it slunk away from the stricken girl and fell over dead. It was Johnny's furious beating, unleashed by the sense that his dear Rachael might lose her life, that had finally brought an end to the cat's attack.

He stood over the carcass, shaking with disbelief at what
he'd done, but also harboring a strange desire to continue
the fight. His adrenaline subsiding, he was suddenly aware
of a groan coming from behind him. He turned to see
Rachael, the sleeve of her dress shredded by the beast's
wicked claws, bleeding profusely. Her dress had almost
been torn off her, and she was dazed and bewildered by the
suddenness of the attack. She didn't move except to utter a
slight whimper. Terror still filled her eyes when Johnny
bent down to take her in his arms. He picked her up and
carried her to a wide patch of grass. Her lips were moving
but nothing came out.

"Shh. Don't speak. The cat is gone. It's going to be okay."
The agony on his face as he looked at the deep claw marks
down her arm suggested he wasn't so sure of that. Time was
of the essence. He had to stop the bleeding and clean the
wounds. He gently leaned her back onto the grass and ran to
his horse to secure a canteen of fresh water. What about
bandages? That thought brought him a rush of panic. He
tore through all the things they'd packed when leaving
Rachael's cabin for the last time. But, being as how they
were afoot, carrying more than the basic necessities had
been out of the question. So there was little to pick through.

When he came to her simple, cotton nightgown, he bit
his lip. She had made a point of bringing it because it held
some sort of fond memory for her. It was the only thing he
could find now, though, that might suffice for wrapping the
worst of her wounds. He would have to rip it into strips,
thus rendering it forever useless as a garment. He cringed
at what she might think of him for taking away something
so personal and dear to her without her explicit permission,
but his choice was limited to strips of nightgown or poul-
tices of mud and leaves.

He began ripping the bottom of the gown into long
pieces of clean, white cotton and wetting some of them
down to wash her arm where the claws had made bloody

furrows. He winced when she made a soft groan at his touch. He swallowed hard and continued washing her flesh.

No tellin' where all those claws had been. I have to get her to a doctor, and for damn sure it can't wait.

Chapter 19

Cotton, Jack, and the two cowboys rode out of Apache Springs in search of Pick Wheeler. They had no idea where he'd gotten off to, so they could but choose the most likely direction a man would head if he were flush with a pocket full of money and a dream of going to Chicago. Cotton's first thought was to start at the mine, since that was where Jack had found the mules, but after some consideration, and armed with the knowledge that Pick had deliberately salted the mine with silver shavings, he doubted the man would have been foolish enough to go near the scene of his crime. Even Pick was smart enough to realize his secret would be discovered at the first turn of a shovel. His best choice would have been to head for Albuquerque, catch a stagecoach from there to Santa Fe, and then head east to the first rail station he could find, probably Las Vegas. Since Pick had spent several years deep in a dark mine shaft, though, Cotton figured it was doubtful the old highbinder had any idea of the railroad's present-day westerly progress.

Should they detect no sign of him before he exited the county, the only thing they could do would be to turn back, since Sheriff Burke had no jurisdiction in any other county but his own. Then he'd just have to send out telegrams to every place he could think of, to be on the lookout for a "fugitive" wanted for robbery—for that's what it was, plain and simple. Pick Wheeler could have been no less a robber than if he'd walked up to a teller's cage and demanded all the cash.

After two hours of steady riding, Cotton reined up at a stand of cottonwoods. He told the two cowboys to spread out, keeping each other in sight, heading in the general direction of Albuquerque. That way, if anyone saw anything indicating where Pick had gotten off to, he'd be able to signal the others. That wasn't the only thing the sheriff wanted them to be on the lookout for. Also *buzzards*. That would be a sure sign of something dead. He was hoping that if they did spot any of the graceful carrion circling an area, it would prove to be nothing more than a dead rabbit or a javelina, the wild boar of the desert. But since Jack had reported seeing blood on the saddle, something violent having happened to Wheeler appeared likely. Sheriff Burke was bracing for bad news. As the cowboys rode out, Jack seemed puzzled by Cotton just sitting his saddle, making no move to join in the hunt.

"You figurin' on sittin' this one out, Sheriff?"

"Not exactly. Just waitin' for the most important member of the search party. Should be here about now."

"Who might that be?"

"What do we need more'n anything else?"

"A good tracker. Why if we . . . Aah, I get it. You sent for Henry Coyote, didn't you?"

"You stay on this job awhile longer and you might be able to figure out what I'm wantin' for breakfast, Jack."

Jack had no more than tossed a disgruntled frown Cotton's way, than seemingly out of nowhere there suddenly appeared a bronze-skinned man with long, graying hair, a colorful cotton shirt, and a bandolier across his chest, full of bullets for the Spencer rifle he carried. The Mescalero Apache held up a hand in greeting. He was afoot.

"Good to see you, Henry. Where's your pony?" Cotton asked.

"Find missing man better this way."

Cotton nodded. "Have you ever met the man we're after, Pick Wheeler? He's an old miner from up near the Dog Creek cut."

"I know him. Foolish man who no like coffee."

Cotton laughed. "Yeah, that's him, all right. He was always partial to rotgut whiskey. Could hang one on with the best of them. Well, he seems to be missing, although we aren't sure of that. Jack, here, found his two animals still saddled up near the mine, a mine which *he* no longer owned. There were signs that something possibly happened to the old man, too."

"Who foolish enough to buy empty mine from man who no like coffee?"

"That's a long story, Henry. But at the moment, Jack's lady friend, Melody, appears to be the rightful owner. We need to find Pick and sort it all out. So far we haven't seen any sign of him along the road north."

"Bring him to *you*, if he alive?"

"Yes. I don't want him harmed; however, do whatever it takes to get him to the jail, unless he's hurt, in which case get word to me so we can get him to a doctor. I'm goin' back to town. Jack's going back with me. There are two other cowboys lookin' also."

Henry nodded and began to sprint away. As he looked back over his shoulder, he shouted, "Have coffee ready, back soon," and he disappeared into the brush.

"He looks to be headed straight for the mine. I thought you said that'd be the last place Pick would go," Jack said, with a puzzled expression.

"Never figured Pick would go to the mine. Henry's goin' to do just what I'd do in the situation, only better."

"What's that?"

"Backtrack the damned mules."

Johnny lifted Rachael from her grassy resting place as gently as he could. Carrying her to where their horse was picketed, he was noticeably nervous about her condition. All his efforts at cleaning and wrapping her wounds had barely slowed the bleeding. He was rattled and worried.

"Where are we going, Johnny?" she said, in a tiny, almost whispering voice.

"We have to find a town with a doctor. I can only do so much. You're pretty badly scratched up, and you got to get care from someone who knows about those things. I can't let anything happen to you."

She smiled weakly, trying to squeeze his hand but finding even that small expression of her faith in him difficult. Johnny's plan was to put her in the saddle in front of him, so he could hold her with one arm around her, while at the same time grasping the reins with the other hand. That way, she could sleep without fear of tumbling from the horse's back. His main dread was that some even greater danger should befall her before he could get her to a settlement where professional help might be obtained, although he had no idea how he was going to pay for such a service.

After she was settled and sitting comfortably, he swung up behind her. He gave the horse a little thump with his heels, and the mare seemed to grasp the need to move with care. It was getting late when they finally got started, and Johnny was praying they might reach civilization before nightfall. He'd seen what happened when wounds went untended for very long, and the most dreaded of all consequences could create terrible pain and finally death, or amputation. *Gangrene!*

He shivered at the thought of Rachael possibly losing an

arm simply because he had failed to keep a more watchful eye out for danger. He should have seen that cat creeping up on them. But he hadn't. And now this lovely young girl was in grave danger. If she died, he'd never forgive himself.

Chapter 20

———◆·◆———

Carp Varner had just finished cleaning a Winchester that looked like it had been used for pounding nails when he heard several horses riding past the front of the shop. Glancing out the dust-covered window, he didn't like what he saw. Three riders in long, oilcloth dusters had reined in their horses and were preparing to dismount in front of the saloon. He backed away from the window so they couldn't see him watching if they happened to look his way. The Callahan Brothers—Black Tom, Stretch, and Dal—were well known in Texas, although not likely as far west as Apache Springs. Was it possible they *had* spotted him back in El Paso, after all, and tracked him here? Perhaps he hadn't been as careful as he'd thought. The hair on the back of his neck felt as if it were afire.

He went back to the bench where he was ready to begin cleaning a couple of sadly neglected Colt revolvers, pushed them aside, and leaned on his elbows to ponder what his next move might be. He had found a perfect opportunity in

Apache Springs, a way to make money and to ingratiate himself with the citizenry; a distinct advantage for when he decided the time was ripe for cleaning the town out. Another fire kind of appealed to him, but since he'd had no chance to see the sheriff in action, he didn't want to make any move that could get him killed. Biding his time had always been what Carp Varner did best. He was a professional at formulating his attack and then making his move when he had every living soul in town pegged for what he was, either a coward or a good prospect for getting backshot. That's the kind of philosophy that helped him kill those who might oppose him, scare those who had no spine into staying indoors or getting shot down, and then burn the town with all but no resistance. He'd lived his whole life with but one dictum: strike those who can't strike back. And do it without warning, swiftly, with no remorse or sympathy.

He sat staring straight ahead, mulling over whether to stay put or actually let the Callahans see him by walking into the saloon like he owned the place. His first confrontation with them had not gone well, at least as far as the Callahans were concerned. If there was to be a second, he'd better be prepared. And this time it would be on his terms.

The need to get a grip on his propensity for volatile outbursts in situations where harm could come was one lesson his mother had failed to instill in the self-absorbed Mr. Varner. And so, after due consideration, and since he'd seen the sheriff and his deputy ride out early in the day and not yet return, he decided to wait for the Callahans to make a move. A move in which he figured to play a part beneficial to himself and to the detriment of the Callahans.

Henry Coyote, the full-blooded Mescalero Apache who worked on the Wagner ranch for Emily Wagner, was keeneyed and deliberate as he began his search for Pick. Henry's life had been saved some years back when Emily and her husband, Otis, came upon him lying near death at the base of a ravine. They'd taken him to their ranch, where Emily nursed him back to health. Shortly thereafter, Otis Wagner was shot down during a bank robbery by a gang of cutthroats who were in turn killed by Sheriff Burke. Henry's allegiance to Emily had become an unbreakable bond, due in part to her caring for him during his convalescence, but also to the responsibility the sheriff had placed on him for her safe return after she'd been kidnapped and held hostage by the plotters of a fiendish train robbery. Henry had also taken a bullet intended for Emily fired by a crazed killer in the pay of another sworn enemy of Burke. The ties between the three of them were strong. And for that reason, Henry was eager to help the sheriff whenever needed. This was one of those times.

Henry slowly wound his way through the thick brush, approaching Pick Wheeler's former mine. He couldn't quite figure what had made Melody Wakefield, Jack's personal whore, invest her money in a worthless played-out silver mine. Even Henry figured Pick to be a blowhard and a worthless dreamer, whose manifold attempts to find silver or gold had led him to nearly every part of the territory, never with significant success. And now he was missing. That thought didn't sit well with the old Indian. He'd seen several men of Wheeler's ilk, none of whom ever stayed around long enough to make good on their boasts. He was thinking about how far the sheriff wished him to go in search of a man whose character was notably suspect. At that moment, he spotted the tracks of Pick's two animals.

He began his quest by squatting close to the first set of prints, nimbly feeling around the indentations, memorizing any quirk that would set it apart from any other tracks he came across. Other than the fact that the prints of the mule were slightly larger than most horses', he also took note of a series of jagged slices missing around the peripheries, most likely acquired by constant travel over the sharp rocks under heavy loads. Looking back at the mine entrance,

Henry also noticed that whatever slag Pick had hauled out had been dumped not far from the mine's opening. That meant one of two things: either Pick was working by himself and was too lazy to haul it farther out of his way, or there was little of significant bulk to bother with. Henry decided it was a puzzle that needed answering before he continued his quest.

When he reached the mine, Henry was instantly aware of Pick's subterfuge. Several yards away from the entrance, behind several large boulders, he found a small number of silver shavings in the soft dirt, along with a discarded rasp. Entering, he struck a lucifer, touched it to the wick of an oil lamp, and started to the back of the tunnel. He quickly discovered that the mine had been almost worked to death years before Pick Wheeler showed up in Apache Springs, with only sporadic evidence of anything more than meager success since then. Cobwebs, mice nests, and rusting cans littered the mine the farther back one went. After about fifty feet and several turns, he found old shovels and picks, rusted and half-buried in dirt where the ceiling had begun to fall from lack of proper shoring.

Some white folks easy to fool, he thought, leaving the hole in the ground, shaking his head, and starting back downhill to again take up his assigned task. The tracks proved easy to follow. The ground was soft from several rains in the weeks leading up to Pick's disappearance, and the mule's hooves sank deep. He'd gone nearly three miles when he came across the road that led northwest toward Albuquerque. The hoofprints showed where the animals had left the road originally to wander aimlessly back toward the mine.

Mules try to go back to place they know.

As he walked farther along the road, looking side to side in a zigzag pattern, Henry came across another set of prints that seemed to be tracking the mules'. *Other rider catch up to old man*. The prints showed they stopped in the middle of the road for several minutes, possibly to talk. Then the horse and rider turned back toward Apache Springs, while the mules stood around for a while, then wandered off into the brush to find food or water.

Old man must be nearby. I sense death.

Within thirty feet of the spot where the two men met, then parted, Henry found Pick Wheeler lying facedown in the dirt with three bullets in him. He'd been back-shot. He appeared to have hung on to the mule's neck for a distance, then fallen from his saddle and crawled off to die. There was no sign of any money on his person. Henry covered the corpse with branches to keep the curious at bay, and then began his sprint back to town. He took a route that, to most men, would have been the most difficult, but to an Apache was the most expeditious. It would be at least a two-hour ride on horseback, but Henry was able to make it in an hour and a half by cutting across slickrock-covered hillsides and cactus- and brush-infested gullies and ravines that horses would have found impossible to traverse.

Chapter 21

———◆·◆———

Johnny was grateful that the night had finally cleared from an early evening wind. The air was calm and he was now able to see a good distance. Too much of their time had been spent fighting dust that swirled around making visibility almost nonexistent. He'd wrapped his scarf around Rachael's face so taking deep breaths came easier for her. He feared she had come close to passing out several times, bringing him to a near panic. After what they'd been through together, he couldn't lose her now, especially not as the result of an attack he carried guilt for not avoiding. When they came to the top of a rise, he spotted dozens of twinkling lights in the middle of a wide valley. *A town, thank heavens we've found a town*, he thought he'd said only in his mind.

"Wh-what did you say, Johnny?"

"I-I guess I was mumbling, Rachael, sorry. I said it looks like there's a town up ahead." He kicked the horse to a trot. *We should be able to make it in an hour or less. I pray there's a doctor there.*

"That's good news, isn't it, Johnny?" Rachael said, barely above a whisper. Her head sank to her chest, and Johnny had to tighten his grip to keep her in the saddle.

"Yes, Rachael, it's very good news. Now we can get you the help you need."

It was after dark when they arrived in a tiny little village along a river. That's when it hit Johnny as to where they probably were, in New Mexico Territory. He hadn't known that they'd left Texas some time earlier and now they had fortunately stumbled upon a collection of Mexican adobes. A low wall surrounded the village, which sat on the banks of what he was soon to discover was the Rio Grande, or Rio Bravo, as it was known south of the border with Mexico.

The small collection of oddly shaped buildings had been built around the residents' most treasured structure, the distinctly whitewashed church with a wooden cross over the main door. The only sounds Johnny heard were the barks of stray dogs, the strumming of a guitar, presumably in a cantina somewhere down the wagon-rutted street, and the cry of a small child demanding its dinner. He had no idea how to locate a doctor, so he did the only thing he could think of, he went up to the closest house and knocked on the door.

The door creaked open about two inches and the light of a candle streamed out. He could see the sleepy eyes of an old woman.

"What is it, señor? Can you not see it is late?"

"Yes, ma'am, I know, and I'm sorry to disturb you, but I have a lady with me who has been badly injured and I am seeking help for her. Do you know where I can find a doctor?"

"No. You have arrived in Mesilla, and we are too poor to have a doctor."

"Where is the nearest help then? I'm desperate."

"Continue on up the road and cross the Rio Bravo. It is

shallow and you'll have no trouble. You will come to Las
Cruces, and there you will find a doctor."

"How far is that, ma'am?"

"Not so far. *Buenas noches, señor,*" the old lady said,
closing the door. He heard a wooden bar slip into place.
Probably figures I'll break in and steal her nightcap.

He hurried back to where he'd left Rachael. He took the
reins and began leading the animal down the road in the
direction the old woman had said. Indeed, he did come to
the river where it was shallow and would be an easy forge.
He hadn't been paying as much attention as he ought since
coming away grumbling to himself about the woman's
refusal to help any more than give a vague set of directions.
His distraction had left Rachael precariously perched atop
the saddle. She was too weak to hang on tightly, and as the
horse stepped into a dip in the rushing river, she tumbled
from the saddle and fell with a splash into the water.

Johnny sprang into action, releasing the reins and making a dive to grab her before she went under. He took her by
the shoulders and lifted her to his chest, as she spluttered
from the intake of river water she'd sucked in. Johnny
couldn't stop apologizing as he attempted to get her back
into the saddle with himself behind her to keep her secure.
They were both wringing wet, and with nightfall had come
chilly breezes down from the mountains.

*If she don't catch her death, more'n anything from my
not watchin' her proper, it'll be a plumb miracle. Fact is,
that's what I need right about now, a miracle.*

The horse sloshed out of the river on the other bank, and
to Johnny's surprise, the old woman had been right. Through
the trees on the bank, he could see lots of lights and hear the
sounds of a town that hadn't shuttered its windows at sunset.
He headed for the center of where he figured the most noise
was coming from. There before him sprang up a lively community of mixed adobes and wooden false fronts. Mostly
the singing and music came from the open doors of several

saloons, but his quest to find a doctor was his priority. Suddenly, a man crashed through the glass window of a saloon and landed on the boardwalk. He cursed, struggled to right himself, and staggered back inside, pulling a revolver as he went, only to find himself right back where he started from a couple seconds earlier. Only this time he arrived with a bullet in the chest. Lying in a spreading pool of crimson, he groaned and fell silent as Johnny looked on in shock. A few people drifted through the swinging doors, saw that the man was no longer in need of help, and disappeared back inside, where the revelry once again kicked into high gear.

"I'm goin' to have to leave you for a moment, Rachael. I'm goin' inside to see if I can find out where a doctor lives. Please don't move. Okay?"

"Uh-huh" was all Rachael could manage in the way of a response. Johnny had no idea whether she had heard and understood him or not, but he had no choice. He tied the reins to a rail and bounded up the three steps to the saloon. When he pushed inside, he was nearly knocked down by the smoke and the sickening smells of beer and whiskey that confronted him. Shouts and hoots accompanied the prancing about of scantily clad females. More whores than he knew existed displayed bosoms spilling out of scoopneck dresses to the delight of all. Girls of all descriptions, sizes, and shapes went from cowboy to miner to merchant in order to secure a paid trip upstairs or to a crib out back for an evening's pleasure.

Johnny approached the barkeep, who busily refilled glasses for a line of cowboys along the bar. When the barkeep asked him what he wanted, Johnny asked where he could find a doctor. The noise was daunting, and he had to strain to hear the answer. Seeing that Johnny couldn't understand him, the bartender pointed to a man in a black coat at a nearby table playing poker with three others. Johnny nodded his thanks and moved to where the man was seated.

"Sir, the barkeep says you are a doctor. Is that correct?"

The man didn't take his eyes off the hand he held.

"Uh-huh. What's your problem, son? You don't appear shot up or nothin'."

"No, sir. It's a young lady. She was attacked by a cata-mount and got pretty badly clawed up. Please, sir, we need your help somethin' awful."

The doctor tossed in a couple chips and said, "I'm in."

The hand was played before Johnny said another word, but inside he was fuming. *How can a man call himself a doctor when he'd rather play poker than help an injured lady?*

Finally, the man scooted his chair back, stood up, and straightened his jacket. "It looks like duty is callin', gents. Don't figure this squirt is goin' to let me play in peace until I have a look at what he brought to town." He motioned to Johnny to follow him outside. Rachael was still astride the mare, but just barely. She was leaning so far that Johnny had to rush to her aid in sitting up.

"Lead your horse down the street to the house with green shutters. I'll go ahead and set the oil lamps afire."

"Yessir," Johnny said, as he untied the horse and led her slowly down the street. He tied up in front of the house with shutters, the only one he saw. He helped Rachael slide off the saddle and carried her onto the porch. At the sound of his boots on the wooden steps, the door swung open and light poured out.

"Set her on the chair next to the table over there, son. And get to unwrapping those strips of bloody cloth." The doctor rolled up his sleeves and carried a pitcher and a bowl over to the table. He then fetched a handful of metal objects, each one of which appeared to the boy to be potentially lethal. Johnny saw Rachael wince at the sound of them being dropped into a metal dish.

The doctor made several distressing grunts as he raised and lowered his head to first look through the glasses that sat on the end of his nose and then go back to looking over them. He reached for a bottle of clear liquid and picked up a folded piece of white cotton cloth. He poured some liquid on the cloth, hesitated, and said, "This is likely to smart some, miss," and then he began dabbing at her exposed wounds.

It must have, because Rachael let out a muffled cry as tears rolled down her cheeks. It looked to Johnny like she might just faint at any time. The boy's frightened expression caught the eye of the doctor.

"I'm goin' to give her a spoonful of laudanum to ease the pain as I sew up the two deepest claw marks. The others will heal fine with a little attention at keeping them clean for a couple days so they can scab over. All in all, she's goin' to be fine. If you're travelin', I'd suggest you plan to stay over for a day or two so I can have another look before you leave."

"We, uh, got no money for a room, sir. Reckon we'd best be gettin' on."

"Now, son, a hasty move might cause her some grief. This kinda thing shouldn't be brushed aside so easily. I have to assume since you can't afford a room, you can't pay my bill, either. That right?" Johnny nodded. "Tell you what, I think I know a way to get you a place to sleep for a night or two."

"Thank you, sir."

The doctor left the room and was gone for several minutes. When he returned, a man with a badge accompanied him.

"There they are, Sheriff. Couple of deadbeats. I think they should rest up in your jail to teach them a lesson. What do you think?"

"Sure, Doc. I'll give them a bed and three meals a day. Just what they need to learn their lesson," the sheriff snorted. He grinned at the doctor, who returned his expression acknowledging their way on the town's dime to help folks in need. Johnny helped Rachael to her feet, and the two of them followed the sheriff to their place of residence for the next two days.

Chapter 22

Cotton had finally had an opportunity to discuss with the mayor what to do about the Burnside Gunsmith Shop now that there was apparently someone interested in keeping the business going. The mayor, always at the ready to step away from anything that remotely resembled taking responsibility, had given his blessing to whatever Cotton thought was fair.

From what little the sheriff had observed, Carp Varner seemed competent at gunsmithing. But there was something that kept eating away at him about the man, and he couldn't seem to set things straight in his mind. On the surface, Varner appeared capable and, as far as Cotton had seen, ready and willing to sit at a bench and repair and clean guns of every type the livelong day. That should have been enough for even a naturally skeptical sheriff, but somehow it wasn't. At least not until whatever niggling doubt that kept rattling around in his head was cleared up.

Cotton was shaken from his woolgathering by Jack's voice coming at just the wrong time.

"Melody is shoving me over the cliff. *I need help!*" Jack said, with a desperate growl.

"Walk away."

"Walk away? How the hell do I do that?"

"Tell her she got herself into this mess, she can get herself out."

"Yeah, Preacher, easy for you to sermonize. You don't have my problems."

"And what problems would those be?"

"If I were to walk away, I'd have no place to sleep, no free food . . ."

". . . and no whore to snuggle up next to."

"Well, uh, yeah, that, too."

"What exactly do you expect me to do about it?"

"We *got* to find Pick Wheeler and get her money back. That's the only thing that's goin' to satisfy her."

"We'll find Pick, don't worry about that. Wherever he is, Henry Coyote will find him."

"Yeah, I reckon I knew that. Sorry to be such a burr under your saddle, but . . ."

"Just make some coffee, Jack, and let's sit back and wait."

"Oh, hell, might as well," Jack said, grabbing the pot off the stove and storming out the back door to get water from the well. When he returned, he dumped some Arbuckles' in it, added a touch of chicory, and set it on the stove. He then stuffed some paper and kindling in the iron door of the stove and lit it with a lucifer.

Cotton stood up and walked to the door. The day was bright with sunshine, with but a hint of a cool breeze. *Good day to go fishing instead of flailing around with my musings and doubts.*

Cotton was standing with his hands on his hips when the old Indian came into view, carrying his rifle across his chest and sprinting down the street. The sheriff blinked a couple of times, not quite believing his eyes. *How the hell did he get back here so fast?* He had often thought Henry had powers beyond his understanding, but he was certain flying was beyond even *his* unique capabilities.

When the Apache stopped in front of the jail, Cotton motioned him inside.

"I assume you found Pick, Henry."

"Find him dead. You got coffee?"

"Almost ready. I'll get you a cup, Henry, just as soon as the water comes to a boil," Jack said as he went to reach for one of the several tin cups on top of a file cabinet, the repository for cups, boxes of cartridges, and stacks of wanted flyers. He placed empty cups in front of Cotton and Henry.

Cotton motioned Henry to take a seat.

"Where is he?"

"He off road in desert. Three bullet holes in back."

"Did you happen to find any money on him, a wad of it?" Cotton asked.

"No find anything."

"Are the other two cowboys still out?"

"No. They ride in. Go to saloon."

Cotton began rubbing his chin, obviously concerned about something, and it probably had little to do with Melody's money.

"Did you happen to spot his old shotgun?"

"No."

"Whoever shot him likely took it." Jack spoke up, as he began pouring coffee into Henry's cup.

"I 'spect you're right. But why would anyone want that old cannon? A ten-gauge isn't an easy weapon to tote around. It's heavy and it kicks like a mule. And it's rather rare, nowadays. Might be worth some money to the right person, I suppose."

"Don't see why you'd care, Cotton," Jack said.

Cotton seemed pensive as he said, "Me either. Let's drink a cup of your fine brew, Jack, and then get our butts out to look upon the recently deceased Pick Wheeler."

"I'll go tell Melody that Pick's dead. That might help get me out of the dung heap."

"No, don't do that, Jack. Let's see for ourselves what we've got before we let the whole world in on it," Cotton said. He took his gun belt off a peg and started for the door. "Oh, and bring along something to wrap the body in."

He put his hand on Henry's shoulder.

"No need to walk, this time, my friend; Jack and I'll pick up horses and a buckboard from the corral and get there the easy way. You can ride my horse and take it out to the ranch afterward, Henry. How far out of town did he get?"

"Where white man's road make two, go to side with knife."

"Uh, what exactly did he say, Cotton? I don't have my Apache ears on today."

"He said for us to go to the first fork, then follow the road to the left, toward the Apache cut. Simple, Jack. You need to learn to listen more carefully. Might learn somethin'."

Jack just grunted and gave him a frown.

A couple hours' ride later brought them to a place where the land dropped away rapidly, a spot of particular concern to stagecoach drivers whenever the rain was coming down heavily. The road washed out quickly and a heavily laden coach could easily slip off and roll for several hundred feet before reaching a level spot. Cotton pulled up as Henry pointed to an area thickly populated with brush and heavy grasses.

Climbing down from the buckboard, followed closely by Henry and Jack, Cotton clomped his way through tugging burrs and unstable slickrock and gravel. He came upon Pick's body, lying facedown, arms spread wide. The corpse had already fallen victim to a few hungry creatures. Cotton looked around, then began a slow encircling of the spot where Pick lay. He widened his circle with each pass. Finally, about fifty feet out, he called back to Jack.

"I don't see any sign of Pick's shotgun, either. Let's try

to get the buckboard down here and pick him up," Cotton
shouted. Jack nodded and sprinted back up the hill.

When they had the earthly remains of Pick Wheeler
securely wrapped in a tarp and loaded onto the back of the
buckboard, Cotton turned to Henry and said, "Henry, many
thanks for your expert help in locatin' this ol' rascal. You
go ahead, take my horse, and return to the ranch. Tell
Emily I'll borrow Jack's horse and be out to see her later."
He waved as the Indian nudged the mare to a trot. He'd
disappeared before Jack could say so long.

"That man is spooky, Cotton, in case you haven't noticed,"
Jack said, as he climbed up beside the sheriff.

"Uh-huh."

"I'm not quite sure how to break the news to Melody
about Pick bein' dead, and also about there bein' not a red
cent to be found. You got any idea how I'm goin' to survive
this?" Jack asked.

"Buy a ticket on the next stage to Albuquerque."

"Uh, yeah, thanks for your help."

Cotton just got a great big grin on his face.

Chapter 23

———◆———

Jack steered the buckboard close to the undertaker's front door so as to make unloading Pick's body easier. He then hopped down and told the sheriff he'd take care of any particulars involved in putting the old weasel in the ground proper. He also passed on the sheriff's request that the undertaker remember to take the bullets out of the body and save them. The undertaker acknowledged the request and set to work. Cotton said he appreciated Jack's taking charge and rode on to the livery. After dismounting, he led the horse inside. He told the kid who regularly mucked out the stalls for the owner, "Don't bother to give her a brush down. I'll be back in about an hour to ride out again."

After leaving the livery, but before he could get all the way inside the jail door, he heard his name being called.

"Sheriff, you got a minute to chat?" It was Carp Varner, and he was hurrying to get there before the sheriff shut the door.

"Uh, sure, Mr. Varner. C'mon in, sit a spell. What's on your mind?"

"Well, I hadn't heard how it went with the mayor. If I'm goin' to be stayin' awhile, I'd like to get a sign up to replace the one Burnside's got there. Folks ought to know there's a new gunsmith in town."

Cotton took off his Stetson and began scratching his head. He looked pensive. He hadn't planned on talking to Varner further until he'd made up his own mind about the man. His uncertainty was palpable. Varner picked up on it.

"Course, if you don't want me, I'll just gather my mea-ger belongin's and sashay on outta town," Carp said.

"Oh, it ain't that I don't want you, Mr. Varner, it's the simple fact that there are a few legal, uh, matters that must be cleared up first, like unpaid bills and the like. It's not as easy as simply turnin' the business over to somebody else. I'm sure you can understand. It has also somehow fallen to me to make sure there won't be any claims comin' from relatives we haven't yet been able to contact. That's the whole of it."

"I thought I heard someone say ol' Burnside didn't have no relatives. Must be I heard wrong."

"I can't say one way or t'other. Fact is I'm goin' to have to search through all the records in the clerk's office and see what, if anything, I can scare up. I've been a little busy, what with havin' to go out in the desert and haul back a corpse and all. I'm sure I can get to it in a couple days, however. If, that is, you can wait that long."

"Uh, you say you found a corpse in the desert?"

"That's right. Pick Wheeler, the miner."

"Did you locate all that money the old bastard stole?"

"Uh, who told you there was money involved?"

"Why that purty little workin' gal over at the saloon, Melody, has been shoutin' it from the rooftops. Got her petticoats in a real whirlwind, she has."

Varner's initial comment had piqued Cotton's interest, but after hearing the man's explanation as to his knowledge in the matter, he was convinced of its logic. Nobody knew of Melody's propensity for shooting her mouth off better than Cotton Burke.

"Yeah, well that's for sure. Listen, Mr. Varner, I promise I shall be through with examining the clerk's records by Thursday. Then I can give you an answer. Is that fair?"

"More'n fair, Sheriff, more'n fair." He tipped his hat to the sheriff and sauntered out the door, whistling.

I appreciate your understanding, my impatient friend; I surely do.

Besides spending valuable time having caustic thoughts about Varner, Cotton decided it might be a good idea to find out what details of her deal with Pick Melody had blabbed. On his way over to the saloon, he met Jack in the middle of the street.

"The undertaker has Pick and we're shut of him and all the trouble he brought to town."

"Unfortunately, that's not quite all of it. I need to talk to Melody. I'm glad you're here so you can kinda come between us if needs be."

"That'll be fine with me as long as I can do it with a glass of brandy in my hand."

"Don't see why not."

"Melody, Cotton's downstairs and he needs to ask you some questions."

"Did the two of you find Pick Wheeler?"

"Yep, we did indeed."

"Wonderful. I suspect the sheriff would like to hand over my money personally, just so he's certain it got to its rightful owner." She pulled a long satin dress over her head and began wriggling one way and the other to get everything in its place. She stood in front of the mirror, turning slightly from side to side, just to make sure she was gorgeous from every possible angle. Jack whistled to make sure she got the point and the proper affirmation. He hated to tell her what Cotton's real reason for wanting to talk to her was, and he'd decided that letting things take their course would work out better for him. He'd already had to spend the last two nights sleeping in the jail because of Melody's wrath.

"I'm, uh, not real sure what the subject is, but I'm sure it'll be damned important to solving the, er, problem," Jack said, grinning without his usual sincerity.

"Good. Let's go," she said, sweeping by him in a flurry of skirts, ribbons, and sweet-smelling perfume. When they reached the bottom of the curving staircase, Melody stopped and looked around. "I don't see him. Where is he?"

Arlo saw Melody's questioning glances, picked up on what it was she wanted, and nodded his head toward the back room. Jack opened the door, allowing Melody to push through. Cotton was staring out the back window.

"So, I hear you've found that busted up old varmint, Sheriff. Where is he? I can't wait to get my hands on him. Where's my money?"

Cotton held up both hands. "Whoa, Melody. You're askin' for things I don't have to give you. I came to get some answers, that's all."

"What! Answers to what? Where are you hiding the old coot?"

"He's down at the undertakers if you just have a powerful hankerin' to see him, but I'd advise against it. He's not in the best of shape right now, flesh torn from his arms, eyes plucked out of their sockets, and three big holes in his back. I don't suppose you know anything about how he came to such an ignominious end, would you?"

"He-he's dead?"

"Colder'n a January frostbite."

"Bu-but what about my money?"

"We searched everywhere for it, but came up empty-handed. Sorry. Right now, I'm needin' to know how much the public knows about what Pick did to you and how he managed to pull it off. Suppose you tell me who all you told about the deal for the silver mine. It could lead us to a killer and the only way to find your money."

Melody's face flushed, and the obviousness of Cotton's suggestion that she might have played a part in Pick's death became abundantly clear. And it embarrassed her. She drew a deep breath, one which pushed her breasts up, showing her most obvious assets above the scoop-necked dress.

"I don't remember. I, uh, might have told a couple folks about, uh, my buying the mine."

"And when you found out you'd been swindled, did you express that with your usual calm demeanor?"

"What the hell does *that* mean?" Melody's eyes flared with her wrath.

"It means did you shoot your loud mouth off like you usually do?" Cotton glared at her, exchanging fire with fire.

Melody could no longer hold her rage back. She exploded in a flurry of expletives that would have made a stone-cold killer blush. And Cotton made it worse by just breaking into a gratuitous grin. She turned and stormed back upstairs. Jack could only blink.

"That seems to have gotten you the information you wanted, Cotton," Jack said, with all the cynicism he could muster.

"No less'n I figured," Cotton said. He gave Arlo a salute as he left the saloon.

Chapter 24

Johnny and Rachael were sitting on a long bench on the porch in front of the jail. The Las Cruces sheriff peeked out and said, "You two doin' all right?"

"We sure are, Sheriff, thanks to your kindness," Johnny said, with Rachael nodding her agreement.

"Doc says you should be able to travel by tomorrow. Where do you figure on headin'?"

"Ain't given it much thought. I've been so anxious about Rachael's comin' near to death, I hadn't figured out what our next move oughta be." He looked over at Rachael and saw nothing but unanswered questions as well.

"I wouldn't doubt but what a nice young couple like you could find employment right here in Las Cruces. Good little town. Peaceable, too. Well, it was until that feller what came though two weeks ago, obviously lookin' for trouble, and upset the applecart."

"What kinda trouble, Sheriff?" Johnny asked, with a curious frown.

"The worst kind. Pure visciousness. Clubbed a man senseless for bumping into him."

"That's terrible. Don't seem a little bump would push a man to do no beatin'."

"That's the way I saw it, too. The man tore outta town with his tail feathers ablaze. I got up a posse, but nothin' come of it. Lost his trail 'bout fifteen miles west of here. Looked like he might be headed for Silver City, but when I telegraphed the sheriff over there, he said he hadn't seen any such individual. Said he'd let me know if he did, though."

"So what did this feller look like?" Johnny asked, his curiosity piqued by the sheriff's story.

"Tall, rangy man with a black duster, flat-brimmed hat, carryin' one of them Smith & Wesson Schofields. Wore a red scarf. Seemed a bit short on patience."

"Didn't nobody get a name?" Johnny's eyes narrowed at the vague description.

"Well, now that you remind me, some of those nearby when our citizen was struck by this feller said it appeared they had words before Mr. Black Duster drew his gun and beat the man with the barrel."

"But nobody heard anything?"

"One lady said the man was sayin' somethin' about a fish just before his eyes jus' rolled back in his head and he went unconscious."

"A fish?"

"Yep. Didn't say nothin' after that."

Johnny's jaw tightened and he began to chew his lower lip. He looked up from beneath a serious scowl.

"Could the man have said, 'Carp'?"

"Why, er, yes. I do believe that's what the lady said. How'd you know that?"

"'Cause that's the man I'm set on killin' myself."

"But you can't leave me here all by myself, Johnny. What would I do without you?" Rachael said. "Please, don't go."

"I have to. Don't you see, Rachael, that's the man that murdered a whole town, small as it was? Those folks didn't deserve to die the awful way they did. But, I tell you, Carp Varner don't deserve to *live* neither."

"The way the sheriff described that Carp Varner, it *for sure* is the same man."

"Well, uh, yeah, I'm sure it was. I *was* on his trail when I come upon you and your cabin."

"Then, after what he did to me, don't I have just as much right to seek vengeance as you do?"

"I, well, I suppose you do, but . . ."

"But nothin'. I'm comin' with you and that's that." Rachael took a firm stance with both feet apart and her arms crossed. She stuck her chin out like she was daring him to say no.

He was trying to hold his ground and not give an inch on his decision to go it alone. But what she'd said did, in a strange way, make sense. Besides, if she could see Varner, and identify him as a thief, then his case against the man would be even stronger. *Maybe it would be best if she came along. Besides, I sure have gotten used to havin' her company.* His expression softened. She knew she had won him over even before he spoke.

"Oh, shucks, all right. We'll go together. But you got to promise you'll not get in the way when I fix my sights on him. Promise?" He wasn't prepared for her answer.

She threw her arms around him and planted a kiss squarely on his quivering mouth.

"Thank you, Johnny, thank you, thank you!" she said as she pulled away. She was all smiles as she scurried back inside the jail.

"Wh-where're you goin'?" he said, puzzled by her sudden retreat. He had been silently hoping she'd want to shower him with even *more* thanks.

"I'm goin' to gather up our belongin's so we can be on our way."

"The doctor said you could travel tomorrow, not today. He wants one more look at your arm to make sure it hasn't begun to fester. Please. There'll be time to find Varner, but we can't travel if you start havin' problems with them stitches or go to bleedin'." Johnny had taken on a decidedly worried demeanor. Now that he'd given his word she could go, he knew he'd have to rein her in. Her enthusiasm for catching the murderous varmint that burned his town seemed to have grown even stronger than his. He didn't look forward to facing a professional gunslinger with nothing more than his one six-shooter, and his doubts were growing stronger now that he was faced with the prospect that Rachael could maybe get hurt in the process. He wasn't sure but what his acquiescence to her going along had been a little hasty. He sure liked that kiss, but was it enough to ward off these new doubts?

"Oh, all right. We can wait. But I'm feelin' much better since the doctor fixed my arm. I'll bet even you can tell that, can't you?" Rachael asked, teasing him. She threw him a look that nearly melted his resolve. Whatever resolve he had left, anyway.

"Yeah, I agree you are much more chipper than when we wandered in here. But that don't make being hasty a good idea. We're stayin' until the doc says you can go. And that's final."

She slowly sashayed up to him and looked up with big, brown, innocent eyes. "Whatever you say, Johnny." She took his arm and began tugging him along.

"Wh-where are we goin'?"

"I thought a nice walk would do us both good. We can look in all the windows and maybe even stop in for a sarsaparilla, if, that is, you have enough money."

"I, uh, reckon I got enough left for one," he said, his voice barely above a squeak.

Chapter 25

Melody, damned if that temper isn't goin' to get you even more problems. It don't make no difference how you feel about Cotton; he's askin' the right questions, and without your cooperation, you could well never see a penny of your money back. And the sooner you get off your high horse, the sooner we can get to findin' whoever stole it from Pick after killin' him," Jack said, after shutting the door to her bedroom. She was sitting with her arms crossed on the edge of the bed, her face so red with anger he thought she might combust. Jack figured he could wait her out. Although, at the moment, she didn't seem inclined to give him the time of day. Hearing no response, he turned and stormed out the door, letting it slam behind him. "*Bitch!*" he muttered to himself as he went down the stairs, taking them three at a time.

"I heard that!" she screamed after him.

Before going back to the jail, Jack figured just one brandy would help settle his nerves. His situation with Melody hadn't improved one bit, and now Cotton was probably ready to give up on helping get Melody's money back. If that were the case, Jack knew damned well he'd be the big loser in the whole mess. He downed the brandy and told Arlo to pour another. He needed something strong enough to bolster his courage before facing the sheriff. When he did finally get to the jail, Cotton was just stepping out the door. Jack was a tad wobbly by then, so he grabbed for the porch post.

"Jack, I see you've been leanin' on ol' Mr. Brandy to help with your woman problem. I suspect I would have done the same thing in your shoes. Go inside and sleep it off. I'm going out to the Wagner ranch to see Emily. I need the gentle hand of a female that *isn't* insane. I'll be back in the mornin' to return your horse."

That wasn't exactly what Jack had hoped to hear from the sheriff, but it would do. He gave Cotton a nod and went inside to occupy one of the cots in a jail cell. First, he sat on the edge of the cot in a liquor-induced haze, contemplating his next move with Melody. His choices were limited. He was fully aware that if prompted, Cotton would eagerly chew him out for even keeping company with a whore. But his life wasn't Cotton's life. In matters of the heart, they were totally different.

He eased back with his hands behind his head. He stared at the ceiling. No ideas were forthcoming. Then, because of nothing he could figure, his thoughts turned to Pick Wheeler's dead body lying in the dirt. For some reason, he began attempting to piece together the old miner's last moments. He envisioned Pick riding one mule and leading the other. He would have had his hands full of reins and lead rope. Even if he did carry a smoke wagon, he would have had little time to use it if someone came up on him suddenly. But he didn't have a revolver. Never had been known to even own one. The only weapon he had was that old ten-gauge shotgun. And he kept that strapped down to the burro's pack.

Suddenly Jack sat straight up. *Where was the shotgun? Cotton said he looked around for it and saw nothing. Henry said he hadn't seen any evidence of anything lying around the brush. No money. And for damned sure, no shotgun. Since it was obvious that whoever killed Pick also took his shotgun, we need a way to smoke the varmint out. What if we posted a reward? If someone comes in with it expectin' to make a few extra dollars, it'd likely be the one who dusted the old goat. Just like settin' a mousetrap.* At the moment his mind was too muddled to know whether Cotton would go for the reward part, but he knew he had to get folks to keep a lookout.

He lay back, satisfied that he'd come up with a logical plan, and was soon asleep.

Cotton rode into the yard in front of the Wagner ranch house right at sundown. Emily came out wiping her hands on her apron. She smiled at him with the warmth of an expectant wife, waiting for her man to come home from a hard day on the range. Except that she and Cotton weren't married, and he had let it be known that riding the range with a bunch of dirty, smelly cattle was the last thing he wanted out of life.

"Howdy, stranger. Just passin' through?" she said.

"Nope. Thought maybe I'd stay overnight while a certain lovely lady beguiles me with her most recent adventures."

"Well, step down off of that saddle and we'll see if we can't come up with an adventure or two that you won't soon forget." Her smile aroused a passion in him that only it could.

"Don't mind if I do. Uh, what's that I smell comin' from the open window?"

"Are you talking about the apple pie or the fresh bread? Coffee? Sizzling steak?"

"I reckon all of 'em," he said. "Hard to separate all them

great smells when the only thing to hit a man's stomach since early this mornin' was a hunk of gristle masquradin' as beef."

"Poor soul. You better come up here and give me a kiss or there won't be anything left in there. The men are already at the table."

He leapt off the mare and wrapped the reins around a rail just in time to catch her before she could slip inside the door, and he left her giggling and trying to keep from tripping on the sill.

After dinner, Emily and Cotton sat on the couch in the living room. He had a cup of coffee in his hand, and she was studying a piece of needlepoint she'd been working on. It was a depiction of the mountains behind her ranch house, the very thing she saw each morning as she stood at the back window while the coffee was brewing. Orange and yellow threads intermingled with dark blues and deep greens depicting the way the sun hit the peaks early of a morning. She was humming softly. He was fidgeting.

Without looking up, she said, "Cotton, what's got you tied in a knot?"

"You can tell, huh?"

"Oh, yeah. I can tell when you're upset, worried, bothered, angry and . . ."

"I'm not surprised. I never have been real good at hiding my feelin's, have I?"

"Nope."

"Then how come it took so long for you to know I love you?"

"I knew the first time we met. Of course, Otis was still alive then, and any such revelation would have been totally improper. But I knew, just the same."

"Well, I'll be damned. Women sure are a puzzlement." He scratched his head and then finger-combed his hair back in place.

She smiled and put the needlepoint in her lap. She stood up, smoothed her skirt, and placed the wooden hoop that contained her artistic endeavor on a table. She motioned for Cotton.

"I'm very, very tired. It's been a long day. So I'm going to bed. If you'd like, you may come tuck me in," she said teasingly.

"Would it be proper?" he said.

"Not on your life."

"Then I'm your man," he said, as he arose from his plush couch and strode across the room to take her in his arms and escort her into the bedroom.

At breakfast, Emily was humming to herself as she scurried around pouring coffee for the hands and slicing strips of bacon for frying. She looked over at Cotton, who was staring out the window, lost in a daze.

"My, you *are* the pensive one this morning, Cotton."

"Not real sure what that means, but I'll admit I have come upon a bit of a puzzlement."

"Am I going to have to drag it out of you?"

"Well, I guess you could say I have a couple things on my mind that don't seem to add up no matter which way I look at them. The first, of course, is finding whoever murdered ol' Pick Wheeler and stole the money he chiseled Melody Wakefield out of. And then there's this new feller in town wantin' to take over the gunsmithin' business from the recently deceased Mr. Burnside. Trouble is, while we sorely need a gunsmith, I've got a passel of reservations about this Carp Varner. And so far, I've not gotten very far with solvin' either problem."

"You've always had a good head for knowing if a soul is living in the wrong column of right and wrong. You read a man better'n anyone I know. As for who killed a crook, maybe that's not as important right now."

"Hmm. You could be right. But I can't seem to make up

my mind whether Varner is suspicious or if it's just that he rubs me a tad raw."

"You've known men like that before. How'd it all turn out when you compare it to what you felt on first impression?"

"I get your drift. I'll cogitate on it." He gulped the last of his coffee and left.

Chapter 26

The doctor in Las Cruces had unwrapped Rachael's bandages and was looking carefully at how well her mountain lion wounds were healing. She closely watched his eyes for any hint of a problem. He unscrewed the lid on a small glass jar, stuck two fingers inside, and began rubbing a dark salve over the stitches of the one wound that was the most severe. He then wrapped new bandages around her arm. He sat back with a smile. Rachael took that to mean good news.

"Well, Doctor, does it look like I'm well enough to travel some?" she asked.

"I'd take it easy for a few more days, but I suppose if you must go, then you must. I'll send along some of this salve for you to administer every day. Then, I think it would be wise to keep the wounds covered with bandages, mostly to keep dirt and dust out. It don't appear there's much danger of any festering now."

Rachael let out a deep sigh. "That's very good news, sir. Thank you so much."

"You were lucky. Mostly because that young man out there cared enough to find proper help. You should thank him, too." The doctor raised an eyebrow and looked over the glasses that barely hung on the tip of his nose.

"Doctor, I, uh, don't know how we'll repay you. At the moment, we're, uh, sort of broke."

"While you been laid up, Johnny has paid off your bill by doing chores for me. He's been hard at work chopping wood, running errands, washing my utensils, and many other odds and ends that needed attending to. He's been a blessing to an old man. We're more than square. Don't you worry none, young lady. I'll tell you another thing, that boy is an honorable young man. You could do a heap worse than hitch your wagon to his destiny."

Rachael blushed at his words. She hung her head. "We're just, uh, friends. Maybe . . ."

"I understand, young lady. But no one ever knows what the future holds." He gave her a fatherly smile. "Now, go along with you. I've patients to visit."

Rachael thanked him once more and wrapped her shawl around her shoulders. She left to find Johnny and give him the good news. She found him standing in the shade of a building, brushing their horse.

"Johnny, the doctor says things are going well. He figures we can travel whenever we wish."

"Yeah, I know. He told me to expect good news. I'm thankful you came through that terrible experience all right. I was scared to death for a while. I'll not let you out of my sight from now on. You can darn well count on it."

"Oh, Johnny, what happened wasn't your fault. It coulda happened no matter what. I'm not made of porcelain, you know. Don't need any special tendin' to."

"Uh-huh. Well, I'm goin' to just the same."

When she walked toward him, Johnny fidgeted with the

bridle, taking far more time than necessary to get the horse ready to travel. Rachael just stood by patiently. He was having a serious problem with taking her along, possibly putting her in even more danger than a run-in with a mountain lion. But he had sort of promised, hadn't he? He'd grown more than fond of her—her smile, the way her hair shone in the sun, the way she walked, straight and proud—everything about her. She wasn't afraid of anything, and that might have been what bothered him the most. He was well aware of the kind of man Carp Varner was and how the man placed no value on the life of another human being. He was a vicious animal, plain and simple. Now that Rachael was well on her way to being healed from her wounds, Johnny was forced to find some excuse to leave her behind, to keep her safe, yet he'd seen no way to do that without destroying all they'd meant to each other.

When he'd first come upon her lying on the floor of that dismal cabin, he'd felt pity. He knew from his upbringing that he could never walk away and leave someone in despair. He was forced by a well-taught conscience to help. But as her strength returned and he'd seen her blossom just by his being around, his feelings had changed. He didn't fully understand any of it, but now he felt so strongly that she must be kept safe—at any cost—he was unsure how to go about telling her she couldn't go with him. He started to speak several times, but each time the words caught in his throat and he stopped without saying a thing.

"I can tell what's goin' through your mind, Johnny Monk, and it won't work," she said, arms crossed, tapping her foot, with an impatient set to her jaw.

"Wh-what are you talkin' about, Rachael? I'm not thinkin' anything."

"You're thinkin' of a way to tell me you're goin' but I'm stayin'. That's what's goin' on in your head, isn't it?"

"Uh, why, of course not. What's put such a thought in your pretty head?"

"Flattery isn't goin' to make things better, you know.

It's about time you understood that I'm not a child who needs to be pampered and scolded from time to time just to keep her out of trouble. I'm a full-growed woman and I can make my own decisions."

"Well of course you can. Whoever said different?" Johnny swallowed hard. *How could she have possibly known what was going on in my head? Reckon I better make sure whatever I do get to thinkin' on don't rile her none.*

"I'd certainly be, uh, pleased to entertain whatever your thoughts are on the matter, Rachael. You know that. I just want to look out for your welfare."

"My welfare is to be best served by keepin' you company on whatever journey you're set on. So, whatever you're plannin' had better include me, Johnny Monk. I'm goin' with you, no matter what. Do you understand?" Her face was getting redder by the second. Her fists were so tightly clenched, her knuckles were turning white.

Johnny took a step backward with both hands in the air, fully prepared to surrender in case she was thinking of using something more dangerous than just words, something like that old broken ax handle resting only inches from her reach.

He was clearly nervous. He knew she could tell by his hesitation to answer her that he was struggling to find a solution, and thus far failing. He'd never known such a strong-willed female; in fact, he'd never really been around any female except his mother and the lady of the evening at the saloon where he worked cleaning up after it closed. She didn't count, he figured, since her job was to bow to a man's will, unless, of course, he couldn't come up with the wherewithal to afford her company.

But here he was, facing the only girl he'd ever really gotten to know, and he was in a decidedly tough situation. He was either going to have to acquiesce to her demands or hightail it out of town as soon as he could. That thought was wallowing around in his head when an important realization came: *the horse didn't belong to him.* By rights, it was *her* horse. The man posing as her father owned it, and when he died it came to her legally as his only kin. Legally, that is, as far as the rest of the world knew. So it appeared that unless he could bring himself to do something as dastardly as to steal a horse from a woman and leave her stranded in the middle of nowhere, he was committed to doing the right thing. Although he was having a devil of a time convincing himself that taking her on a dangerous mission *was* the right thing to do. Decision time had come. He nodded.

"I reckon there'd be worse things that could happen to a man than to be travelin' with a beautiful young lady. We'll start out at first light tomorrow mornin', if that's all right with you." His eyebrows shot up in anticipation of her affirming answer. What he got, however, was anything but expected.

Rachael surprised him by running forward, grabbing him around the neck, and starting to plant kisses all over his face—on his lips, cheeks, eyes, and anywhere else she could.

"Thank you, Johnny. You'll not regret takin' me, I promise," she said still clinging tightly to his neck.

As she giggled with happiness, Johnny thought to himself, *Maybe this will work out all right, after all.*

Chapter 27

Stage just dropped off the mail at the hotel, Cotton. Here's one for you. I sure wish they'd hurry up and get that post office built like they been promisin' for a month of Sundays. We're gettin' big enough for one," Jack said, strolling into the jail.

Cotton took the envelope, turned it over to see who it was from, then tore one end off and blew into it to hold it open. He fished out the letter with his thumb and forefinger, unfolded it, and began to read. Silently. After his eyes had traveled the length of the missive three or four times, Jack's patience had run out.

"Well, what's it say? You come into a fortune from a deceased uncle back East or something?"

"No, nothing like that. But it is a surprise of sorts, and it seems those letters I sent out have paid off. Here we were in the dark about any Burnside kin, and now there's the fellow we found in Burnside's papers claimin' to be his nephew. And I'll bet you can't guess what he wants."

"Probably thinks he's got a gunsmithin' business comin' to him. Am I on the right scent?"

"You got 'er sniffed out, pard."

"I figure since you haven't officially turned it over to Varner, you can always backtrack."

"First, I'd better make certain this man *is* Burnside's legal heir."

"How do you figure on doin' that?"

"I'm goin' to send him a telegraph message to ask him to come to Apache Springs and bring everything he can to prove he is who he says he is."

"What if he can't prove such a thing?"

"He'll have to scout out another line of work. Besides, what if he doesn't know a damned thing about bein' a gunsmith? We can't afford to have some inexperienced fool takin' folks' guns apart and screwin' things up, can we?"

Jack scratched his head. "I see what you're drivin' at, but I still don't . . ."

"You're goin' to have to trust me, Jack."

"I guess you're right."

"Good, that's settled. Now, I been thinkin' on Melody's money and Pick gettin' himself shot to death. Even if we should come across a wad of greenbacks, there's no way to prove it's Melody's. The only link I see is Pick's old ten-gauge."

"I been thinkin' on that very thing myself, Cotton."

"That shotgun was surely taken by the man or men who shot Pick. If we find that gun, we got at least a trail to follow."

"Yeah, I got to agree. But where do we start lookin'?"

"First, I want you to start askin' around town to all the merchants—and that includes Melody's saloon—for folks to keep an eye out for anyone spending lots of cash. Especially those who aren't known to have been flush before. And you can tell 'em to keep an eye out for that blunderbuss, too."

"I already came to the same conclusion. Got to thinkin' offerin' a small reward for anyone who's seen it might be a good idea, too," Jack said. "Okay if I get a few posters printed?"

"Go ahead. Start at one end of town and stop at every store and shop all the way to the other end."

"Sounds like thirsty work. Mind if I fortify myself with a quick brandy?"

"Suit yourself. A man should always be at his best." Cotton gave him a cynical grin along with one raised eyebrow.

Jack returned the favor with a salute and left quickly. He headed straight for the saloon.

"Get me a brandy, will you, Arlo?" Jack asked the bartender. "Melody around?"

"I saw her about an hour ago. She said she was going to the gunsmith's shop."

"Why would she do that?"

"Said something about that peashooter she carries around not having the firepower she figured she needed."

"What the hell does she need firepower for?"

Arlo nervously continued wiping the polished surface, mopping up spills.

"I, uh, don't know. All I can figure is she's scared of something."

"Like what?"

"Don't have any idea. But I know she's real shook up about something, especially after Pick Wheeler took her for a wad. Maybe she figures someone else might try takin' advantage."

"When did you say she left?" Jack swigged his shot of brandy.

"An hour or so. Something like that."

"Thanks, Arlo. I think I'll wander down to our friendly gunsmith and make sure she's not trying to buy dynamite."

Arlo snorted at the thought. He continued his cleanup as Jack slipped out the batwings.

* * *

When Jack got to the gunsmith's, he peeked in through
windows so dusty he had to wipe a spot to even see if anyone was inside. He didn't see Melody. He opened the door
and went inside. He called out.

"Mr. Varner, it's Deputy Stump. You here?"

He listened for a moment, then began scanning the
place. He first noticed a glass case that had been left open,
where new handguns were usually kept, at least they had
been when Burnside was still alive. On the velvet lining he
could make out a distinct impression, that of a revolver. A
much larger revolver than Melody had ever carried before.
That's when he heard the shot. It came from out back. He
raced to the back of the store and opened the door. There he
saw Melody and Carp Varner standing very close together.
In fact, Carp had one arm around her shoulder and the
other hand helping her hold up a .45-caliber Smith & Wesson six-shooter. Smoke was trickling skyward from the
barrel.

"I don't mean to interrupt such a cozy gathering, but
there's an ordinance in town that prohibits the discharge of
a firearm within the town limits," Jack said, walking
toward them. "What's the idea?"

"Oh, sorry, Deputy, I didn't know of such a rule. We're
done here anyway."

"What're you doin', Melody?"

"I'm buying a new gun. I don't feel that safe anymore.
Figured I ought to be prepared, just in case. Especially
since it doesn't seem the law hereabouts can protect its
citizens." She glared at Jack like he was some inept dolt.

"Melody, this doesn't make any sense. Who haven't we
protected?"

"Your being a deputy didn't keep Pick Wheeler from
robbing me, did it?"

"Even after I advised against it, you made your deal
with him. Then, Pick left town. He was no longer in our

jurisdiction. There was nothin' we could have done to prevent him gettin' robbed and killed, either."

"And all *my* money being stolen!" she blurted out, spun around, and stomped off.

Varner called after her. "Miss Melody, shall I bring the shooter to your establishment, later?"

"Whenever you've a mind to, Mr. Varner," she hollered back, hiking up her long skirt to step onto the boardwalk. "I'll even buy you a drink."

"Thank you, ma'am," Varner called out, then tipped his hat to Jack and went back inside his shop, closing the door behind him.

Jack followed Melody out front and was left standing there, alone, fuming. His eyes followed her down the street. If looks could kill, Melody Wakefield would have been dropped on the spot.

Chapter 28

———— ❖ ————

As Jack returned to the jail, Cotton could see he was about to explode. The deputy came storming in, went straight for the first cell, lay down, and rolled over toward the wall. Cotton had known Memphis Jack long enough to see the signs of an anger so intense that any attempt to mollify the situation could get a man shot. He decided to keep quiet and let things settle out. He continued reading the week-old newspaper he'd been perusing when Jack came in. Since asking Jack what the problem was seemed out of the question, he decided to wander over to the saloon and listen in on any conversations that might touch on the subject. Clearly, whatever it was that had his deputy so steamed, Melody had played a part. And knowing Melody, as Cotton did, it was likely a huge part.

He'd no sooner entered through the batwings than he heard Melody shouting orders down to Arlo, the barkeep. "Bring me up a couple bottles of that Kentucky Bourbon and send Mr. Varner upstairs when he gets here!" She slammed the door to her bedroom.

Looks like Mr. Varner has made himself a friend . . . and an enemy. Not sure I'd want to be in his shoes in either instance.

When Arlo came over to the sheriff's table and asked if he wanted anything, Cotton said he'd have a beer. There were almost no customers at that time of day, so when Arlo brought the glass of beer, he pulled out a chair and sat down.

Cotton had chosen a table along one side of the room. He almost always sat alone, not being one to engage in conversations with strangers, especially when one of them might someday turn out to be confrontational when drunk. Cotton thanked the barkeep and took a sip.

"What was that all about?" Cotton asked.

"Don't know for sure, but I think Miss Melody is pretty upset with Jack because of the loss of her money."

"How does she figure Jack could have done anything to prevent it? After all, even though he tried, he couldn't stop her from making a foolish investment in a worthless mine."

"I know. One minute she can be sweet as sugar, and the next minute, a she-cougar defending her cubs couldn't compare to that lady," Arlo said, looking down at the floor. He was obviously shy talking about Melody behind her back.

"I'm not clear on why she'd take up with Carp Varner, though. He hasn't been here long enough to get to know her."

"First day he wandered in here, covered in trail dust and thirsty as a desert rat, he saw her prance through in one of her fanciest dresses and he said to me he had every intention of bedding her. I told him that'd be the stupidest thing he ever did. I figured that'd be the end of that, but he swore to me he'd make good his desires sure as there's fires in hell."

"Sounds like he may get his wish."

"Hard to say. I never figured she'd turn on Jack. And certainly not over something that wasn't his fault. She's a puzzle, all right." Arlo scooted his chair back as a couple cowboys wandered in. "Time to get to work. See you later, Sheriff."

Cotton held up his glass to the barkeep, then downed the contents in one long swallow. Having set the glass on the table, he slowly walked to the door and, stopping to glance up to Melody's bedroom, turned and left. When he started off the boardwalk, he saw Varner coming toward him with a big grin on his face.

"Business must be looking up, Mr. Varner, at least judging by the look on your face."

"You noticed, huh? Yep, Sheriff, things are giving every indication of getting even better minute by minute now." Varner didn't stop to chat but breezed by, straight up the steps and into the saloon like a man on a serious mission. Cotton noticed he carried a Colt .45 stuck in the front of his gun belt. He seemed unusually well armed.

I wonder what that Colt is for. Shaking his head, he turned and walked the dusty street toward the telegraph office. *Probably something quite innocent. Right now, I reckon it's time I contact Burnside's nephew, if Burnside really did have a nephew.*

"Thank you, Johnny," Rachael whispered. She sat behind him with her arms wrapped around him so tightly he couldn't have escaped if he'd wanted to. "Thank you for letting me come with you."

"Huh?" Johnny said, the wind whipping around them and making it hard to hear. The chattering sounds of birds usually filled the air, but today they were strangely silent, their cheery calls blown to the four corners of the earth by mini tornadoes swirling across the sands.

"I said, thank you for bringing me." She hugged him tighter.

"Oh."

The wind seemed to be picking up, and within minutes

dark clouds started appearing over the mountains to the west. That wasn't something he looked forward to. A late summer storm often blew up winds carrying sands that could strip the paint off a building, or sudden showers with their attendant flash floods. He sniffed the air. It was there. You couldn't miss it. All the signs of a monster storm were building. The breeze picked up more and brought with it the unmistakable smell of rain.

This one looks to be about to drown us. We better get to cover. But where? There doesn't look to be anywhere that won't put us in worse danger. Time's running out. That gully washer will be on us in less than a half hour, I'd bet my britches on it.

"What is it, Johnny? You seem tense all of a sudden," she said. With her face buried in Johnny's shirt, she was protected from the dust and the smell of rain. "What's got you bothered?"

"We got to find some shelter, and fast. We're about to be visited by one of them huge summer blows."

"I don't see anything. Where?" She was now on alert also, scanning the sky and the desert from side to side. He leaned over so she could see what he'd been looking at for a while. What lay ahead was black, swirling, mountainous billows of towering storm clouds.

"Oh, my!" she said, her eyes wide. "What'll we do?"

He swung his head ninety degrees in each direction. The prospects were bleak. Few trees. Where he did see trees, they were obviously along a small creek, the last place to seek shelter when the heavens opened up and dumped an ocean's worth of water on the earth. Suddenly, he stopped and stared, squinting to sharpen the image of what he saw. Or, at least, what he thought he saw. Off to the south about a mile there was what appeared to be a cave on the side of a rock-strewn hill. It was about halfway up the incline and far enough away from where water might reach to safely ride out the storm.

"There! That looks to be a likely spot. We'll head for

that dark opening," he shouted. She could barely hear him above the increasing winds.

He kicked the mare to a run. Obviously aware of the danger herself, the horse didn't hesitate. They rode against the wind, covering their mouths and noses with kerchiefs to keep from ingesting half the desert's sand.

Johnny reined in a hundred feet from the entrance to what he'd presumed to be a cave. Between them and the entrance was too much loose rock and too many tight squeezes for him to take the horse farther. He hobbled the animal as far up from the base of the hill as he dared, took his rifle and Rachael's hand, and started up the slippery incline. Getting close enough to the opening to peer in, he was nervous about the possibility of coming upon another puma. He let go of Rachael's hand, lifted the rifle, checked that it had a cartridge loaded, and stood just outside the gaping dark hole. He raised the Springfield and fired a smoky blast into the dark hole. The blast lit up the interior, showing it going back only a few feet, too shallow to harbor any large animals. Rattlesnakes, however, were always a danger. He listened intently for any sound coming from the darkness. Fingering another cartridge, he loaded it in preparation for whatever might come next. No sounds emanated from the shallow cave, so he called to Rachael to come back. Things would be all right.

Johnny and Rachael ducked inside just as the storm broke over them.

Chapter 29

Arlo pointed at the curving staircase with a long, bony finger, directing Carp Varner to Melody's quarters. In an obvious hurry, Carp took the stairs two at a time, arriving in front of her door with the quickest of strides. He removed his hat, licked his fingers, and slicked down his hair, then knocked.

"Who is it?" came a syrupy voice from inside.

"Uh, it's me, ma'am, Carp Varner, the gunsmith."

"Why, do come in, Mr. Varner," she answered, in a voice a Southern belle would envy. "I hope you brought what I asked for."

He eased open the door, to find Melody lounging on her bed, propped up against a half dozen fat pillows. She wore a revealing gown that fell open sufficiently to display her ample pulchritude. Her white legs were crossed at the ankles, and she seemed to be fussing over what was once a long necklace, but which had now become merely a tangled pile of silver links.

"I'll just bet a gunsmith is very clever with his hands, wouldn't you agree, sir?" Melody flashed him a coy smile.

"I would indeed. Would you like for me to take a look at that mess you're fiddling with?"

"Oh, I surely would. Why don't you come sit next to me here and I'll just place the whole job in your capable hands?" Melody's voice had lost any semblance of subtlety and was now quite blatantly offering up an invitation to sample her charms. Her gown fell off one shoulder as she wriggled to one side, allowing Carp the space he might need to accomplish the task at hand.

Jack had tried unsuccessfully to take a nap, in hopes of calming his frayed nerves. His anger at Melody over her unreasonable reaction to his revelation that they'd had no luck finding her lost money had not diminished. Too frustrated by her attitude, he decided to confront her head-on. He was through trying to keep the peace by giving in to her every demand. He rolled off the bunk, pulled on his boots, strapped on his gun belt, and strode out the door. Cotton eyed him suspiciously as he passed the desk without a word.

His purposeful gait might suggest to anyone he passed on his way to the saloon that he'd firmly adopted a new attitude. He drew in a deep breath to shake off the effects of his restlessness as he barged into the saloon.

Arlo looked up and immediately broke into a wide-eyed, panicked stare, overcome by fear of what Jack might do if he found Carp Varner in *his* bed with *his* woman.

"Melody upstairs, Arlo?" Jack asked, stopping briefly at the bottom of the staircase.

"Melody? Uh, well, I . . ."

"You *do* remember Melody, don't you, Arlo? The one who pays you to dispense cheap booze and stare at deputies with dumbfounded expressions? That Melody."

"Yes, of course, I know who Melody is, uh, how about

if I go up and knock on her door and see if she's there and tell her that you'd like to see her and . . ."

"What the hell has you so spooked? I don't recall ever seeing you at such a loss for words, unless she's got some-one with her. Is that it, Arlo? She entertaining a guest?"

"I-I-I don't, uh, know, Jack. Why don't y-you let me find out? Okay?" The barkeep's nervousness had spoken vol-umes, even though he'd tried to keep from blurting out words that he knew could easily get a person killed. He didn't favor any possibility of him being that person.

His patience stretched to its limit, Jack spun around and launched up the staircase. When he got to the top, he grabbed the doorknob to Melody's room, twisted it, and burst inside. There he saw Melody lying wrapped in an embrace with Carp Varner, whose pants had somehow fallen down around his ankles. Varner was kissing her and grabbing at her breasts with lustful vigor. In less time than it would take a man to blink, Jack's Remington .44 was in his hand, cocked and pointing directly at the gunsmith's buttocks.

"You son of a bitch! You have five seconds to get your ass out of that bed and away from *my* woman. Failing that, you'll be spending the rest of your life with a serious hitch in your git-along. One . . ."

Completely caught off guard, Carp fell off the bed try-ing to gather his wits and pull his britches up. His gun belt was lying on the floor beside the bed, too far for him to make a reach for the Smith & Wesson that rested in his holster. He scrambled to pull himself together.

"Two . . ."

Carp took hold of the mule ears of one of his boots, tug-ging as hard as he could before discovering he had it on the wrong foot.

"Three . . ."

Varner scuttled toward the door. Finally, he fumbled to get a grip on a chair and pull himself to a full standing position. He still had to hold his pants closed with one hand while he limped through the open door, one boot on, the other in his empty hand. Jack scooped up Carp's gun belt and threw it at him.

"Four . . ."

"I'm gone! I'm gone!" Carp yelled over his shoulder as he started down the stairs, lost his footing, and tumbled all the way to the bottom. Fumbling to get himself together and stand, he'd barely made it through the batwings when he heard Jack's shout.

"Five!"

"What the hell do you think you're doing, Jack!" Melody screamed at him, trying without success to gather the front of her gown together.

"I'm gettin' ready to make one less whore in this town!" He pointed the Remington at her.

In a panic, she began pulling pillows all around her to create a fortress to somehow stop Jack's shot. She sat wide-eyed and shivering with fear, tears streaming down her face as she clung to anything she could find for protection. She whined pathetically, choking back a cry. Her breath had been reduced to short, sorrowful gasps.

Jack glared at her with fire in his eyes. "Reckon *your* time has come, bitch!"

"No! No, please! Jack, Jack, honey, it was all a mistake. You know how much I love you. He just came up to, uh, sell me a gun. I swear!"

"He needed to jump your near-naked body to point out the finer points of a six-shooter? What kind of a fool do you take me for?"

"He started to take advantage of me for whatever reason I cannot imagine. I tried to fight him off, but as you could see, he was much stronger than me. I just couldn't—"

"Stop it, Melody! I'm sick of your lies, your selfishness, your wildly stupid schemes."

When he turned to leave, she pleaded all the more.

"Don't leave, Jack, please. Come here and make love to me. I promise I'll never stray again. Please!" Completely naked, Melody swung her legs off the bed and got down on her knees, pleading.

Jack gave a huge sigh, reached down, and pulled her to her feet. He stared at her for a second while his anger subsided. Then he pushed her back on the pillow-strewn bed and dove on her. He couldn't get out of his clothes fast enough. The Remington clattered to the floor. They made love for the first time in a week—at a fever pitch.

Chapter 30

The next morning, as Cotton was sweeping the floor inside the jail, Jack strode in whistling for all he was worth. He went straight for the coffeepot and poured himself a cup. The sheriff watched with a wicked grin as his deputy pulled back a chair, swung his feet up on the desk, and began blowing the steam from the cup of Arbuckles'. He switched from whistling to humming once he began sipping the coffee.

"Nice to see you back, Jack. For a while I thought you might have fallen into a bottomless pit of self-pity. Glad to see that didn't happen. Uh, it didn't, did it?"

"Nope."

"The way you been actin' the past few days, I figured whatever was ailin' you had to have somethin' to do with Melody."

"Yep."

"I take it things have straightened themselves out."

"Yep."

"Good. Now we can get back to the business of keepin' the peace. You up for that?"

"Yep."

"Then the first order of business is: Did you talk to the folks hereabouts concernin' anyone seein' any sign of Pick's old shotgun?"

"Nope, not yet. But, now that you bring it up, I'm about to." Jack got up, gulped down his coffee, hiked up his gun belt, and went out the door almost as cheerfully as he'd come in.

I don't know what happened to change Jack's attitude, but I'd be in favor of more of it.

Jack went from one shop to another, sticking his head in and always asking the same question: *Have you seen that old ten-gauge shotgun that Pick Wheeler always carried, or anyone flashing a wad of bills?* By the time he got to the end of the street, covering both sides as well as the half dozen shops on a side street, he'd talked to everyone he could find. Neither hide nor hair of the old blunderbuss had been seen since Pick left town. Jack had purposefully avoided stopping by the gunsmith's shop. He didn't want to renew the confrontation with Carp Varner. Besides, he hadn't liked the man from the moment he'd first laid eyes on him, and since Melody had pulled one of her famous foolish moves in an effort to get her hands on a Colt .45 without any cost to her, except a roll in the hay, he thought it best to let sleeping dogs lie. Not that he would ever forget the man's audacious and purposeful attempt to undermine a relationship he'd been well aware of. Situations like this almost always require a reckoning at one time or another. Jack would be certain to keep his eyes open.

As he made his way along the boardwalk back toward the jail, he had no way of knowing that behind the filthy

windows of Burnside's shop stood a man with two shotgun
shells in one hand and a double-barrel scattergun in the
other. He opened the breech and slid each shell into a
chamber. He snapped the old ten-gauge shut and slid it out
of sight under the gun case.

*Poetic justice is headed your way, Deputy. And it'll
come when you least expect it.*

Cotton was buoyed by the quick response he'd gotten from
the man claiming to be Burnside's nephew. The telegram
said he'd arrive in town in one week and would be carrying
sufficient documents to substantiate his claim. He'd added
that he, too, was an accomplished gunsmith and could prove
it. He at least hinted at a desire to take over his uncle's business.

Cotton mulled the realization that this news wouldn't sit
well with Carp Varner. Then, out of nowhere, a devious
thought crossed his mind. *I probably should let things be
for a few days. On the other hand, it might be a good time
to let Varner know someone is arriving in town to take up
where Burnside left off. It'd be interesting to see what
effect such news might have on our new gunsmith.* Since
he had had second thoughts about Varner from the beginning, he felt no guilt about putting him to the test. In fact,
the more he thought about it, the more it seemed exactly
the right thing to do. *If he takes the news in stride, maybe
I've been wrong about him. But if he flies into a rage, that
might prove to be an opportunity to take him down a notch.*

The feelings Cotton harbored about Varner puzzled him.
Every time he saw him, the sheriff had an itch, and it only
went away when the man was out of sight. Being a sheriff
naturally made a man suspicious of others. It was an occu-
pational hazard. But there was a niggling suspicion in Cotton's mind that this particular man harbored darker secrets
than he would ever voluntarily disclose. It was up to Sher-

iff Burke to track down any such secret and bring it to light. And the sooner the better.

After the storm had passed and they could see there would still be sufficient daylight left to get closer to Socorro, Rachael and Johnny started down the hill to gather up their horse and rejoin the road. When they found her, their hobbled mare was nibbling on shoots of grass, seemingly unaffected by the big blow. Off to the south, they could see the effects flash flooding was having on the previously dry creek beds. Water rushed down the snakelike tributary, carrying with it all manner of debris—downed limbs, broken cacti, dead animals. Rachael was mesmerized by the sight of such destruction.

"Look, Johnny, over there. Isn't that an empty boat like fishermen use, all smashed on the rocks? Where could it have come from? I've never seen anything like that. All that stuff being pushed along to who knows where? I'm glad you were wise enough to guide us uphill and out of its way."

"You're sure right about that. Why, I once heard a fellow up in Colorado got caught up in a deluge like that on a Sunday, and the rushing waters carried him all the way to Mexico, where he ended up on Tuesday. Of course, he wasn't all that upset because Mexico's where he wanted to go in the first place, and he'd had himself one helluva free ride," Johnny said, with a smirk.

Rachael punched him in the back. "Laugh all you want to, mister, I'll admit I'm a little new to the more violent side of things out here, but I'll catch on, don't think I won't."

"I'm sorry. I shouldn't have teased you."

"Oh, it's all right. I've been teased before, and it don't hurt none, leastways not so's a body'd notice."

As they rode, Johnny kept an eye out for any hint they were getting close to Socorro, the place where the sheriff

in Las Cruces had suggested Carp Varner might have
headed. Of course, the elusive killer might have gone only
a few miles, then changed direction and gone to Lordsburg
or Silver City, instead. A man like Carp Varner didn't often
do things the way most folks might figure. Johnny was
acutely aware of that. Varner didn't shy away from trouble,
either. He'd seen the man shoot someone for a mere slight,
but then that kind of thing wasn't really anything out of the
ordinary for small, dirty frontier towns. Violence was everywhere. But for a man to kill another man for no reason at
all, then turn around and burn a whole town to the ground,
taking innocent citizens with it, well that bespoke a man
without a soul. A man inhabited by a demon so dark, no
light could ever reach inside him.

That was a perfect description of Carp Varner, a man
with Satan squeezing the very life out of him.

But pay it no mind, you bastard, Johnny thought, *because
I'll catch up to you, and when I do, that demon better duck
or he's goin' down with you.*

Chapter 31

———◆◆◆———

Black Tom Callahan looked over with sleepy eyes. He and his two brothers, Stretch and Dal, had been in Apache Springs for a mere day and a half, spending their time staying to themselves, out of the public eye, and trying their best to be very subtle about keeping an eye on the comings and goings at the bank. They had set up camp outside of town, in a dense copse of trees by a creek, to avoid arousing suspicions as to their intentions, and when they came to town, they stayed far away from the saloon, where trouble often gathered.

"What's goin' through your mind, Tom?" asked Stretch, the tall, skinny brother whose nickname was an obvious reference to his appearance. All three Texas outlaws did their best to blend in and not bring undue attention to themselves, mostly spending the days lounging on a bench in front of the hotel pretending to read a newspaper or whittle a stick.

"That bank seems pretty busy. Another couple days and

it'll be ready for the Callahan Brothers to stage a withdrawal. A big fat one. Any objections?"

"None from me," Stretch said.

"I'm not near as sure as you two are," Dal said. He sat forward and unfolded a well-read newspaper he'd picked out of the trash, shielding his comments with the paper held in front of his face. "I recognize that sheriff. Saw him in action a few years back in Texas. Not a man to mess with."

"There're three of us, Dal, and only one of him. What's the problem?" Stretch said.

"He's got a deputy. Memphis Jack Stump. I've heard of him, too."

"So what?"

"Makes it two of 'em we could have to face. And we don't know if there might be more with itchy trigger fingers," Black Tom said. "And, I *mighta* made a mistake, but I could swear I caught a glimpse of a man that looked a lot like that son of a bitch Carp Varner walking out of the sheriff's office yesterday. Couldn't swear to it, though."

"Varner? What the hell would he be doin' here?" Stretch asked.

"Who knows? I can't imagine he'd throw in with the law, more'n likely just the opposite. But if there was money to be made, who knows? With Varner, there's just no sense to be made of him or his ways," Dal added.

"I can't figure out why the man's still alive. Shoulda been gunned down a long time ago, far as I'm concerned," Stretch said.

"I'm thinkin' the same. But folks do seem to put up with a lot of hell-raisin' before they get down to doin' somethin' about it," Dal said. "I give you Dirty Dave Rudabaugh as an example of what I'm sayin'. Now, can either of you tell me why that filthy pig is still runnin' around free as a bird?"

"The man's got nine lives, like a cat's supposed to have. Although, I never really believed that," Stretch said.

Black Tom rolled his eyes.

Dal just shook his head.

"How about if I go into the bank, maybe ask about how safe the place is? I could act like I'm thinkin' of movin' a large sum of money to a bank that'd be safer than that tin box they got in Socorro," Stretch said.

Still shaking his head, Dal said, "Now, pray tell what banker is goin' to believe you got two cents to rub together, let alone a 'large sum'?"

"If I snuck into one of them stores at night and stole myself some nice duds, I'll bet they'd believe me," Stretch said.

"All right, enough! Bickerin' ain't goin' to get us anywhere. I say we continue to lay low for a few more days, at least until we can size up who all we might be up against. Can't be in a hurry when there's big money at stake," Black Tom said, biting his lip and looking off into the distance.

Carp Varner was keeping a keen, but clandestine, watch out for the Callahan Brothers, where they went and where they were at all times. He was spooked by what their presence might mean to his own plans for Apache Springs. They were the only ones who knew him and his reputation from back in Texas. He made sure he left his shop only after dark, and then he went out the back way, staying close to the buildings and remaining in the shadows. Fortunately, during the day he could spot them as they rode into town and took their places on the hotel porch.

As he was ramming a rod with a cloth down the barrel of a Sharps rifle that had come in the day before, he got an idea. He'd noticed the Callahans rode in early and left town late in the day. It was almost as if they were coming and going on a schedule. But why? The only reason he could think of was to make sure no one followed them to learn where they were holed up. But who would care? Maybe someone in town had recognized them and knew them for what they were: outlaws. As far as Carp knew, however, they weren't wanted in New Mexico for anything. At least not yet. He *had* noticed they stayed away from the saloon and seemed to spend an inordinate amount of time lounging around on the porch of the hotel or on the public bench outside the mercantile.

Maybe they don't want to draw attention to themselves for some particular reason. That's it! They're plannin' on robbin' the bank, and, if so, that could interfere with whatever plans I may come up with for this town.

He pondered that idea for a while, not certain if sharing such information with the sheriff would be beneficial to him or not. If he voiced his suspicions, the sheriff would probably only keep an eye on the Callahans, since he couldn't arrest them based on hearsay of a citizen, and a recent one at that. Sheriff Burke would ask him why he had misgivings about the men, who, to that point at least, had caused no trouble, even if they were wanted in Texas. Then there'd be more questions about how he knew them and then the inevitable digging into his own past. He didn't need any of that. While he'd been very careful not to leave any trail that could be followed by anyone except an Indian, he could never be too careful about what information he shared with anyone.

He set about changing some of the furniture around in the shop and cleaning the dirt off the front window. He scooted the display case around so instead of a customer walking up to it as soon as he came in, he'd have to turn to the left. He then put the workbench at a ninety-degree angle to the counter. That way he had a better view outside at all times. He also kept two loaded revolvers in the desk drawer and the ten-gauge shotgun under the counter. He never went anywhere without his own sidearm, either. His Smith & Wesson Schofield had served him well for a long time. Besides, he felt naked without it strapped on and ready.

Looking over the new layout, he smiled to himself, satisfied he'd done all he could to thwart any danger the Callahans might conjure up on his behalf, if on the off chance they spotted him. He wasn't about to leave himself vulnerable to whatever mischief those notorious gunslingers might be considering. Another thought then popped into his mind.

What if he was to jump in and help take down the Callahans when, or if, they *did* attempt something as audacious as robbing the bank? Of course, he'd have to be sure none of them lived to say anything about him. Would that make him a hero in the eyes of the community? Could becoming an instant hero erase the doubt that he'd clearly seen in the sheriff's eyes? He pulled the ten-gauge from beneath the counter and leaned it against the workbench.

If those three boys are fixin' to do what I think they are, this old ten-gauge scattergun will come in handy. Why, I might even be asked to consider becoming a deputy. Now, wouldn't that just speed my future in the community right along?

Chapter 32

———❖———

Johnny and Rachael arrived in Socorro late in the day. They were dirty, tired, and hungry. As Johnny helped Rachael off the horse, she groaned and stretched. They were both exhausted from being in the saddle for such a long time. She looked around for a place to get some food while he tried to locate the livery. They hadn't eaten much more than a rabbit he'd shot and some biscuits they'd wrapped in a checkered napkin back in Las Cruces. Knowing they were broke, the sheriff in Las Cruces had slipped Johnny a couple dollars for helping keep the jail swept and the trash taken to the dump. Johnny slipped the bills into his pocket and promptly forgot about having any money. He was so used to being completely broke, having even a few dollars seemed foreign.

"There," Rachael said, pointing down the street to a small adobe building. "That looks like it might be a restaurant. Maybe there's somebody still there. I'll go have a look while you get the horse some grain and put her up for the night."

Johnny was too tired to say anything. It was all he could do to keep from collapsing in the street, curling up, and going to sleep right there. He just nodded and started leading the mare down the street in search of a corral.

When Rachael got to the little restaurant, which turned out to be not much more than a hole-in-the-wall, she peeked in the open door. There were no customers. The only person she saw was a short, rotund Mexican lady clearing the four small tables in readiness for the next meal. She figured that would be breakfast. The lady broke into a cheery smile when she saw the young girl and motioned her inside.

"Good evening, señorita. Would you like some tortillas and beans? Plenty left. Come, you will enjoy," the lady said.

Rachael looked around to find Johnny, but he was nowhere to be seen. She took one step inside. She was hesitant since she had no more than fifteen cents left. She figured that wouldn't go far, certainly not far enough for two. If Johnny couldn't eat, she wouldn't either. The smells coming from inside instantly reminded her of how little she'd had to eat in the last few days, and the journey had been difficult at times. She sighed and started to leave, giving the lady a weak smile.

"No, do not leave, señorita. I can see you are hungry. There is more than I have sold today and I don't want to throw it out. You probably have no money, but that is *bien*. *Por favor*, come and sit with me. I don't often get another *mujer* to talk to."

"I, uh, I have a friend. We are traveling together. He went to find a corral. We are riding together on one horse and have come a very long way. But I couldn't eat without him sharing. Thank you anyway, ma'am. You are very kind."

"Feed one, feed two, what difference is one more mouth? Bring him and I'll feed you both. *Prisa*, I prepare some *habas* for you."

Rachael's eyes lit up at the woman's words. To find food and be able to share with Johnny was a thrilling stroke of luck, especially in a place where she knew no one. She stepped outside, glancing around. She'd about given up when she spied him coming from between two dark buildings. She called out to him.

"Johnny, hurry. There is food here."

Just the word "food" quickened his steps. When he got to the little restaurant, he whispered, "Rachael, you know we don't have any money." He'd completely forgotten what was in his pocket.

"Don't worry. I do have fifteen cents, but a very kind lady has offered to feed us for free. Come inside, quickly."

He put his arm around her waist and they walked in together. When the restaurant owner saw him, she gave him the same warm smile she'd given Rachael. They went over to a table that had not yet been cleaned, so as not to disturb the lady's hard work at setting up for the morning meal.

"No, no, sit here, *mis amigos*. I have set out nice silverware and plates just for you, my *huespedes especiales*." The lady waved them to a different table, nearer the kitchen. The two of them looked at each other as if they'd never experienced such kindness before and no one had ever considered them special. If they'd thought about it, they'd have realized that wasn't really the case, for in every instance where they'd found themselves in need, someone had stepped up to lend a hand, asking nothing in return. When the lady placed a bowl of beans and a plate of steaming tortillas in front of them, it was all Johnny could do to keep from grabbing a handful of the refried beans and stuffing it in his mouth, foregoing the use of any utensils. He didn't, however, but instead, gathering all the control he could muster, he sat with hands folded in his lap like an obedient son awaiting a mother's signal that it was okay to dig in. Rachael found his tentativeness amusing and covered her mouth to keep from giggling.

Before joining them, the lady went to the door and shut it. She threw a colorful shawl over her shoulders and then sat at the table with them. "The nights are becoming cooler. I fear a hard winter."

"We have seen signs of that very thing all the way from Texas," Johnny said. He had yet to touch anything on the table.

The lady leaned forward on her elbows and, with narrowed eyes, said, "Well, young man, do you eat or must I treat the pigs to a *fiesta*?"

"Oh, uh, yes, ma'am," he said, and plunging his spoon into the beans, he dug in. The look on his face said just how enjoyable it was. As they both ate, the lady looked away as if she were trying to find the answer to some dark secret. Johnny was too busy shoveling food into his mouth to notice, but Rachael was alert to the lady's drifting off.

"Ma'am, is there something wrong?"

"Oh, no, nothing *niño*. It will pass as all things evil do."

"Evil? What kind of evil happened?"

"*Sí*, I forget you just arrive. I should not trouble you with such news. You eat and forget the ramblings of an old woman."

That got Johnny's attention. "Well, if it's something we can do to help, we'd be obliged to try. You sure been kindly to us, and we'd like to return the favor."

"You can do nothing. It is done with. Even the sheriff says so, a man who has never been disposed to trouble himself over a couple of poor *Mexicanos*."

"Can you tell us about it?" Johnny asked, between bites.

"It happened to my brother, José. He was knocked down two weeks back."

"Is he, uh, okay, though?" Rachael asked, timidly. She'd put her spoon down and was now more interested in the lady's story than in filling her stomach.

"He fell and hit his head on the doorframe. He died from his wound, I'm afraid. We lay him to rest in the cemetery outside of town, even though they do not put our kind with the whites. But we got a plot in the back and it's not so bad." She dabbed at her eyes with a napkin.

"Who hit him and why?" Johnny asked, now intensely interested.

"He did not get out of a man's way when told to, and the man struck him, right in front of the restaurant. The man was very angry."

"That's what he got shot for? Not movin' fast enough? What kind of an animal would do such a dastardly thing?"

"Don't know his name. Somebody said it, but I don't remember it. He was tall, thin. Wore a dark duster, a pair of tall boots, and a big red bandana, like cowboys wear. I swear his eyes were black as coal. There was a devil inside that man."

Johnny's rage, excitement, and bloodlust all converged on him at the same time. He felt full to bursting with an urge to yell, "Hurrah!" *We're finally on the right trail.* His expression took on the look of a madman.

Carp Varner! I'm comin' for you. And don't think for a minute I won't catch you and blow you straight to hell, myself.

"Did the sheriff arrest the man?" Rachael asked, hoping the lady wasn't frightened by Johnny's suddenly dark countenance.

"Oh, no. *Thees* killer just ride away free as a bird. Didn't even have no posse sent after him." The lady hung her head and sobbed.

"Anyone see which direction he went?" Johnny asked.

"Took the west road is all I know." The lady continued dabbing at her tears.

Rachael put her hand on the lady's arm.

"I'm so sorry for your loss, ma'am. But I figure he'll get his comeuppance before long."

"You can just about bet on it, "Johnny said through gritted teeth.

After they thanked her for her kindness, the lady tearfully watched after them as they left to find a place to bed down for the night. They headed for the livery stable where Johnny had boarded the horse. Straw would make for a pretty decent bed for the two of them, as well.

Chapter 33

———◆◆◆———

Cotton muttered to himself as he stopped leafing through some new wanted dodgers. He didn't like what he saw. Three brothers wanted for a bank robbery three months ago in Texas. It hadn't happened in New Mexico Territory, but they had shot a teller, and that might just make it his business, especially if the three men sitting on the bench in front of the hotel were those very same wanted men. No picture accompanied the description, but it fit them pretty well. It said they were the Callahan Brothers, from Amarillo. What were they doing here? Planning to rob another bank, maybe? He needed to make sure they were who he figured them to be without making a fuss that could end in someone getting shot. As soon as Jack got back from checking to make sure doors had been locked along the two streets comprising the town, Cotton figured to lay out a plan to get one of them to give up a name.

Jack came through the door looking beat and plopped into the chair across the sheriff's desk. He stared at two piles of wanted papers, one wadded into little balls and the other piled neatly.

"What you got there? Why the wadded up dodgers?"

"They're either in prison or dead."

"We kill any of 'em?"

"A couple. Sure takes a while to get the posters out to all the sheriffs and marshals. It *would* help if they got here *before* we were forced to gun 'em down."

"Who's that one in your hand for? Anyone we know?" Jack got up and took a cup from atop a file cabinet. He poured a cup of coffee, then returned to his chair.

"Maybe. Here, take a look. You recognize these three?"

"Callahan Brothers, hmm, don't sound familiar but . . . wait! There're three hombres sittin' in front of the mercantile right now. Kinda fit the description. Been here a day or so. You think that's them on the poster?"

"Don't know. Need to find out. I saw them when they rode in, but they seem to be stayin' to themselves. Before we march over there and arrest some innocent cowboys on a pretty thin description, we'd better make sure."

"How do you figure to do that?"

"Have they seen you?"

"I 'spect."

"Then I can't have you take off your badge and go down there to ask who they are."

"Maybe not. But I could ask Arlo to keep his ear out for any loose conversation. He gets a lot of folks in the saloon that might hear somethin' useful."

"That's a good idea. Do it. Oh, has Melody cooled off enough to talk to me in a reasonable fashion yet?"

"Not likely. Maybe I can make another run at her. Gotta be careful how I go 'bout it or I'll be back here sleepin' in a jail cell again."

"You can always throw your bedroll on the floor at my house if you need to. Just let me know before you walk in."

"'Fraid I'll catch you, uh, entertainin'?" Jack said with a knowing grin.

"You never can tell, Jack. Now, go tell Arlo what we want him to do."

Jack looked around the near empty saloon. It was the middle of the day in the middle of the week. Customers tended to come in the evenings or on the weekend. He walked casually over to the barkeep and leaned on the bar.

"What'll it be, Jack?"

"Brandy, and I have a job for you."

"As long as it don't involve using that shotgun on someone again, I'll do it."

"Nope. No shotgun this time. I want you to ask around to see if anybody recognizes three men sittin' either on the hotel porch or in front of the mercantile. Came in one, maybe two days ago. We may have some paper on them, but we have to make certain we got the right ones," Jack said, leaning over the bar and keeping his voice low.

"I can do that, Jack. I'll let you know as soon as I get something." Arlo turned to get a bottle of brandy and poured a shot glass full. Jack thanked him and went upstairs. He could tell Melody was in her room because he heard her humming some song off-key. He opened the door and went in.

"Hi, sweety, where've you been?" she asked.

"My job. You remember what I do, don't you?"

"Oh, that's right, you fetch and do errands for the sheriff, uh, Bark or Beak, or . . . now what was his name?"

"Stop it, Melody. I'm not here to fight. I'm tired and hungry. I thought we could get a bite to eat."

"Ah, that would be very nice. Let me put something on I can be seen in and we'll go to the hotel," she said, moving away from her mirror to an armoire, wherein hung dozens of fancy dresses.

He helped her into a long blue dress with satin bows and a lacy neck and cuffs. She slipped into shoes with silver eyelets and highly polished pointy toes. As they left the room and started down the staircase, he took her arm and pulled her near.

"Do you know anything about three men who came to town a day or so ago? They seem to be spending a lot of time watching the bank," he whispered. She stared at him for a second.

"No. Should I?"

"Not really, but you usually make an acquaintance with everyone who comes to town."

"Sorry, not this time. Haven't noticed them around the saloon. Just drifters, I'd guess. Why do you give a damn?"

"They kinda fit the description on a wanted dodger that Cotton got this mornin'."

"Oh? What might they be wanted for?"

"Bank robbery. A killin', too, I think."

"This town sure does seem to attract the worst type of people. Lordy me, what's this old world coming to?"

"I am also curious about that thing Cotton asked you about. Remember? He wanted to know who all you told about givin' Pick Wheeler a lot of money?"

"You asking because you want to know, or did Cotton put you up to it?"

"Nope, he didn't. It's still his idea. But I want you to take another look at it without worryin' about whose idea it was. It's good solid reasonin'. Whoever you might have told could play an important part in my, uh, investigation."

"All right, if it's for *your* ears only. First, of course Darnell Givins knew, since he's the one handed all that cash over to that old reprobate. And there was some fellow sitting on the bench outside the bank when we came out. I s'pose he could have overheard our conversation, but I was so excited I didn't really take notice of him. I mighta said something then that could have been important. Oh, and I reckon I was a little over-ecstatic about owning a silver mine, so I think I let something slip to the ladies at the dress shop. And the waiter at the hotel restaurant. And a few cowboys that suggested I go upstairs with them for some touch and tickle, but I shut them down telling them I now owned a silver mine and didn't need their measly dollars," she said, drifting off in thought. "I think that's all. Maybe. I'm not sure. Things were happening pretty fast and . . ."

"And you got caught up in the excitement."

"Uh-huh. Did I blow my chances for getting my money back?"

"I'll let you know. First, I need to follow up on those people you talked to and see who they talked to. You see, something like this can spread like a wildfire. Somewhere in that string of folks might be whoever shot Pick and stole your money. See, simple."

"I, uh, never thought about it that way. I figured Cotton was just trying to make me look like a fool."

"Shall I tell him you're sorry?"

"Must I go that far?" she said with a sheepish grin.

Chapter 34

———◆———

"Cotton, I got Melody's list of folks she shot off her big mouth to. Oh, and she says she's sorry." Jack lied, handing a folded piece of paper to the sheriff who opened it and began reading.

"There could be something in here that will help. I reckon we'll see."

"Yeah. I was particularly suspicious of the lady at the dress shop," Jack said, with a smirk.

"Uh-huh, that one struck me, too." Cotton folded the paper and stuck it in his shirt pocket.

"What do we do now?" Jack asked.

"The man claiming to be Burnside's nephew is supposed to arrive this afternoon. News of him wantin' to take over where his uncle left off should prove interestin'. Now that we're for sure he's comin', I think I'll saunter over and talk things over with Carp Varner. You want to come along?"

"Why not? Never know what might turn up when you shuffle a new deck."

"My thoughts exactly."

Varner was jamming an oily cloth down the barrel of a Springfield rifle. A drop of the oil landed on the desk as he pulled it out. He looked up as Cotton and Jack entered.

"Well, Sheriff, I hope you're coming with good news," Varner said. "Ahh, I see you brought along your impulsive deputy, too. I hope nobody's lookin' for trouble."

"Why should there be any trouble?" Cotton said quizzically.

"The last time me and the deputy spoke, he was pretty riled up about me and a certain lady."

"I get it. Jack failed to tell me you two had a run-in." He looked at Jack, who looked away. "I reckon whatever went between you is over. Anyway, I'm here with some news about the shop."

"Good. I'm eager to hear what you've got to say," Varner said.

"I doubt you'll see it that way. I received a notice from Burnside's nephew, a man we didn't know existed, and he says he might want to take over his uncle's business. He's supposed to be arriving on the afternoon stage. Since I've never seen the man, I'll have to wait until we've talked to know if he has a legitimate claim and is even capable of repairing firearms."

"I, uh, reckon that means I'd better start clearin' out."

"Not yet. Give me a chance to see what kind of critter we're dealin' with. I'll let you know."

"Fair enough, Sheriff. I'll wait to hear from you."

With that, Cotton and Jack went to the hotel for lunch and an opportunity to talk over what would happen if the nephew turned out to be a good prospect to run the gunsmithing business.

* * *

*Looks like I'm going to have to make something happen.
Can't just sit here and twiddle my thumbs while that fool
sheriff decides whether I go or stay.*

Carp Varner stared out the window of the shop. His expression was as dark as a looming thunderstorm. He had
only a couple of minor jobs to do, neither of which was due
to be done anytime soon. Taking time to look out the window wasn't keeping him from completing anything that
would bring in any quick cash. After seeing the Callahan
Brothers ride into town, he'd been biding his time. He knew
they were up to no good, and if he could put a stop to their
misdeeds before the sheriff caught wind of their plans, he
figured to be a hero. And towns like Apache Springs didn't
have the stomach for tossing out a hero. *What the hell's taking them so long?*

Almost as if responding to Varner's silent question, just
after noon, the Callahan Brothers left the hotel porch and
began a slow walk toward the bank, looking around like
mice wary of being spotted by a cat. They split up, two
walked down one side of the street, and the other took the
side where the bank sat, diagonally across from the gun
shop. Few people were in town at this time of day, it being
near lunch. Some were at the hotel, eating, and others were
staying inside their shops, avoiding the midday sun. As
they got close to the bank, Black Tom stopped and signaled
the others to cross the street and join him. They gathered in
front of the millinery store, which sat on the corner of the
alley next to the bank.

"All right, one more time, here's how this is going to go
down. Dal, you go stand at the entrance to the alley, back
enough that you don't attract attention. Stretch, get our
horses and bring them around back of the bank. As soon as
I see you're in position, I'll go into the bank and wait for

any customers to leave. When I come out with the money, Dal will step up and cover me from the alley entrance alongside the bank. Stretch, when you see me come out, you bring the horses up to the front of the bank. We'll tear out of here to the south. Any questions?"

"Where you figure on us makin' for, Tom?" Dal asked.

"There's plenty of good places to take cover in those rough hills. If the sheriff gets up a posse, it will take him at least an hour, maybe more. We can easily shake him off our trail if we make it through the first south pass."

"And if we don't?" Stretch asked.

"Then we're in for one helluva gunfight. Unless you've got some other half-assed questions, let's get this soiree started."

They each headed for their places, all under the watchful eyes of Carp Varner.

Looks like I won't have to wait much longer. Varner chuckled as he took the shotgun and went to the front door. His shop being at ninety degrees to the bank's entrance, across the main street, guaranteed him both a front row seat and the first shot, if it came to that. And he knew damned good and well it would, at least if he had anything to say about it.

Carp checked the loads in the shotgun one more time, closed the breech, and cocked the hammers. His Smith & Wesson Schofield sat comfortably on his gun belt. He was ready for a small war. He watched Stretch make a run to the livery stable, go inside, and come back out minutes later with three horses in tow. Halfway down the street, he led the horses down a side alley. Probably goin' to meet up at the back of the bank. *Dumb plan.* Carp smiled.

Dal positioned himself at the entrance to the alleyway beside the bank, turned, and stood near the entrance to the street. When it was obvious Black Tom was preparing to enter the front door of the bank, Varner stepped onto the boardwalk and stood in the shadows of the portico—and waited for the first move to be made. He didn't have to wait long.

Luckily, there was no one in the bank except the manager. When Black Tom entered, the man stood up and extended his hand. "Good afternoon, sir. How can—"

Tom didn't wait to hear the entire greeting. He held up his six-shooter, pointing it directly at Darnell Givins, and said, "No bullshit, mister. Start cleanin' out that vault."

"Y-yessir." Shaken, Darnell moved as fast as he could, which obviously wasn't fast enough for the robber. Black Tom gave him a very sharp stab in the back with the barrel of the revolver. "Move it! I'm not a patient man, mister, and I don't intend to tolerate no shenanigans."

Givins began stuffing money in the gunnysack Black Tom had tossed to him. He started to perspire profusely upon hearing Tom cock the hammer. He dropped several of the money packs, then had to scramble to gather them and shove them in the bag. He handed the bag to Black Tom with trembling hands.

Black Tom smiled and said, "There now, that wasn't so hard, was it?" He turned suddenly to leave, then looking back momentarily, he said, "Don't holler for the law before we get gone and I won't have to shoot you. Understand?"

Givins was nodding his head so hard his teeth were chattering.

Black Tom burst out the door and started for the alley. He hadn't gone fifteen steps when he noticed a familiar face across the street.

"You! You son—"

"This just isn't your day, Callahan," Carp Varner hollered and then let loose with one barrel of the shotgun, striking Black Tom in the face. Dal pulled his gun, but to no avail. He, too, was cut down instantly by the second barrel of the ten-gauge.

Seeing what was happening, Stretch came thundering

down the alley. He'd just begun to pull his revolver when a voice from behind yelled.

"That's far enough, mister! Unless you want the same as your brothers got." Cotton Burke was behind him, coming fast from the rear of the bank. Stretch threw up his hands.

"D-don't shoot, Sheriff. I give up. All I did was fetch the horses. That's all, I swear."

Cotton took his revolver from him and marched him to the front of the bank, where his two brothers lay covered in blood. Stretch stared in disbelief at the corpses. He began to tremble. He was so shocked at seeing his brothers lying in pools of blood he didn't even look up to see who'd pulled down on them. Cotton looked over just as Carp Varner was slipping back into the gunsmith's shop and shouted, "Nice shooting. Thanks for your help."

Varner smiled as he called over his shoulder, "You're welcome, Sheriff. Anytime," and then he popped back inside to return the shotgun to a safe place.

Cotton pushed the tall, skinny Callahan along in front of him. Jack came running toward them, Remington at the ready.

"What the hell happened, Cotton?"

"Tell you when I get this hombre locked up. Oh, and make sure Givins is all right and take him back the bank's money, then fetch the undertaker."

Chapter 35

———≻•≺———

Stretch sat morosely in his jail cell. The sheriff and his deputy were in the other room talking about what had befallen the other two Callahan Brothers. The remaining brother was nearly in tears as he overheard only bits and pieces of their conversation.

"So what happened out there, Cotton? I heard what sounded like a cannon goin' off. Figured we were at war all of a sudden."

"Those three we figured for the Callahan Brothers? Well, they were, and they cleaned out the bank. Nearly got away with it, too."

"So you got the other two."

"*I* didn't get the other two."

"Uh, I saw them lying in the street. What happened, they fall down and start bleedin' from fright at seeing you thunderin' toward them?"

"The only one that saw me was the one I got locked up in back."

"What was it made you go back there in the first place?"

"I noticed them leave the hotel porch, stop, and put their heads together for a minute, then head down the street in the general direction of the bank. I got curious when one of 'em went straight for the livery. When he came out with their horses, I went around the back way to see what was goin' on, just in case we'd been right about 'em."

"Those two blasts were louder'n what a Colt puts out."

"Uh-huh. Seems our gunsmith stepped out of his shop at just the right moment, saw what they were up to, and started blastin' away with a scattergun. Got those two in the street before I could catch 'em tryin' for a getaway."

"Handy." Jack scrunched up his mouth in a doubtful frown. "Real handy. Almost *too* handy."

"My thoughts exactly."

"You haven't had time to talk to your prisoner yet. While you do that, I'll make sure the undertaker has hauled away the mess, if you'd like."

"I'd like."

Jack left, and Cotton poured coffee into two cups. He opened the door that separated the cells from the office. Stretch was surprised when the door opened, and he sat back on the cot quickly. Cotton handed him a cup, which he took, although reluctantly.

"So, what's your name?" Cotton asked, blowing the steam off his coffee.

"Name's Stretch and don't try being nice to me, Sheriff; I ain't up to none of your questions. What about my brothers, Tom and Dal?"

"What about them?"

"I could see they was bad wounded in the dirt. Did you send for a doctor?"

"Nope."

"Why the hell not? You folks ain't no better'n us."

"Bein' good or bad doesn't make any difference. But bein' dead trumps all manner of reasons not to fetch a doctor."

"Dead! You sayin' *both* my brothers was dead lyin' there?"

"Deader'n a skunk in a stampede. Undertaker'll take good care of 'em, though."

Stretch sniffed back a tear. He wiped his nose on his sleeve and looked away.

"Wh-what's goin' to happen to me? I didn't rob nuthin'."

"You were in on it, weren't you?"

"I, uh, s'pose. But it was all words, nuthin' like really doin' . . ."

"You might as well stop there. All three of you were in on robbin' the bank. Two of you didn't make it out alive. Just because the others are dead doesn't let you off the hook."

"What's that mean?"

"Means you'll be stayin' with us until a U.S. marshal can come pick you up."

"Don't I get a trial?"

"If you want. The judge won't be around for a couple weeks. Besides, the marshal will be takin' you back to where the original wanted poster came from: Texas. Better get comfortable."

Stretch Callahan stared at the sheriff like he'd been handed a death sentence.

"Undertaker took 'em. Reckon they'll be stood up in front of his place for a day or two, then he'll plant 'em." Jack said, as he glanced at the prisoner, who stood holding on to the bars with an iron grip. "What d'ya figure to do with him?"

"If he behaves himself, he'll get a trial back in Texas, and the judge will likely send him off to prison. If he doesn't, maybe we'll take him out back and *hang* him," Cotton said, plenty loud enough for Stretch to hear. The reaction was instantaneous.

"I ain't never killed no one! You can't hang a man for just *thinkin'* on doin' a robbery," Stretch yelled from his cell.

"I'd surely have a problem with that, indeed I would, but

there's no tellin' what a bunch of liquored-up yahoos with a rope might conjure up," Cotton hollered. "That was their money you were fixin' to make off with."

"Then you gotta get me out of here. Take me down to Silver City or . . ."

"Calm down. I'm not takin' you anywhere. You're as safe here as you can be."

Stretch thought on that for a minute before speaking again.

"Uh, Sheriff, if'n I'm to be your guest, don't that mean you gotta feed me?"

Jack leaned over and whispered to Cotton. "He's got a point. I don't know about you, I'm thinkin' I don't want to wet-nurse this hombre for a couple weeks waitin' on a judge."

Cotton scratched his head. Fact was, he didn't favor the situation, either. Then an idea came to him. He got up and went back to the cells. He leaned against the wall facing Stretch and drew his Colt.

"Here's the lay of the land. You're goin' to answer some questions. For every one that's a lie, I pop a cap into the cell. Now, you may not get hit, but on the other hand, you may. A stray bullet has a mind of its own."

Stretch began to perspire. "You-you can't do a thing like that. It's illegal."

"Or just an unfortunate accident."

"I, uh, wh-what is it you want to know?"

"First question: you got any past trouble anywhere here in New Mexico?"

"Why'd you want to know that?" Stretch said, a little hesitant with giving information to a lawman. "No-no . . . er, well, yes. We did sorta have a little trouble in Las Cruces."

"That was a close one. Wanna tell me what sort of trouble?"

"There was this fella we'd tangled with one time before. He up and stole what was ours. Black Tom said if we ever run on him ag'in, we was to gun him. Spotted him in Las

Cruces. 'Bout the time we was all fixin' to draw down on the hombre, the sheriff stepped in. Told the other man to get the hell out of town. On his way out, he bumped into a Mex. Reckon his anger got the best of him 'cause he up and clubbed the fellow senseless. Then he mounted up and lit a shuck to hell an' gone."

"Sheriff go after him? Get up a posse?"

"No, sir. He just let him leave. I figured he didn't want anything more to do with that gent. As I think on it, he may have just saved our lives that day."

"What was the man's name?"

"Can't rightly remember, uh, Varmint or somethin' like that."

"So what did you do to get you into trouble?"

"We was broke, so we broke into a hardware store that night and took the cash drawer. Don't know if there was a posse after us, either. Kinda felt like that sheriff didn't really want to leave town much."

"Second question. You ever kill anybody?"

"I never did. Never had the stomach for a killin'. But my brother, Black Tom, he had to put a couple fellows in the ground."

"Where was that?"

"Missouri. Texas."

"Self-defense?"

"Uh, not really."

"Then I reckon he got what was comin' to him."

Stretch gave him a sad look. Dark circles of despair suggested he'd never been on his own and wasn't sure he liked the way things were shaping up for him.

"The wanted dodger I got on you three didn't say anything about murder, just robbery. So until I figure out who to contact to come get you, you best get used to this cell, because you're goin' nowhere," Cotton said. He walked back into the office, holstered his Colt, and sat down.

"Get what you wanted?" Jack asked.

"Got what I expected. I'd like you to go to the telegraph office and send for a U.S. marshal to come get this fool."

"All right, then what?"

"The stage is due in an hour. Burnside's nephew ought to be on it. After I've talked to him, we can make a decision about what, if anything, we can do with Carp Varner. That fellow still bothers me. And I need to talk a bit more about him shootin' down those two Callahans. Can't go lettin' citizens gun down folks on a hunch."

"Pretty good hunch though, wouldn't you say?" Jack said, with a smirk. "You figure there's more to it?"

"I'd bet on it."

Chapter 36

—◆—

Johnny and Rachael sat picking straw out of their hair. She leaned against one of the stalls while he sat with his legs curled under him. He was pensive. She looked over at him questioningly.

"What're you thinking about, Johnny?"

"I'm thinkin' we don't have no idea where that rattlesnake Carp Varner headed. The road the Mexican lady said he took could take him to Lordsburg, Silver City, Apache Springs, even Albuquerque. Or he coulda cut back and gone to El Paso. It's a big country out there."

"What are we going to do?"

"I don't know, but I'll come up with a plan somehow. One thing's for sure, we better stay here for a while, at least until we find out where he likely went."

"We're going to need more money than the three dollars you found in your pocket. That nice lady isn't going to keep feeding us for free, you know."

"I know. I'll have to scrounge around, see if I can get a job at one of the stores, or even here at the livery."

Rachael thought that over for a minute, then spoke up. "I'll see if there's anything I can do. No sense in you taking all the responsibility on yourself. And I don't want to hear that girls can't do anything, either. Understand?" She balled her fist in preparation for an argument.

Johnny said nothing. Instead, he got up, brushed himself off, and took off for the big double doors at the front of the livery. On his way, he ran smack into the owner, Abe Olson, nearly knocking him over.

"Whoa, there. What're you in such an all fired hurry for?"

"I-I got . . . to . . . uh, find a . . . job."

"A job? What do you need a job for?"

"We are . . ."

"Broke? That what you're tellin' me, boy? Can't pay your bill for feedin' that hay burner of yours, that it?"

Johnny hesitated. "Well, you see, Mr. Olson, uh . . ."

"Never mind. I got it." Olson sighed and looked off, rubbing his chin whiskers. "Tell you what, son, if you'll muck out the stalls, brush down horses when they come in, make sure there's feed for all of 'em, you two can stay here, and keep your horse here, too. No charge. How's that sound?"

"Would it leave me enough time to find some other odd jobs so we can get enough together to eat?"

"I suspect so. In the meantime, you can eat with me'n the wife, just till you find somethin' else."

"Thank you, sir, that sounds fine. Mind if I go tell Rachael?"

"You go right ahead. Then come on back here and we'll get you started."

Johnny nearly stumbled over his own feet rushing to tell Rachael the good news. They wouldn't starve after all.

Rachael stopped in the first shop for women she could find. There were several ladies picking up rolls of cloth, cards with buttons, and packages of needles. There was a whole display with spindles of thread, dozens of them. A lady saw her looking around and came over to her, arms crossed.

"Is there anything I may help you with, young lady?" the woman said.

"Uh, no, not exactly. I was just wondering if—"

"If you could slip a couple of these pretty things in your pocket and rush out of here with them? That what you were wondering?"

"Oh, no, ma'am. I was wondering if you might have need for some help in your beautiful store."

"I'm sorry, but I have no need of help. You best run along now. I suspect someone is waiting for you."

"Thank you, anyway," Rachael said, disheartened and angry at being taken for a potential thief. *I guess I don't look very proper in these rags I'm wearing. Can't blame the lady one bit.*

She left the store and wandered until she came to the hotel. At the side of the building a bedraggled woman came out of a door carrying a pan of soapy water and potato peelings. Rachael started toward her just as the lady tossed the pan's contents on the ground. Some of the water splashed Rachael's feet. The lady looked startled.

"Oh, my dear, I'm so sorry. Bless me, sometimes I forget to look around before tossing the garbage. You come inside and wash off.

"Thank you, ma'am. But I'm fine. I was on my way to see about some work, maybe in the kitchen, or serving customers. I've fetched for folks before," she said.

The lady looked her over for a minute. "Well, you look strong enough to handle being on your feet all day, but we'd have to put you in something more appropriate than that, er, whatever that is you're wearing."

Rachael gave the lady an apologetic smile. The lady turned and motioned her inside. The back room was stuffed full of sacks of potatoes and beans. Cans of tomatoes, peaches, and pork and beans were piled high on shelving that ran the full length of one wall. On the opposite wall were baskets of eggs and carrots and sacks of flour. All that food made Rachael's mouth water, something the lady picked up on immediately.

"When was the last time you ate, child?"

"Oh, just yesterday. A nice lady at a Mexican cantina fed us, my friend and me."

"That would be Mrs. Morales. Yes, she *is* a fine woman. But I suspect you'll be needin' more than an occasional meal to keep you goin'. You say you're traveling with a friend?"

"Yes, ma'am."

"Well, in exchange for two meals a day for the two of you, plus a little extra to take care of other things you'll be needing, you may help out in the kitchen for a spell. After I see how you handle that job, and it *is* hard work, mind you, we'll see about something more regular."

"Thank you, ma'am. When shall I get started?"

"There's a pile of dirty dishes in the tub. They need to be washed and dried for the evening meal. You'll find a box of soap shavings on the counter and a kettle for boiling water on the stove. First, let's put an apron on you, so you don't get soaked with soapy water. Although, I must say, those duds you're wearing look like they've seen better days."

Rachael. "Yes, ma'am, I reckon they do at that."

Late that evening, two very tired young people huddled in a stall, barely able to keep their eyes open. Johnny had told Rachael about his arrangement with Mr. Olson, and Rachael had shared her story of how they were going to eat for the next few days, at least until they found a reason to move on. That reason, at least in Johnny's mind, was finding out where Carp Varner had gone.

Chapter 37

For nearly two weeks, Johnny and Rachael had gotten up at dawn and begun their day. Each was filled with enthusiasm when starting out, but by late evening, both were worn clean to the nub. Rachael thought the skin on her arms and hands was going to turn as coarse as tree bark from being in water and harsh soap chips all day. And Johnny had had all he could take of manure and straw dust. He was coughing and sneezing constantly. They had, however, earned enough to keep them in food and a place to stay after they continued on their journey. All they were waiting on before setting out was information about Carp Varner's whereabouts.

Johnny thought about the prospects of finding the murderer and taking him down. His anger filled him almost to overflowing. It hadn't helped that Rachael had told him on several occasions that hatred can eat a man up, make him unable to get past that dark poison that keeps you from being the sharpest you can be. In fact, Johnny was slowly beginning to realize just how right she was. His work, while satisfactory, wasn't his very best effort. He knew it, but he couldn't seem to get Varner out of his mind. Until the day a stranger came straggling into town late one day dragging a saddle and looking like he'd been trampled by a herd of cattle. His clothes were worn and dirty, the pants torn and faded from exposure to the intense sun. The man made it to the front of the livery before falling in a heap in front of the double doors, right where Johnny happened to be at that very moment. Johnny rushed to help him to his feet.

"Sir, let me help you. You look like you could use a drink of water. Sit here on this bale of straw and I'll fetch some from the well."

The man shuffled to where he could sit and fell awkwardly onto the straw. Johnny tried to hold his arm, uncertain whether the man could even sit unassisted. When Johnny returned, the man had taken his beat-up, dusty hat off and was fanning himself with it. The man's face was red from too much sun, but his forehead and the top of his balding head were nearly white.

"Here you are, sir," Johnny said, handing him the cup. "You look like maybe you came from a ways off."

"Started out in Silver City. Had a horse, a revolver, and a rifle. Had a bedroll and saddlebags with food, too. Until that lanky son of a bitch throwed down on me and took everything I had. Told me I'd best start hoofin' it or I'd likely die from sunstroke. Damned near did, too."

"Would you like me to go get the sheriff? He can maybe gather a posse and apprehend the rascal."

"Too damned late now. I've been on the road for a spell without a cent to my name and no way to pay for a ride on the stagecoach even if one happened by. Only one I got sight of was off in the distance just before he took the cutoff to Albuquerque. I couldn't get his attention. Slept in a rancher's barn and ate with his family for several days. Didn't have the money to buy a horse from him, though. So, after a while, I started hoofin' it here."

"That's terrible. You sit there and rest awhile, and I'll go fetch the sheriff. If you'd like more water, the well is just out back," Johnny said. He scooted out of the livery before the man could object. Johnny knew the old man thought it had been too long since he'd been accosted for the sheriff to be of any help, but he had to try. Someone needed to try.

He returned in about twenty minutes with the sheriff in tow. The lawman wore a rumpled pair of wool pants and a yellowed cotton shirt, spotted with stains of tobacco that hadn't been spit hard enough or far enough to avoid blowback.

"Here's the gent I told you about, Sheriff. He looks to be in awful shape. Been robbed and left to die in the desert, I reckon." The sheriff nodded and stepped inside the dark barn.

"Good day to you, sir," the sheriff said, holding out his hand. The only reply he got was a weak attempt at a "howdy." "Boy here tells me you were robbed out near the road to Albuquerque, that right?"

"That's the way it was, Sheriff. Took everythin' I owned: my rifle, gun belt and revolver, saddlebags, and ever' last cent I had to my name. Then he had the gall to shoot my horse so's I couldn't track him down."

The sheriff rubbed his whiskered chin and pushed his slouch hat back on his head. The look on his face suggested he didn't intend on doing much other than listen to the man's complaint and maybe jot down a few particulars. Mostly, that was so that in case something similar ever came up, he could say he'd heard of another instance that was just like it.

"Reckon you best come on down to the jail and give me all the particulars. I'll make note of 'em. Got no paper or pencil with me." He started to walk away as Johnny helped the old man to his feet.

"This jail very far, young man?"

"No. Just a few doors down on the other side of the street. Think you can make it with my help?"

"I'll give it a try. Here, take my arm and steady me till I get my legs under me."

Johnny helped the man all the way to the jail. When they got there, the sheriff was already seated at his desk, had a piece of paper in front of him, and was licking the lead of a stubby pencil.

"Have a seat and tell me what you can."

"Well, like I told this here youngster, I was comin' from Silver City, bound for Las Cruces, when this tall, rangy feller rode up and asked if I had the makin's. I said I did, and whilst I was fishin' around in my pocket for the tobacco pouch, he up and threwed down on me. Told me to get my hands high or I wouldn't see another dawn."

The sheriff was trying to keep up with the story he was being told, but he clearly couldn't, since he had to stop every few words to remoisten his pencil. When the man stopped talking, the sheriff continued until he was up to where the old man had left off. He looked up and said, "I don't suppose you could describe this gent, could you?"

"Well, of course I can describe him. Hell, it ain't every day I get robbed. Doubt I'll ever forget it. Nor the man who done it, neither."

"Good. What did he look like?" The sheriff prepared to begin writing again.

"Like I said, he was tall, rangy. Wore a dark duster and a large, bright red bandana. Carried one of them Smith & Wesson Schofields. Forty-five, if I saw correctly. Ridin' a mare."

"You see which way he was headin'?" The sheriff narrowed his eyes.

"Took the road west. Probably goin' to Apache Springs, unless I miss my guess."

The sheriff looked at Johnny. "That's sounds a lot like the man that hit the Mexican lady's brother, don't it?"

"It sure as hell does. And it's for sure the man I'm goin' to kill the second I lay eyes on him again." Johnny jumped up, put his hat on, and ran from the sheriff's office. The sheriff called after him, but to no avail. He went straight for the hotel restaurant where Rachael worked. He could hardly contain himself. When he burst in, Rachael was stacking some newly washed dishes on a shelf.

"Rachael. I know where he's goin'."

"Where who's going, Johnny?"

"Carp Varner. And we're goin' after him just as soon as you can get your things together and I can saddle the horse."

"But, but, Johnny, I can't just up and leave now. These good folks are relying on me to help out. Besides, it's too late in the day to start out."

"I know, but we may never get this chance again. I *have* to go after him. And right away before he gets too far ahead of us. He murdered all my friends, folks that fed me, clothed me, give me a job in the stables, taught me how to use a gun. I can't let 'em down. He did you wrong, too, you know. We both got to make him pay, don't we?"

"I-I s'pose, but . . ."

"But nothin'. Get your stuff together and let's get a move on. Hurry, I'll meet you at the livery." Johnny ran out the door before Rachael could utter another word in protest. She was suddenly torn between joining Johnny in going after Varner and staying with people who'd shown her that she could make it on her own. She was hoping to build a future, something she'd never thought she could do. But then she owed Johnny so much. He'd saved her life—twice. He'd treated her with respect, never asked anything of her she wasn't willing to give, and now he needed her to accompany him on a journey that could easily cost them their lives. It was a lot to ask of anyone.

Her head was abuzz with conflict. She was staring at the open door when she heard a voice that startled her.

"What is it, dear? What's bothering you?" asked the restaurant owner.

"Uh, oh, it's nothing, ma'am. My friend Johnny is leaving and he asked me to go with him. I-I'm kinda twisted up inside, I'm afraid. I'm sorry to be a bother."

"A bother? Pshaw. There's nothing in this world more important than friendship, young lady. If you're holding back for fear of disappointing me, don't you dwell on that for a moment. I'll get along fine, always have, always will. But, child, you've a chance for more than friendship with that young man. I'd take it and not even look back."

"Thank you, ma'am. I'll always be grateful for your understanding," Rachael called back as she rushed out to find Johnny.

Chapter 38

Johnny and Rachael pointed the mare in the direction of Apache Springs, with their sole aim a rendezvous with a killer.

After having given more thought to the lateness of the hour, they'd decided to stay that night at the livery in order to get a fresh start in the morning. But soon after sunrise, they rode out of town with Rachael's arms tightly around Johnny's waist. She leaned her chin on his shoulder and tilted her head just enough to nuzzle his ear. A chill ran up his spine. *What the hell is that all about?* he thought. In the little time he'd known her, he had felt something growing inside, something he couldn't explain. He saw in her eyes that she, too, was becoming more than a friend. But what? The last night they'd spent on the trail, he'd looked over at her when she bent over at the stream to wash her hair. To keep her shirt from getting soaked, she'd slipped it off her shoulders, letting it cling to her upper arms and breasts. He thought his heart was going to burst in his chest. He was so shaken, he quit washing himself and went back to build a fire. Ever since that night, he'd been having strange feelings. He was afraid of what it might be. He remembered his father saying once that Johnny would know when the right woman came along, because he'd start to tingle all over and get sweaty whenever he thought about her. His father had called it: love.

Rachael whispered something in his ear. The wind was blowing hard enough that he didn't quite get the gist of what she was saying. He ignored her with a nod and a grunt and kept on riding. Suddenly, she punched him in the back. That stopped the tingles and made him pay closer attention.

"Wh-what?"

"Can we stop and rest for a while? I'm tuckered out. I need to get down and tend to . . ."

She needn't explain further. Johnny understood and reined the mare off the trail and into a copse of trees. She slipped from her perch behind him and rushed into the thick brush. Following her lead, he dropped from the saddle. He stretched his arms and took the saddlebags over to a clearing. There were plenty of rocks to use in making a fire ring. Since there didn't seem to be any water nearby, he had to be very careful lighting a fire without some protection from the wind. A brush fire in the desert could decimate an area hundreds of miles in all directions. Sufficient deadfall would make a fire easy to build, and he set about doing just that.

When Rachael emerged from the brush, she walked over and sat on a fallen tree trunk. "Thanks," she said.

Johnny had a nice little fire going and had dropped some coffee in the pot. He added water from his canteen and set it on a rock right next to the blaze. He was rubbing his hands together to get the circulation coming back after so long gripping the reins.

"Sure," he said. "I'll have some coffee in a few minutes. And I think there are still some biscuits left." Rachael got up and lifted the flap on the saddlebags and peered inside.

She rummaged around through the collection of items they'd cobbled together for their trip. They had no idea how far they would have to travel before locating their quarry: Carp Varner.

She pulled out a couple of the biscuits and handed one to Johnny. "Guess we might as well eat 'em. They're starting to get hard."

"Maybe by tonight we'll find a town or ranch house where we can bed down on something easier on our backs than pebbles and burrs," he said.

"Doesn't it seem like we should have come to a sign or something telling us where Apache Springs is?" she asked.

"Uh, yeah, I think so, but . . ."

Just then the sound of a wagon rattling along the dusty road caught their attention. Johnny stood, cupped his hand over his eyes, and squinted into the afternoon sun. He saw a buckboard loaded with burlap bags being driven by a woman. A very attractive woman at that. Alongside her rode an old Indian on a paint pony.

Johnny and Rachael ventured out to where they could be seen by the lady. He held up a hand to attract attention. The lady reined in the buckboard, while the Indian eyed them warily.

"G'day, ma'am. We were wondering if you knew the way to Apache Springs. I think we may be lost," Johnny said, taking off his hat, something he'd been taught to do when greeting a lady. Rachael shuffled up behind him, looking trail weary.

"You two traveling together, are you? Where are you from?" Emily Wagner asked.

"Yes, ma'am, we are," Rachael said shyly. Johnny had started to answer, but Rachael beat him to it. She stepped in front of him to speak her piece. "We came from Texas."

"That's a pretty long trip. How many days have you been on the trail?"

"I-I'm not real sure. Seems like a year. I . . ." Rachael said, but she was cut off by Johnny jumping in.

"Been out several weeks, I reckon. Don't know exactly how long. Had to lay over in Las Cruces because a catamount jumped Rachael and near tore her arm off. Had to get a doc to patch her up."

"Goodness! Are you going to be okay, child?"

"Yes, ma'am, I'm well on the mend. Thanks to Johnny."

"I must say you neither one look like you've had a bite to eat for days."

"Uh, yeah, well I s'pose it has been a while," Johnny said, drawing a circle in the dust with the toe of his boot.

"Then we must do something about that. My ranch is only about a mile up this road. You come along with us and I'll make sure you get fed and rested before you continue on to town. How does that sound?"

Before Johnny could say a word, Rachael blurted out, "That sounds wonderful, ma'am."

Emily suggested Rachael climb up beside her and ride in the buckboard. It was a suggestion that was met with mixed emotions by Johnny. He knew it had been hard on the mare to carry two people all the distance they'd traveled, but he sure did like having the feisty young girl clinging to him like an apple refusing to fall from the tree. He liked the feel of her body and the smell of her hair. Nevertheless, without complaint, he wheeled the mare around and fell in behind the wagon. He was joined by the scary-looking Apache wearing knee-high deerskin boots, a cloth headband wrapped around his forehead, and a bandolier of cartridges for the Spencer rifle he carried. Johnny looked over and smiled at the old Indian, but was met with a blank expression and black, suspicious eyes.

When they pulled up in front of the Wagner ranch house, Rachael couldn't believe her eyes. It was just what she'd always dreamed a ranch house should look like. It had a large, wide porch, with real glass windows and a huge chimney coming right out of the middle of the roof. Even after Emily got down and called out for some of the hands to come unload the buckboard, Rachael sat mesmerized by the size of this fine house.

"Come on, dear, and let me show you around. Henry Coyote can show your friend where he can unsaddle your mare and get her fed and rubbed down. I'll bet a little attention won't hurt her feelings. Oh dear, I've forgotten a very important part of my manners. I hope you'll forgive me. I'm Emily Wagner. I own this ranch."

"I'm Rachael and he's Johnny."

"Are you brother and sister?"

"Oh, no. He's, uh, well . . ."

"Never mind, dear; it's not important. Come in and sit while I fix something to fill your stomachs."

Rachael followed obediently. She looked back quickly to see Johnny reluctantly trailing the Apache. She could tell Johnny wasn't certain how to adjust to having an Indian so close without fearing the loss of his scalp. But there was something about the old man she found reassuring, almost comforting. As she sank deeply into the leather couch, her eyes danced from one fine thing to another. *Oh, to live a life like this.*

Then she heard something sizzling in another room, and the smells of fresh bread invaded her senses. She was certain she had just stumbled into heaven.

Chapter 39

Mayor Orwell Plume strolled into the sheriff's office as casual as you please. A stranger would assume it was an act repeated on a regular basis between fellow town officials. But a visit from the mayor was anything but a usual occurrence. Cotton sensed a note of negativity about to explode across his desk. He didn't stand, but stuck out his hand. They shook as he motioned the mayor into the chair across from him.

"This certainly is a rare visit, Mr. Mayor. I take it you got somethin' on your mind."

"You sure do get to the meat of things in a hurry, don't you, Burke?"

"I've had to face down some of the worst hombres this territory has to offer; didn't give me much time to dance around. When a gun's about to be drawn, that's not the time for askin' questions."

"I see your point. Well, then I best get to it. The reason I'm here is to make mention of the fact that the new gunsmith took

over *your* responsibility for a moment and drilled a couple of
would-be bank robbers. Caught 'em in the act, so to speak.
I'm wonderin' where you were while all this was goin' down."

"Not real sure what you're gettin' at, Mayor. Never figured I was expected to sit outside the bank to ward off evil
if it should stop by."

"Not at all, not at all. However, it shouldn't be left up to
the citizenry, either."

"And the point you're tryin' to make is . . . ?"

"The thought crossed my mind that, since the election
for sheriff, clerk, and mayor is comin' upon us in a rush,
perhaps it wouldn't be such a bad idea for there to be a little
competition for a change to make the race more interestin'."

"And who did you have in mind to run against me?"

"Right offhand, I'd say that Varner fella might take a
few votes out of your column, bein' as how he's a hero of
sorts right now. Looks like he can shoot, too. That's the
kind of sheriff we need. A decisive one. No nonsense.
Shoot and be done with it."

"Uh-huh. Anybody suggested they make a run at the
mayor's office?"

"Now that you mention it, no. It's not likely, either."

"How do you figure?"

"Bein' mayor takes someone with a business head, good
with keepin' folks happy about the way the town's growin'
and lookin' out for the little fellow."

"And you don't figure there is such a person here in
Apache Springs, right?" Cotton asked.

"That's about the size of it."

Cotton rubbed his chin and smiled.

"I take it you disagree."

"I do."

"I'm pretty certain *you* aren't interested in the job, seein'
as how you hate makin' speeches and such."

"You're absolutely correct there, Mayor. I'm not the
least interested in takin' over your desk."

"But you do have someone in mind, don't you?" The mayor scrunched up his face.

"Uh-huh."

The mayor waited and waited. Finally, out of patience, he blurted out, "Well, spit it out, man! I don't have forever. Who is it?"

"I was thinkin' that we might need someone who has a real feel for the community. Someone who knows almost everyone by their first name, at least all the men. After all, it's the men who spend most of the money and make all the big decisions, like electing a mayor, and all."

Plume squinted. His forehead was so wrinkled it looked like a prune. "Who would that be?"

"Why the only logical choice: Melody Wakefield," Cotton said, with a huge grin as he raised both eyebrows.

Plume stood up in a flash, knocking over his chair, his fists balled so tightly his knuckles were turning white.

"What! What kind of bull are you spreadin' around, Sheriff? There's no way in hell that damned whore could get elected mayor! I don't have to listen to any more of your crap!" He turned to storm out. Cotton silently watched after him.

Don't count on it, pard. Don't count on it. He leaned back in his chair and interlaced his fingers behind his head. He was shaken from his thoughts by the rumble of the afternoon stage. He got up and walked to the door. As the coach pulled up in front of the hotel, a man Cotton guessed to be about thirty stepped off, looked around, and went inside.

By the time the sheriff got to the hotel, the man was signing the guest register. Cotton walked up to him. The man turned, saw the badge, and smiled.

"You must be Sheriff Burke. Good to meet you. My name is Turner Burnside. I wrote you about my uncle's gunsmith shop."

Cotton extended his hand. They shook.

"Glad you're here, Mr. Burnside. Let's go over to the saloon and chat before I take you over to your uncle's shop."

"Fine. I'll just take my bag upstairs and join you in a minute."

The desk clerk handed the man a key and pointed to the first room at the top of the stairs. Burnside disappeared into his room, returning within seconds.

"I'm ready, Sheriff. Lead the way."

"At the moment, another man is using your uncle's shop to repair guns. He came to town the day before your uncle died. Kind of a coincidence, I'll admit, but we couldn't find anything suspicious about that. The thing is, that man desires to stay on and keep the business open. But, of course, if you have the same desire, then obviously the business must go to you. That's the reason I wanted us to chat before you went down there."

"I understand, Sheriff. Good of you to warn me. My uncle taught me well in the art of gunsmithing. I'm no slouch at repairing, even building weaponry. In fact, I had my own shop in Boston before coming out here. The business of personal weapons has dropped off quite a bit back East, so I figured since the frontier is still relatively wild, maybe the time was right for a move."

"'Wild' is a pretty fair description, I'd have to say, Mr. Burnside," Cotton said.

"Call me Turner, Sheriff. Please."

"All right, Turner, I suggest we have ourselves another beer before surprising Mr. Varner."

"Varner? Did you say Varner? Would that be Carp Varner?"

"Why yes, it most certainly is. Do you know him?"

"That dirty, thieving piece of lowlife trash nearly ruined my family. That's how well I know him."

"I reckon you best tell me the whole story, Turner. I'd be most interested in hearing it."

Turner Burnside leaned across the table so they could talk without being overheard. Cotton asked Arlo to bring over two more beers. He leaned on his elbows. When the beers came, Arlo nodded to them both and returned to his post behind the long bar. Cotton took a long sip.

"Well, Turner, I'm all ears. What can you tell me about Mr. Varner?"

"My uncle set up shop in St. Louis a number of years back. He was doing well. He and my aunt had a profitable store selling and repairing all sorts of weapons. One day, Carp Varner came by asking my uncle for a job. There wasn't enough business to support three gunsmiths, since my uncle already had a helper. It wasn't long before Varner opened his own shop right next door. The difference was he put a big sign in his window. It said: ALL GUNS REPAIRED FREE! I don't suppose it takes much imagination to figure what happened."

"Yeah. Your uncle's business dried up in a hurry."

"That's right. Offer someone something free, and he'll take it every time over having to shell out hard-earned cash. That's when my uncle moved his business out here, in an attempt to get away from such underhanded business tactics."

"Did you ever hear of your uncle having any health problems?"

"Not that I ever heard of. Why do you ask?"

"Just curious. He died shortly after Varner showed up in town," Cotton said.

"Hmm. Any chance he could have seen Varner and it shook him up bad enough to cause his death?"

"Could be. Maybe both your aunt dying and seeing Varner played a part in his untimely death. I'm sure goin' to miss that man."

"Yeah." Turner drank down his beer, looking wistfully off in the distance. "Me, too."

Chapter 40

"D id you two get enough to eat?" Emily asked.

"Oh, yes, ma'am," Rachael said, while Johnny nodded his approval and wiped his mouth with a napkin.

"Now, you must tell me what brings you to this part of the country."

Reluctant to tell anyone his real purpose for coming to Apache Springs, Johnny did more than his share of hemming and hawing. Rachael, noticing his reticence, jumped in and came up with a story she hoped Mrs. Wagner might find acceptable.

"It all started with me, Mrs. Wagner. My, uh, *father* left me alone to go find work. Our ranch was failing and he saw no other way to get money. He was gone for such a long time, I was running out of food. Then a man came along and robbed me of everything I had left. I was about done in when Johnny happened by and saved me. He got me back on my feet, went out and hunted game to feed us, and as soon as I was strong enough, we took what we could carry and went in search of another ranch. It seemed like we'd walked for days before we came to a ranch. They were such nice folks. They fed us, and when they went to show us a horse they could lend us, it turned out to be my *father's* horse. The rancher had found a man dead along the road. Turned out to be my, er, *father.* The rancher took the horse and put her in their corral in hopes one of the dead man's family would come along and claim her. It was just fate, I reckon," Rachael said.

"My goodness, young lady, that was some story. Lucky for you this boy came along."

"Yes, ma'am, it surely was."

"Well, exactly what was your purpose in coming to Apache Springs then? Especially since there must have been a dozen towns bigger that you came through."

"We, uh, heard of some opportunities here," Johnny blurted out, and was almost immediately sorry he had.

"What kind of opportunities, Johnny? There's not too much I can think of for two young folks looking to get a start."

"What Johnny means is that we talked between ourselves and decided we should start small, then maybe build up," Rachael said.

"What experience do either of you have that would make someone want to take you on?"

"Johnny knows a lot about horses, and I, uh, can cook and sew and . . ."

"I see. Well, then, I have a proposition for you. Johnny, I'll have Henry show you our stable of horses, and maybe you can help out around here, just until you feel comfortable to move on, of course. And, Rachael, you can certainly be helpful in feeding the ranch hands. They can get a powerful hunger on, and it's sometimes difficult for me to keep up with feeding all of them."

Johnny looked at Rachael and she eyed him back. Emily couldn't quite get a handle on what was transpiring between them, but she was certain they hadn't been completely honest with her. It was obvious they had come a long way, and few people would embark on such a journey without a powerful reason for doing so. All she had to do was bide her time and pick up on the little things that often pass between people without them even knowing it.

Finally, Rachael spoke up. "That sounds like a wonderful opportunity, ma'am. We'll take you up on it. Oh, can you tell me how far it is to Apache Springs? That's just in case one of us needs to go into town for, uh, supplies or something."

"It's about two hours down the road. But I doubt you'll want to make it a regular trip, since you'll both have duties here. We can certainly go in on Saturday to stock up on beans and flour and the like. That'd be a good time for Johnny to go along and help load the wagon and have a look around. That sound all right?"

"Yes, ma'am. That sounds like a wonderful idea," Rachael said, watching Johnny's frowning reaction out of the corner of her eye. "Johnny thinks so, too, don't you?"

"Huh? Oh, uh, yeah. Real good."

"Fine. I'll have Henry show you around, Johnny. You just wait here and I'll go call to him." When Emily left the room, Johnny jumped on Rachael, taking care not to be overheard.

"What's the idea? We got to get to town to find Varner. He ain't goin' to come nosin' around out here in the sticks," he said in a loud whisper.

"We need to watch and wait. We'll get our opportunity. But if we go running around like a chicken with no head, without knowing where he is or what he's doing, well, he could get wise to us and be waiting. You need to learn patience. That's something my ma always told me. And I believed her. It worked for me and it'll work for you."

Johnny was sitting with a dark frown when Emily returned with Henry right behind her.

"Tell you what, Turner, what say we go to the hotel for some dinner. That'll give us time to put together a plan so's we don't spook Varner. If he's guilty of anything illegal, we need to bide our time and be ready. That sound all right to you?"

"Yessir, sounds just fine to me. Only real food I've had for a spell was at the last relay station, and that was questionable."

"Well then, I hope you're hungry because the hotel puts on a pretty hefty feed bag," Cotton said. They left the saloon and headed straight for the hotel. The route would take them within sight of Varner's shop. That wasn't by accident. Cotton wanted Varner to get a look at Burnside's nephew, to see if he recognized him. And if he did, what might his reaction be?

The sheriff didn't have to wait long. As they passed by, Varner could be seen standing in his doorway glaring at them both as if they were his mortal enemies. For all Cotton knew, they might just be. He didn't hesitate or stop to talk but, instead, kept the pace up, chatting with Turner about nothing in particular. When they entered the hotel, Cotton took a quick glance back to see if Varner had watched them the whole way. He had, slamming his door only after they had nearly disappeared inside. *Temperamental bastard, isn't he?*

"You work on ranch?" Henry asked Johnny as they entered the barn. Johnny followed him to where he picked up a bucket and filled it with grain from a bag. He carried it to one of the stalls and poured it into the trough.

"Uh, no, not really. I mostly did odd jobs here and there, at least until my father brought me to Whiskey Crossing," Johnny said. "That's kinda where I grew up."

"Where this Whiskey Crossing?"

"It is, er, *was* a small town in Texas. That was, uh, before Varner showed up."

"Where town go?" Henry seemed not to understand the boy's hesitant words. Yet he could tell there was much more inside the boy's head, and he'd probably have to drag it out of him to get a complete picture.

"It burned up. Killed every living thing—people, animals, everything. All up in smoke; the most terrible fire you can imagine. Now there's nothing left out there on the prairie but charred remains of buildings and bones of the dead." Johnny looked away, as if it was all too painful to remember. Henry decided not to push.

Chapter 41

When Henry left Johnny for a few minutes to return to the ranch house, he called for Emily to step out on the porch. She could tell he had something important to say and didn't want to be overheard.

"What is it, Henry?" she said, wiping her hands on a towel.

"Boy tell bad story. Many people die in fire. He see it all. Not good for boy so young."

"Did he say where this happened?"

"He call place Whiskey Crossing. Say it white man's town, place he call Texas."

"That's all he said?"

"Yes."

Puzzled by the boy's story, Emily decided she'd see what Rachael knew of this "Whiskey Crossing." She asked Henry to try to keep the boy busy with chores, anything to keep him occupied for a while, and to find out anything more that he could. Henry grunted and shuffled back to the barn. When he got there, Johnny was brushing down the mare he and Rachael had ridden all the way from where Rachael's "father" had died in Texas.

As Emily entered the living room, she stopped to watch the young girl standing on tiptoes and struggling to reach a book on the shelves next to the fireplace. For a moment, at least, Emily saw herself in that youthful exhibition of curiosity and a desire for learning.

"See one that interests you?" Emily said.

Startled by Emily's voice, Rachael nearly lost her balance. Fortunately, she had a firm grip on the edge of the shelf.

"Y-yes, ma'am. I-I hope you don't mind, but I've always been fascinated by books."

"I don't mind at all. In fact, I'm pleased to find someone so young with a desire to learn. Come sit on the couch and show me what you've found."

Rachael sat beside her and held up a copy of *The Leatherstocking Tales* by James Fenimore Cooper. The book was bound nicely with a pressed leather cover and gilt edges on the pages. The title was embossed in gold leaf.

"This one is so beautiful. And there's this man with a very strange name: Natty Bumppo. I've never heard such a funny name. It makes me giggle."

"Cooper was a wonderful author. I have several of his. You're welcome to read any of them you'd like. He's somewhat of a favorite of mine, too."

Rachael began leafing through the first few pages. Whenever she came to an engraving of the story's action, she stopped, mesmerized by the wonderful illustrations. Emily sat for a while and watched the girl as she was caught up in the beauty of the book, moving her lips silently as she read occasional passages, and turning pages with the careful respect of a librarian.

"Rachael, what can you tell me about what happened to Johnny before he found you?"

Rachael put the book in her lap. Her eyes became distant and sad.

"I only know what he told me, but from what he said, it must have been horrible. Much worse than what happened to me."

"I suppose I don't really know what happened to you, either. Why don't we talk about it? Sometimes, when you are able to discuss terrible memories with someone who understands, it makes the memories less painful."

"Well, all right. I'll try."

Rachael launched into the story of her treatment by an older man to whom her mother and father had sold her into servitude. He'd insisted she call him "Pa," mostly because of the age difference. But since he wasn't really her father, she felt little or no affection for him. As she began to develop into a young woman, the man began to make advances on her, which she had always been able to fend off. But things began to go bad with the livestock and what few crops they had in. That's when her phony father decided he'd go into the nearest town to find work. When he didn't return for weeks and the food had all but run out, Rachael didn't know what to do.

"I'm sorry I led you to believe it was my real father that died," Rachael said.

"That's all right, dear. Go ahead with your story."

"Well, as I said before, a stranger stopped and stole what little I had left. That's when Johnny happened on me lying on the floor of the small cabin. He saved my life, that's what he did. And he never asked a thing for the help, neither. He's been a good friend."

"It sure sounds that way. You've had a pretty hard time of it. I'm thinking you should stay around here for a spell, at least until you have a notion as to where you'd like to go and how you're going to get there. You know, the both of you riding that poor mare out there is sooner or later going to take its toll, and she'll break down. Then you'll find yourselves afoot and in an even worse situation."

"But I don't know nothin' about ranchin', Miss Emily."

"Oh, my dear, believe me, you can be a heap of help to me. Why, just having another female around to talk to is worth its weight in gold."

"Well, yes, ma'am, I reckon I can see how it might be, at that," Rachael said, giving Emily an understanding smile, the first smile she'd displayed since arriving at the Wagner ranch.

"I never knew a real Injun before, Mr. Henry. I hear you people can find things that's been hid better'n anyone. That true? Could you really find this penknife of mine if I was to hide it real good?" Johnny said.

A wry grin came over the old Apache's face. He liked the idea of being challenged by this young white boy. He gave an affirmative nod. Johnny eagerly took up the challenge and in an instant tore out of the bunkhouse to find a suitable hiding place. On his way, he thought it clever to try throwing the Indian off his trail by removing his boots and setting them on the stoop of the ranch house. Then, trying to think even farther ahead, he wrapped his feet in two cloths that were hanging on a clothesline. He looked around until he spotted a gnarled mesquite a hundred yards away. *The old man will never find it in the crotch of that tangled mess*, he thought, and proceeded to stick it down as far as he could into a hole hollowed out by birds or insects.

When he came sauntering back into the bunkhouse, apparently quite pleased with himself, he leaned on the doorpost and peered in. Sitting at a table, the old Apache looked up from taking a sip of coffee.

"I'm ready, Mr. Henry. I hid it. And I'll bet you don't find it." Johnny's smug expression amused Henry, and he chuckled all the way out the door.

Outside, the Apache stood momentarily looking at the ground, shaking his head. He lifted his head, cupped his weathered hand over his eyes to cut the glare of the searing sun, and slowly, deliberately began sniffing the air.

"Why are you doing that, Henry?"

"Smell direction of boy," Henry said.

Needless to say, Henry Coyote was not fooled by the boy's supposedly clever devices and, instead, walked straight for the mesquite tree, reached down into the maze of limbs that came together at the trunk, and pulled out the knife.

Johnny's eyes grew wide as he saw all his cleverness go for naught. As Henry returned to hand him the knife, the boy was spluttering.

"H-how'd y-you do that? Are you a magician? You got eyes in the back of your head or somethin'?"

Henry grinned big before returning to his coffee. He took a sip.

"You not see window in side of building?"

Chapter 42

———◆———

Emily stood on the porch and called to Henry. When he ran up to her, she whispered that she wanted him to go into town and ask Cotton to come out to the ranch. She was convinced the sheriff needed to hear the story of what Johnny and Rachael had been through directly from them. She was quite certain there was more to it, and she had become alarmed by some of what she'd overheard from the boy, mingled with what Henry had been able to glean.

When the Indian left, Johnny came out of the barn, after pitching hay to several horses.

"Where's Henry goin', Miss Emily?"

"I sent him into town to invite someone for dinner. Someone I'd like very much for you and Rachael to meet."

"Oh, who's that?" he asked.

"You'll see. He's a special friend of mine. You'll like him."

There was something about the secretiveness with which she'd sent Henry off. Johnny had noticed her whispering to the Indian, and he'd felt a tingle run up his spine. *What's she up to? I wonder if it has anything to do with us.* His natural inclination to trust no one was once again gripping him, and his youthful imagination began to soar.

"You go on back to whatever Henry had you doing, and I'll start fixing something special for us all. I'll call you soon to help with getting some wood for the stove. Okay?"

"Uh-huh. I mean yes, ma'am," Johnny said, with a hint of suspicion in his voice.

He went back to the task set for him, but he was increasingly concerned about Henry's sudden departure at Emily's bequest. *Why isn't that old Indian here to show me what all my duties might be?* He hurried through the task of turning horses out into the corral, including the mare he and Rachael had ridden in on. He patted the horse's neck. Still puzzled by Henry's leaving, he decided to find Rachael and confer with her. *Maybe she's overheard something. She might know what's going on.*

Stabbing the pitchfork into a pile of straw, he started for the house. As he rounded the corner to the back door, Rachael stepped out with a pan full of dirty water and dumped it on the ground, narrowly missing Johnny.

"Hey! Wh-what's the idea?"

"Ohmigosh! Johnny, I'm so sorry. I didn't see you. Here, take this towel and dry off whatever splashed on you."

"Actually, I don't think I got any on me at all. Reckon I was just surprised."

"Good. What're you doing coming to the kitchen door, anyway?"

"I needed to see you. Henry left in a hurry after talking in hushed tones with the ranch lady. I need to know if you've heard her say anything that might make you think our mission is in trouble."

"I don't understand."

"She was whisperin' to him and then he rushed off, mounted up, and tore outta here like the cavalry was chasing him. I need to figure out if it has to do with us."

"And if it does?"

"Okay, here's the way I see things. What if Carp Varner *is* in Apache Springs like we figured? And what if he's worked his way into the confidence of important people? I'd bet he's good at that. Miss Emily is one of those *important* people, at least as close as I can figure, what with her owning this big ranch and all."

"So what? First of all, Carp Varner doesn't know we're on his trail. And Miss Emily doesn't know that, either. We've never even mentioned his name. Unless, of course, you opened your mouth to the Apache."

Johnny gave her a scowl. "Of course I didn't say anything. Not a word." At least not a word he could remember. He *had* told the Indian that he'd come from a town that got burned to the ground. But no particulars were discussed, and nothing about Carp Varner. He was damned certain of that. Well, pretty certain.

"Then I don't see what you're so worried about. Besides, what can we do about it anyway?"

"I, uh, don't reckon I know. But the—"

"But nothin'. Now, I have work to do and I need to get back to it. I suggest you do the same. If Miss Emily is affordin' us a nice place to stay, feedin' us good food, and all she's askin' in return is a little help here and there, then I say we owe her. Now, scoot." Rachael turned on her heel and hurried back inside. The door closed behind her. Johnny was left standing there alone with nothing more than an unsettling feeling that something wasn't quite right. He was a bit unsettled by Rachael's dressing him down, too.

"Turner, I'm gettin' a strange feelin' about what happened to your uncle. It might be best if you don't meet up with Carp Varner just yet, at least not until I do a little more checkin' up on the man," Cotton said. "Do you mind puttin' off seein' the store for a spell?"

"After finding out that Carp Varner is here, I'm eager to

follow your lead, Sheriff. And I have no wish to meet him face-to-face. The man is a viper, of that I am certain."

"Good. And if you wouldn't mind, make it a point to keep out of his way, just in case he has plans to keep you from movin' in. If he's as devious as you say, he might be capable of most anything."

"From what I heard about him from my uncle, I'd say you're right."

"Well, you kinda settle in, enjoy the town, and keep your ear to the ground."

As Turner Burnside left Cotton's office, Henry Coyote reined in out front. The old Indian slid from his pony's back and eased through the door as silently as a wraith. Cotton hadn't heard him arrive and was startled when he looked up to see the Apache's grinning face.

"Got message from Miss Emily."

"Have a seat, Henry, and tell me."

Henry refused the offer and proceeded to give him the message.

"I must return to ranch. Miss Emily say you come to ranch tonight. Two people come and she say you must have talk."

"Two people, huh? Who are they?"

"White-eyes. Young colts. Boy and squaw. I go now. You come soon. I tell Miss Emily."

"Two young white yearlings, huh? That's interesting."

Henry grunted acknowledgment and turned to leave.

"Do you think they spell trouble?"

"Trouble for someone maybe." Henry left before Cotton could probe further.

The sheriff stared after the Indian, puzzled by the cryptic message. He chewed his lip for a moment before drawing his Colt to check his loads.

Chapter 43

Johnny watched another young cowboy backing a horse into a wagon's shaves. He didn't appear to be much older than Johnny himself. As Johnny leaned on the doorframe, an idea came to him. He walked over to the cowboy and stood watching for a moment before speaking.

"Howdy, name's Johnny. You work for Miss Emily, too?"

"Teddy Olander," the boy said, as he stuck out his hand. "Yep. Been here awhile, I reckon."

"Need help?"

"If you want to, you can put the harness on and get her all cinched up. I'll hook up the chest strap."

"You like it here?" Johnny asked, as he set to fitting the harness and hooking up the old mare to the buckboard.

"Sure do. Best outfit this side of the springs."

"Springs?"

"Yeah, the springs. That's where Apache Springs got its name. It's the source of the town's freshwater. Don't you know nothin'?"

"I, uh, reckon not all that much. Not about this country, leastways," Johnny said.

"Well, that's all right. I didn't know diddly when I first came, either."

"Looks like you're fixin' to go somewhere."

"Yep. Miss Emily is sending me into town to pick up some tools and such. A couple of boxes of nails and several rolls of fence wire."

"You figure they'll be pretty heavy?"

"Yeah, I suppose. Why?"

"Just thinkin' maybe I should go with you. To help with the liftin' and all."

Teddy rubbed his chin as a frown came across his face.

"I don't know. Better ask Miss Emily. I wouldn't want her to get angry," Teddy said.

"Aww, she said I was to do the chores that old Indian gave me, and I've done all of 'em. So, until he gets back from wherever he got off to, I'm just sittin' around. I like to keep busy, you know?"

"Yeah. I feel the same way."

"C'mon. I won't get in the way, and I can lift pretty good, too. I'm stronger than I look. I'll bet you wouldn't mind an extra hand."

Teddy took off his slouch hat and wiped his brow with his sleeve. He glanced about, as if thinking that going against his better judgment wasn't such a good idea. Finally, he motioned Johnny to climb aboard the buckboard. Teddy took the driver's seat and slapped the reins to get the mare moving. They rattled off down the slight hill to join the road to town, jostling about with every rut the wagon could find. The rough ride came near to tossing Johnny out on his backside more than once. Teddy couldn't shake his concern, but he'd made the decision to let the boy come along, and it was too late to change his mind now. Johnny sat tightly gripping the side rails to the seat while trying to hide a satisfied grin and looking off toward the hills that ran along the road to the west.

"How far is it to town?" he asked.

"Couple hours. Not very far."

Johnny just nodded. He reached down with one hand to check the revolver on his hip.

"I'm goin' out to the Wagner place, Jack. Be back in the mornin'. I'm takin' the long way to get one more look at the place we found Pick's body. Keep an eye on things, will you? Especially that Carp Varner fella."

"You learn anything more 'bout him?"

"Nope, except that apparently Turner Burnside's uncle had a run-in with Varner back in St. Louis. Turner didn't have anything good to say about the man."

"What happened to our prisoner? I don't see him," Jack said, glancing about as if there'd been a jailbreak.

"Yeah, while you were getting reacquainted with Melody, a U.S. marshal from Texas came to take him back for trial. I told you he'd be showin' up sooner or later after I sent a telegram. They musta wanted him pretty bad 'cause they didn't waste any time comin' for him."

"You want me to air out the mattress in that cell? That Callahan brother seemed to have damned little regard for bathin'."

"Not a bad idea."

On the ride out to Emily's ranch, Cotton had some time to think about the Carp Varner situation. If he'd had bad thoughts about the man when he first arrived in town, finding out that he'd likely been the reason for Joshua Burnside's untimely exit from St. Louis made him even more suspicious about whatever happenstance had brought Varner to Apache Springs. Too many coincidences discomfited him. *Just what the hell is his real reason for being here? And his jumping in to stop a bank robbery was damned convenient, too.*

After mulling around his doubts about Varner, he turned up the collar on his coat to ward off a chill that had begun to drift down from the hills. The sky had gone from bright blue to charcoal gray, and a blustery wind was picking up. *I'll bet we're lookin' at our first snow before the week's out.*

When he reached the place where Pick Wheeler had been shot, Cotton dismounted and began wandering around, trying to find something, anything that might point to the guilty party. He spent over an hour, kicking rocks and brushing aside the tall grass and dried-up shrubs. The hoofprints of the horse that met Pick and stood while the two riders talked were unremarkable, but just then he saw a piece of paper caught in some brush and being wafted by the breeze. He bent over and plucked it from the grip of the leafless branches. It appeared to be a receipt from a business in Las Cruces. Cotton could think of no reason for its being there. He shrugged and stuck it in his shirt pocket. After an hour of his search for anything that might appear to be a clue, he gave up and went on to his intended destination.

Arriving at the Wagner ranch, he reined in by the corral. He dismounted and began to remove the mare's saddle. He was ready to take off the bridle when Henry came out of the bunkhouse. Henry came up to him looking grim.

"You see Teddy and other boy on way out?"

"Uh, no. Didn't pass anyone from the ranch. Why?"

"They go to town for nails and wire. Miss Emily worry there be trouble."

"I'll check on her. Thanks, Henry."

Stepping onto the porch, the door swung open and Emily Wagner rushed out to hug him.

"Thank goodness you're here. You must meet a young lady and hear her story. And the boy she arrived with, well, actually at the moment he's missing."

"Missing? Henry said he probably went to town with Teddy. I'd hardly call that 'missing.'"

"Wait till you hear what Rachael has to say. She's in the back. I'll get her."

Cotton got comfortable on the big leather couch. There was a small fire in the fireplace, just enough to take the chill out of the air, something he'd not seen for several months. It felt good. It felt like home. He casually glanced around the room, at the books that lined one wall, at the overstuffed chairs with doilies on the arms, at the pictures hanging by long wires from a strip of polished wood that went all the way around the room about two feet down from the ceiling.

He was dreaming of a life of leisure and how he might fit into it, when out of the corner of his eye he caught a movement. He turned to see a pretty young girl, whom he guessed to be no more than sixteen or seventeen, standing in the doorway. Her brown hair was gathered on top of her head and then wrapped in a scarf. She wore a simple cotton work dress with an apron he'd seen Emily wear a dozen times before. The girl was barefoot. She looked at the floor shyly.

"Rachael, this is a very close friend. He's the sheriff of Apache Springs, and I'm sure he'd be interested in hearing what you and Johnny have been through."

Cotton stood and smiled at the girl. He stuck out his hand, although he could tell she was reluctant to get too close to anyone wearing a badge. Finally, awkwardly, she gave a timid shake accompanied by a weak smile. Emily guided her to a chair that faced the couch, taking the seat next to Cotton herself.

"It's nice to meet you, Rachael. Where are you from?"

"Texas."

"Did your parents have a ranch there?"

"Uh, not really."

"Do they know where you are?"

"Doubt it. Besides they don't care."

"Oh, I'm sorry. So, you're all alone?"

"No. I got Johnny."

"Johnny's the young man you arrived with?"

"Yes."

"Is he a relative?"

"No."

"How'd you two come to meet up?"

"He saved my life."

Chapter 44

———◆———

Rachael wrung her hands as she tried to avoid looking the sheriff straight in the eye. He could tell she was scared, but of what he had no idea. Although it wasn't uncommon for young folks to be leery of the law, he could discern no reason for this shy girl to fear him. He self-consciously ran his fingers through his hair in case it was in such disarray as to give the appearance of an ogre. Emily, seeing the tension between them, suggested it was time for some coffee or tea. Rachael jumped up, volunteering to make some. Cotton started to say that it wasn't necessary, but Emily put a finger to her lips to shush him.

"That would be fine, dear. There is also a box of store-bought cookies on the first shelf. Bring them with you when you come back. If you'd rather not have coffee, make some tea. You saw where I put the tea, right next to the little ceramic pot, didn't you?"

"Yes, ma'am," Rachael called from the kitchen.

"What's goin' on, Emily? That poor girl's scared to death. And where *is* this Johnny she mentioned?"

"I don't know exactly. One of the other hands said they saw him riding off in the buckboard with Teddy Olander. He didn't tell me he was going, though. And it isn't like Teddy to let a stranger ride with him without first saying something to me. That's got me concerned."

"Yeh, Henry asked if I'd passed them comin' here. Are you certain they were headed to town?"

"I assume so. I sent Teddy into Hargreaves' Hardware for some rolls of fencing I'd ordered so we can expand the corral. The old corral can't hold all the new stock I've acquired recently. I asked Henry to give the boy a few chores to keep him busy. I'd told both him and the girl I'd let them stay, feed them, and give them a bed, and in return they were to help out with chores. Looks like he worked faster than I figured. After he'd finished up, he must have spotted Teddy getting ready to leave."

"Sounds like this Johnny was real anxious to get to Apache Springs. I wonder why."

"If you can get the girl to say more'n a few mumbled words, you may have your answer."

"Tall order."

Rachael returned with a plate of cookies and two cups of coffee. She was carrying them all on a silver tray. Placing the tray on a table next to where Emily was sitting, the girl resumed her own chair and sat silently with her hands folded in her lap.

"Thank you, Rachael. That was very nice. Coffee, Sheriff?"

"Yes, thanks," he said. "Now, Rachael, can you tell me about how Johnny came to save your life?"

Rachael's nervousness returned. It was clear that if Cotton wanted anything out of the shy girl, he was going to have to be very patient. Her story wasn't going to come easily. That's when he noticed what appeared to be wrappings or bandages showing beneath her simple cotton dress.

"What happened to your arm? Were you injured?" he asked.

"Yes, sir. A mountain lion jumped me. Nearly tore my arm to shreds."

"Is that when Johnny saved you?"

"Yes . . . the second time."

"He saved you more than once?"

"Yes, sir."

"That must have been quite an ordeal for a young lady. Are you pretty much healed up?"

"A doctor in Las Cruces fixed me. He sewed up the gashes and put some stuff on there to help it get better. I still wear some wrappin's to keep the dirt out. He said if it festered I could lose my arm, so I'm bein' real careful."

"Goodness!" Emily said. "If I'd known all this, I'd have taken you into town to have Doc Winters look you over. Can't be too careful about something so serious." She was clearly shaken by Rachael's revelation.

"I'm sure it's goin' to be fine."

"You said that the catamount attack was the second time Johnny saved you. When was the first?" Cotton narrowed his eyes, hoping to draw out more revealing information about the mysterious Johnny.

"That was when he first found me. I was near done in. Hadn't had nothin' to eat for quite a spell. I was sprawled out half in and half out the door to the cabin where I lived."

"You lived alone?"

Rachael sighed before launching into the story of the man pretending to be her father and what he'd done to her. Emily's expression reflected the terror this young girl must have gone through. She'd never experienced anything so traumatic; even her kidnapping by the Cruz gang had left her with fewer emotional scars than those Rachael was describing. Emily was so disgusted by what she heard, she put her hand over her mouth to keep her anger from showing.

"I wasn't always alone. Just after my 'father' took off," Rachael continued. "He said he would come back, but he never did. When Johnny and I went to look for a way to earn some money to live on, that's when we found out he'd been killed. The nice people that buried him kept his horse. When they heard that the horse should rightfully belong to the man's next of kin, they didn't know I wasn't really, so they insisted we take her. While havin' to ride double is kinda hard on the horse, it was sure better'n walkin'. I'd just about worn my legs down to nubbins after several days."

"So, the two of you left your cabin and started walkin'? Did you have an idea where you were headed and how far it might be?"

"No, sir. We just put one foot in front of the other and let the good Lord guide us. Reckon he did, too. After all, we're here and we're both alive."

"You've been through a lot of hardship, Rachael. You were lucky to find this ranch. How'd you come on it?" Cotton asked.

"We was headed for Apache Springs. We took a wrong turn and ended up on the road where we met Emily. She was so kind to let us stay and give us food. I have to say, I love it here." Rachael looked with a sigh. "And, I . . ."

"You're welcome to stay as long as you'd like, child," Emily interrupted.

"Thank you, ma'am. I'd like that. But I suppose I'd better ask Johnny."

"Unfortunately he seems to have gotten off somewhere," Cotton said.

"He left? Without me?"

"I don't imagine he'll be gone long. Appears he hitched a ride into town with one of Emily's cowboys. I'm sure he'll be back this afternoon."

"H-he went into town? Oh, my god! If he runs into the man he's aimin' to kill, he may not come back at all. He could be dead in the street." Rachael burst into tears.

"He's aimin' to kill someone? Who?" Cotton asked, his expression turning dark with surprise. "Damn!"

"He's after the man who killed all his friends. Murdered them!"

"Where'd this murder take place?"

"I-I, uh . . ."

"Tell me, girl! Now!"

Emily grabbed Rachael and held her close. She glared at Cotton. "You're scaring her. Don't yell!"

"But if I'm goin' to save a life, I need to know whose life it is. And that boy, I don't need to have him shot down in my town, either."

Rachael continued to sob uncontrollably as Emily patted her and tried to calm her down. Emily motioned for Cotton to go outside. She mouthed the words to wait and she'd get what he needed. He realized she was probably right. He had no experience with teenaged girls and he guessed maybe yelling wasn't the best way to get answers. He sheepishly went out on the porch and took a seat on the first step to wait for a calmer approach to prevail.

Chapter 45

As soon as the buckboard pulled up to the rear of the hardware store in order for them to load their supplies from the dock, Teddy wasted no time jumping down from the spring seat to climb the three steps to the dock. He stopped before entering the back door to look around at Johnny, and was surprised to find an empty seat where the boy had been only seconds ago. He shrugged his shoulders and went inside to tell the owner he was ready to load the Wagner order.

"G'afternoon, Mr. Hargreaves. It's Teddy Olander, and I'm here to pick up some fencing for the Wagner ranch."

"Ahh, yes, young man. Pretty late in the day for ridin' all the way back to the Wagner place, ain't it?"

"Aww, heck, I've done it plenty of times."

"Well, as you wish. I have three rolls of heavy-duty fencing on the loading dock. I believe the lady said she wanted a small barrel of ten-penny nails, too. That sound right?"

"Yes, sir, exactly right. I brought someone to help load up, but he seems to have disappeared on me."

"That's all right, I'll give you a hand soon as I tally up some things for Mrs. Dunwoody." Hargreaves chuckled. "Be just a minute."

"I'll just be out back, sir." But Teddy was puzzled by Johnny's strange disappearance. His curiosity was too much for him, and he wandered down the alley and out to the main street.

Johnny had no idea where to even start looking for Carp Varner. If he was in town, the most likely place to start would be the saloon. Carp seemed to spend most of his time leaning on the bar, sucking up whiskey, beer, or whatever he could find that was liquid and made him feel tough. Johnny walked around the side of the hardware store and found himself only about five buildings from what he figured to be a saloon. It was a fancy place with a large, painted sign out front, covered in gold leaf and lots of swirly letters. While the fancy lettering was difficult to decipher, he thought it spelled out *Melody's Golden Palace of Pleasure.* The thought struck him that, considering the name, the establishment might cater to those seeking female companionship—for a price, of course.

He hadn't said a word to Teddy about his real reason for coming to town with him, and that was why as soon as the buckboard came to a halt, he hopped off and tore around the building. Of course, if for some reason he didn't return before Teddy found it necessary to get back to the ranch, he would likely be stranded in a strange town. This was beginning to look more and more like a bad idea. As he stood staring at the saloon, he heard a voice behind him.

"You lost, son?"

Johnny spun around, his hand inadvertently going for the handle of his six-shooter. That's when he came face-to-face with a rough-looking man with a serious look on his face, wearing a badge and a Remington .44.

"Uh, no, I-I'm just looking for someone."

"Well, I know about everybody in Apache Springs. Perhaps I can point you in the right direction. Name's Memphis Jack Stump. I'm the deputy sheriff here. Who is this person?"

Johnny swallowed hard. He was at a loss for words. Just at that moment, Teddy Olander came around the side of the hardware store and, seeing Johnny talking to the deputy, called out.

"Hey, Johnny, there you are! This wire isn't goin' to load itself. Get your scrawny ass over here and help out!"

"Ahh, so you must work out at the Wagner place, too?" Jack asked.

"Uh, yessir. And, er, I better go help Teddy."

"Sure. Next time you're in town maybe I can help you find who you're lookin' for." Jack touched the brim of his hat and strolled on along the boardwalk. The two young cowboys disappeared down an alley.

Carp Varner was beginning to get anxious. He hadn't heard a word from the sheriff on a decision about the gunsmith shop, even though he was pretty sure the man claiming to be Burnside's nephew had arrived on schedule. He'd never been good at biding his time, and this occasion was no exception. He liked to hurry things along. He was running an oiled rag over his Smith & Wesson, trying to conjure up a plan wherein Burnside's nephew might have an accident, a fatal accident. As his twisted mind wrangled with several possible scenarios, the one that appealed to him most was to set fire to the hotel—*burn the damned place down around that scamp's ears.* An evil, self-satisfied grin came over his face.

He knew his plans would have to wait, however, when he heard the door open and in strode Mayor Plume. Varner laid the six-shooter on the workbench and moved to greet the town's highest-ranking official.

"Good day to you, Mr. Mayor. What can I do for you?"

"Been meaning to stop by and congratulate you more fully for your superb handling of the attempt on the bank."

"It wasn't anything that most folks hereabouts wouldn't have done."

"Quite the contrary. It was a feat of masterful timing, something I might add is sorely lacking in our fair community. In fact, the whole affair has me thinking. You know there's an election for sheriff comin' up in just a couple days. It seems to me that you might be just the right fellow to give the folks a real choice, for a change."

"Oh, well, that's something I hadn't ever considered. Sheriff, hmm? I'll think on it. Thank you for the vote of confidence, Mr. Mayor."

"Now I figure if you'd agree to throw your hat in the ring, a gesture like that might just shake things up real proper," Plume said. The mayor gave Varner a wry smile and a nod. He thrust out his hand and Varner shook it. The mayor spun around and strutted through the door with a satisfied smile. Varner watched as he went toward his office, stopping briefly at every window along the street. He was greeting each passerby like the true politician he was.

Varner stood, pensively watching the antics of the pompous mayor all the way until he disappeared back inside the building that housed his and his clerk's offices. Varner sat at his workbench to ponder this newest twist to any future he might be considering in Apache Springs.

I wonder how Plume might feel if he knew what happened the last time I ran for an elected office. He snorted as he thought back to the day when he left Whiskey Crossing nothing more than a pile of blackened charcoal and twisted nails; his ruminations brought renewed confidence that after his handling of the robbery he might, indeed, hold more sway over this town than he'd thought. But he knew *exactly* what the mayor was driving at.

I am impressed by your idea, you pompous fool. And your misguided attempt to get a handle on gaining more control of Apache Springs is an interesting proposition. I believe I will run for mayor.

Chapter 46

"How come you left me to do all the work myself? I thought you offered to come along to help?" Teddy's words carried the sting of disappointment with them. He was noticeably perturbed by Johnny's hasty withdrawal.

"I'm sorry, but I had something that needed doin'. Won't happen again."

"Darn tootin' it won't, because I'll be comin' alone the next time." Teddy looked straight ahead as he angrily slapped the reins on the horse's rump to hurry her along.

"I said I was sorry."

"Yeah, well what's more important than doin' what you say you're goin' to do?"

"Oh, I fully intend to do what I've said. Count on it." Johnny glowered straight ahead as the buckboard pitched and rolled with the added weight of three rolls of heavy fencing wire.

"And just what would that be?" Teddy's response to Johnny's elusive answer was snappish.

"I'm goin' to even the score with a snivelin', belly-crawlin' snake. I'm goin' to put him in the ground sure as I'm sittin' here. And that's somethin' *you* can count on."

Teddy chose to discontinue the conversation at that point. He figured this new hand wasn't quite right in the head. He went back to making certain they got back to the ranch in one piece, even if a couple times in the waning sunlight that seemed unlikely, as a result of one or another of the wheels dropping precipitously into ruts that drifted too close to the edge of the often washed-out road and its attendant steep drop-offs.

"I'd better go into town and see if I can find this wayward lad, Emily. I'll bring him back and you can figure a way to deal with him, just as soon as I get some answers about this supposed killin'."

Emily stood with arms crossed to keep away the chill. She had wrapped a crocheted shawl around her shoulders, but the breeze still carried with it a nippy warning of things to come.

"If you don't get back tonight, I'll assume you have him safe and sound."

"Let's hope it's that easy."

As he reined the mare around, there came the distinctive sound of the buckboard straining under a load. Down at the end of the lane, Teddy jumped off and began to lead the horse uphill. Johnny, too, had gotten out to lighten the load. The horse was lathered and wheezing. As they got closer, Cotton stepped down from his saddle and retied the reins to the rail. He walked out to help the boys unload the wire.

"You fellows need a hand?" Cotton said.

"Howdy, Sheriff. Yessir, it'd be nice to have a pair of reliable hands to help with the unloading," Teddy said, with a clearly sarcastic tone to his voice. Johnny said nothing. He was staring wide-eyed at Cotton. The fearful look did not go unnoticed.

"Reckon I'm the only one that don't have other duties. I'll grab a pair of gloves and be right back." Cotton wandered off toward the bunkhouse. He came back in seconds with a pair of heavy leather gloves suitable for handling rolls of barbwire that could slice a man's hands to shreds if mishandled. Johnny continued to keep a close eye on the lawman.

Cotton and the two boys got the job done quickly, with the wire stored beside the barn. It would have to wait for the next day to be used to build onto the corral. When they'd finished, Emily called them to come in for supper, but insisted they not forget to wash up first. Cotton was amused at the expression on Johnny's face. It appeared the boy was none too fond of being mothered. Teddy, on the other hand, loved being thought of as a part of the ranch family.

When all were seated, Emily set bowls of potatoes, beans, carrots, and canned tomatoes out for everyone to take what he wanted. She then came around with a platter of sizzling meat, rare and juicy, and smelling like heaven. Cotton rose to fetch the coffeepot, when suddenly Rachael jumped up and said, "I'll get it, sir. Sorry I forgot my manners."

Cotton thanked her, sat back, and cut into a hunk of steak. He chewed extra slowly in order to decide the best way to get the conversation going in the direction he desired. Emily had given him a talking to about rushing into the subject of killings and such. She had sensed the deep conviction both of these young people held of delivering justice to one who deserved it in the strictest terms. And Cotton had firsthand knowledge of dispensing justice. He had only to look back on his own recent past to conjure up an example.

"Emily tells me you're from Texas, Johnny. What part?"

Johnny made sure to swallow before speaking, just like he'd been taught.

"When my pa and me got to a little spit of a town, he said it looked a fair to middlin' place to settle, for a while, at least. It was called Whiskey Crossing, mostly 'cause it wasn't much more than a saloon, a general store, and a livery. The livery had a blacksmith, though."

"Sounds like most towns hereabouts that started from dust and cactus, then grew to lots more dust and cactus. Just added a few sticks."

That made Johnny crack the least bit of a smile, which spread to Rachael.

"How long did you live in Whiskey Crossing?"

"Oh, about four years, I reckon. On the way through Texas, my ma caught the fever and died. It wasn't long after we arrived my pa got bit by a rattler. He died before I could get him help. The townsfolk put up with me and made me feel welcome. So I stayed, since I really didn't have nowhere else to go."

"What did you do there?"

"I swept out the saloon every night. Then I helped at the livery, muckin' stalls an' such. Even helped stock shelves and carry in boxes when they was delivered at the general store."

"And you got paid to do all this?"

"In a manner of speakin', yep. They fed me three meals a day and let me sleep in the back room of the saloon."

"Was there a school?"

"Uh, no, there weren't no schoolhouse. But the whore, er, sorry, the *lady* at the saloon could read and write some, and she took the time to teach me to cipher and make my letters."

"So, what was it that made you decide to leave? It doesn't sound like a bad place to live."

"No, sir, it wasn't. Fact is, I felt like I belonged. Those folks was my family."

"But you left."

"Not 'cause I was of a mind to. There weren't nothin' left after that bastard burned the whole town to the ground.

Killed every livin' thing. All gone in a horrific blaze. An inferno!"

"That's terrible! How did you escape?"

"I was down the hill dumpin' a load of manure from the livery when I heard the shouts and the shootin' and the screams and cryin'. I crawled back to the top of the hill and saw it all, but that lowdown snake didn't see me."

"Why would somebody do such a terrible thing, Johnny?"

"I figured it was because he lost the election for mayor and folks laughed at him. He was evil when he came to town, though. Didn't just up and get that way overnight. Why, he shot four men over several weeks, most for back-talkin' him. Worst man I ever did see."

"Who is this man? Is he the one you're lookin' for?"

"How'd you know I was lookin' for someone?"

"I-I reckon I, er, let it slip, Johnny." Rachael spoke up. "I'm sorry."

Johnny looked into Rachael's eyes, eyes that were plead-ing for his understanding.

"That's okay, Rachael. It don't matter. I'm still goin' to get him."

"You haven't told me who this man is, Johnny," Cotton insisted.

"Name's Carp Varner. That's who. And I figure he's in Apache Springs."

"Carp Varner!" Cotton's mouth dropped at the news. He'd thought all along that there was something rotten about Varner, and now it appeared he was right.

"What do you figure to do, Cotton?" Emily asked, her face shadowed with fear.

"First thing in the mornin', Johnny and I are goin' into town."

"You arrestin' me, Sheriff?" Johnny said.

"Not exactly."

Chapter 47

———✦———

Early the next morning, Cotton sauntered into the dining room. All of Emily's ranch hands were already there, each eagerly chowing down on the day's fare. They paid him no mind, having become comfortable with him showing up at unexpected times. He looked around to see Emily coming from the kitchen with a bowl of freshly baked biscuits. She smiled at him. He noticed Rachael sitting next to an empty chair, looking nervous.

"Good morning, Rachael. Where's Johnny?" he asked as he took a seat and unfolded his napkin.

"I, uh, I'm not sure. I haven't seen him this morning."

Cotton was clearly concerned about the young man's absence, especially after his confessing the previous evening to a deep desire to seek out and kill Carp Varner. The sheriff placed his napkin on his plate and walked out of the room. He went to the porch and looked around. Seeing no signs of the boy, he jogged across the yard to the bunkhouse. Throwing the door open, he wasn't surprised at what he found. Or didn't find. Johnny's bunk was empty. His gun belt and six-shooter were also missing. Peeking inside the corral, he saw that the mare the two young people had ridden in on was gone, along with the saddle. He gathered up his own horse and then ran back to the house. He called inside to tell Emily he had to leave and that he'd be back later. He was just clearing the front gate when she stepped out onto the porch with a look of concern.

Henry Coyote came around the corner of the house. Seeing him, Emily asked, "Do you know where Cotton has gone off to?"

"No. Go in hurry. No words."

"Never mind whatever you were going to do today. I want you to go after the sheriff. Find out what's going on. He may need help. And if you see Johnny, tell him to come in for breakfast."

"Young boy no here."

"What do you mean, not here?"

"He go early. Take horse. Go in direction of town."

"Damn! So that's where Cotton went, to catch up with that young adventurer. Go find them, Henry. Find them and keep them safe."

Henry must have anticipated something akin to the orders he'd just been given because he had no sooner disappeared into the barn than he emerged almost instantly, mounted on his pony and ready to ride. He was carrying his Spencer rifle, and a bandolier of cartridges was draped across his chest.

As Emily turned to go back inside, she came face-to-face with an anxious Rachael. "He's gone, isn't he? He's gone to kill that awful Carp Varner," Rachael said, nearly in tears.

"I don't know, dear. Kill-or-be-killed seems to be a way of life out here. Pray Cotton gets to him before he does something terribly foolish," Emily said, pulling Rachael close and hugging her tightly.

* * *

Cotton spurred his mare to run for all she was worth. *Got to get there before that fool does something we'll both regret.* He decided to cut through Chiricahua Pass, a place known to harbor all manner of dangers, to reduce the time it normally took to get to town. Only a single horse and rider could expect to get through the impossibly narrow pass the walls of which were festooned with jagged thrusts of flesh-ripping rock jutting out like fingers waiting to grasp the unwary. The trail itself was littered with fallen debris from small landslides brought on by spring rains and winter ice. All in all, the sheriff's choice of a fast route to Apache Springs was questionable at best.

Damned good thing that kid didn't know about this pass; I doubt he could have made it. Come to think of it, I'm not so sure I can. He ducked suddenly, just missing being knocked from his saddle by a scraggly juniper branch that seemed to come out of nowhere, long dead from many a harsh winter. *Hmm, best keep my mind on getting there in one piece.*

Carp Varner had decided he'd been brooding long enough. It was time to make his move. He must get rid of the man calling himself Burnside's nephew. After deliberating for hours, he'd come up with a plausible plan, at least to his demented mind. He stuck his Smith & Wesson .45 in his holster, slipped on his black duster, and closed and locked the shop door behind him. He strode purposefully to the hotel. When the desk clerk saw him and asked if he could be of help, Varner said no, he was going into the restaurant for a bite to eat. The clerk turned back to whatever aimless task he'd been pursuing when he was interrupted by Varner's arrival.

But Varner merely went into the restaurant, passed through to a rear entrance, and continued outside. *That little maneu-*

ver should get me an alibi, at least for a bit. He climbed the outside rear stairs to the second floor. Earlier that day, he'd gotten Burnside's room number when the clerk went out back to take care of business. Carp just ducked behind the counter long enough to glance through the register, take note of the room, and leave before anyone noticed he'd even been there.

When he got to Burnside's room, he tapped lightly on the door.

"Who's there?" came a voice from inside.

"Telegram for Turner Burnside."

The door opened quickly. "I'm Turner Bur— What the hell! It's *you!*"

Turner tried in vain to shut the door before Carp could get inside. But, being a much larger man, Varner shoved Burnside aside and closed the door. He put a finger to his mouth. Turner got the point. *Keep quiet. Or else.* He got that second part when Carp drew a finger across his throat as he pulled open his duster to reveal the hilt of a very large knife, known to all as an Arkansas toothpick.

"Yep, it's me, Carp Varner."

"Wha–what do you want, Varner? Haven't you done enough to my family?"

"Not quite yet, sonny. Pack your bags, you're leaving town. Now!"

Although he kept his voice down, Varner's intentions were clear: "Do my bidding or die."

Burnside stuffed everything he had into two suitcases. He carried no gun, which Varner had taken note of as soon as he entered the room. When Burnside was done packing, Varner made a quick survey of the room, and seeing nothing to indicate anyone had ever inhabited number 6, he pushed the younger man toward the door, then grabbed him by the shirt collar and shoved his face against the frame.

"Here's what's goin' to happen. You'll do exactly as I say or this extremely sharp dagger will be shoved through your back and into your heart, at which time you will feel horrendous pain . . . but only briefly. Then, a split second later, your life will be ended. Understand? I've seen a man die that way, and it wasn't a pretty sight."

Burnside nodded that he understood.

"Good. Go down the hallway toward the back stairway. Do it very quietly. If we should meet anyone along the way, you are to do or say nothing, not even a look that might suggest you are in a tight spot. When we get downstairs, we'll follow the back alley down to the Butterfield Stage office. I'll purchase your ticket so there's no reason for you to converse with anyone. Now, move."

Burnside was shaking so hard he was struggling to get himself and the two suitcases through the narrow hall without banging against the walls and causing other residents to step out of their rooms to see what the commotion was about. Varner didn't seem to care how they got to their destination, only that they arrived before the stage was scheduled to leave, twenty minutes from then. He gave Burnside some incentive, a sharp jab in the shoulder blade with the point of the stiletto.

Chapter 48

———◆———

Carp Varner and Turner Burnside arrived at the rear door of the Butterfield Stage office just ten minutes before the stage was scheduled to leave. Varner paid for a one-way ticket for one, then they walked swiftly past the counter and straight through to the awaiting coach, Varner's stiletto still in Burnside's back. Varner took the suitcases from Burnside and tossed them up top, into the waiting hands of the shotgun guard. He shoved Burnside into the coach, closed the door, and gave the reluctant traveler a bone-chilling glare. Burnside swallowed hard and looked away.

"I hope you have a good trip. Don't *never* come back." Varner stayed put until the driver snapped the whip and the team of six bolted forward. The coach made a dusty trail as it departed straight out of Apache Springs, bound for Silver City.

Varner hastened back to his shop to further hone the next part of his plan. He had written a note to the sheriff telling him that Burnside had made a decision not to take over his uncle's gunsmith shop. Varner forced a signature from Burnside before leaving the hotel room. Now he had but to deliver the note to the sheriff's office when no one was there. He planned to leave it on the sheriff's desk.

He hadn't seen Burke since the evening before and assumed he'd gone to the Wagner ranch to stay. When Deputy Memphis Jack left the jail to go over to the saloon, that was his signal to drop the fake note off. If all went as he'd hoped, the sheriff would undoubtedly offer him the gunsmith business and all the contents, and there'd be nothing standing between him and his goal of making himself important in the town. That would be right after he won the race for mayor, of course. He figured to be a shoo-in.

A vicious smile crossed his lips as he strolled down the street to the print shop to have some posters printed announcing his upcoming candidacy. Completely unaware of youthful eyes watching his every step, taking care to remain unseen behind some crates stacked in an alleyway.

When Cotton reached the town limits, he began his scan of every person he saw. He figured the kid shouldn't be hard to spot, even though he'd surely try to make himself less than conspicuous. As the sheriff rode slowly down the street, looking left and right, hoping to catch sight of Johnny coming out of a store, he saw not one glimpse of anyone who could even *pass* for an eighteen-year-old boy. Not unless, that is, the lad had found some women's clothing and been able to struggle into a corset and get someone to cinch him up.

Cotton dismounted in front of the jail, drooped his reins over the rail, and had started inside when he saw Jack coming across the street.

"Didn't expect to see you for another hour or so," Jack said.

"I'm trying to track down a troublesome young man who seems destined to get himself killed or hanged, one or the other." Cotton leaned against a post and hung a thumb in his gun belt.

"What's he look like? Maybe I've seen him."

"Skinny, about what you'd expect from a kid with too little to eat and too much energy to spend. About five-ten, a hundred and twenty pounds, maybe. Brown hair that's too damned long and brown eyes. Likely wearing ratty jeans and a too-big shirt with the sleeves rolled up."

"Yup. I did see someone like that. Yesterday, if I recall correctly. He was standing at the entrance to the alley by the general store. I asked him if he was lookin' for someone and he said yes. But he never got a chance to tell me who. That young fella Teddy something-or-other yelled at him to get his scrawny ass around to the back and help load some wire."

"That's the boy I've got to find before he gets himself gunned down. You haven't seen him today, have you?"

"Nope. If I do, what do I do with him?"

"Arrest him."

"For what?"

"His own safety. Lock his scrawny ass up tight and then hunt me down."

"Sounds serious."

"Bet your ass it is. He's lookin' to gun down one of our erstwhile citizens."

"Now, who'd that be?"

"Carp Varner."

Jack looked at the sheriff like he'd lost his mind. Cocking his head and narrowing his eyes, he said, "Do you really figure I'll jump over a barrel to save that scoundrel's life?"

"We can't sit by and allow someone to cut him down in the street, can we? No matter what we think of him. Besides, from what I'm gatherin', Varner's damned good with that Schofield. And I don't want to have to bury some snot-nosed kid before he's had a chance at life."

"All right. I'll do it, but I won't like it," Jack said.

"I'm not askin' you to like it, just help me save an innocent soul," Cotton said, standing next to his deputy.

"When do you figure on him gettin' here?"

"I think he's already in town. We just can't see him. He
knows I'll stop him if I can, so he'll stay hidden until the
right opportunity arises. It could happen anytime. And we
need to keep an eye out for Varner, too."

"What're you gonna be doin' while I'm savin' the world?"

Cotton had started to say something when he looked
down the street and saw Mayor Plume headed his way.
"Looks like I'm goin' to be busy defendin' some dereliction
of duty on my part, sort of a regular occurrence accordin'
to him," Cotton said, pointing to his oncoming and constant adversary.

"I see what you mean. I'd rather not be subject to the
talk of a fool. I'll be lookin' around for the boy, and keepin'
an eye out for Varner, too," Jack said, slipping around the
corner, availing himself of the short span of time before the
mayor got to the jail.

"Mornin', Mayor. You look like a man with somethin'
on his mind."

"Not particularly. Nothing of any real importance anyway. Just thought you'd like some time to think about your
predicament. Got any coffee?"

"C'mon in and I'll rustle you up some and you can elaborate on the hidden meanin' to those cryptic words."

They went inside, and Cotton pulled a clean cup from
atop the filing cabinet. He poured a cup full and handed it
to the mayor. That's when he noticed the folded paper lying
on his desk. He pushed it aside until he was through with
the mayor.

"Take a seat and tell me about my 'predicament,' and
what you're *really* here about." Cotton sipped some of his
own half-full cup.

"I been talking to that new gunsmith, and the fact that I
think he's figuring on running against you in the election.
Reckons he's done the town proud by shooting down those

two bank robbers, enough that folk'd be grateful enough for a change in the law." Plume sipped his coffee, watching the sheriff like a hawk, obviously awaiting some reaction from him.

Cotton didn't even blink. "Well, I must say I've been havin' second thoughts about continuin' to put my life on the line for a bunch of ingrates, as well. I might not even oppose Varner's decision, if, that is, he follows through with what you're suggestin'."

"Uh, well, I'm not certain it's official." Plume took another hurried sip from his cup, apparently uncomfortable with the obviousness of his position in the matter.

It was no secret the sheriff and the mayor had seen many differences of opinion during Burke's three years as sheriff. The way Cotton gave Plume a look like he knew exactly where the suggestion that Varner run for sheriff had come from caused the mayor to break out in a sweat.

"Well, I can tell you're a busy man. I'm sure you've got many things need attending to, Sheriff, so I'll be running along." He pushed himself up from the chair, set the cup on the corner of the desk, and skittered out the door like a mouse discovered in the cupboard.

Cotton's mouth curled into a wry smile. *Just how stupid does that jackass think I am?*

Chapter 49

———◆———

Johnny was taking no chances on being seen. He knew that by now the sheriff would probably be out looking for him. In fact, he figured he could already be in town. The sheriff and his deputy both knew Apache Springs from top to bottom. That put him at a disadvantage, but he figured the one thing he had going for him was his youth and resourcefulness. Since he wasn't known by anyone in town, though, he'd stick out like a sore thumb. Staying out of sight would have to be his main objective.

It was only by a stroke of luck that he'd spotted Varner soon after riding in that morning. The man he wanted to see dead in the street had come out of a gunsmith shop and walked to the sheriff's office, then on down the street. *Bold as you please. I'm going to enjoy putting him in the ground, no matter what happens to me afterward.* His plan not yet formed, Johnny began looking for some sort of a pattern to Varner's wanderings about town. How well did he know the sheriff? Did he go to the hotel on a regular basis? Did he have a room there? What was his connection to the gunsmith? The answers to these questions would go a long way toward showing Johnny his best shot at catching the gunslinger off guard—the only way he'd ever get the first shot off. That first pulling of the trigger was essential. Varner wasn't merely one mean, heartless bastard, he was also the fastest shootist Johnny had ever seen, not that he'd actually ever seen a real gunslinger in action. But then, with all the men Varner had gunned down, the man had to be good, didn't he? Johnny tried his best to move from place to place as unobtrusively as possible, using crates and water barrels up and down the alleyways to conceal his presence from townsfolk. He was doing pretty well keeping out of sight of Varner and felt good about his plan to follow the man until he fully understood his daily schedule. That knowledge would undoubtedly reveal the best time and place to confront the killer before plugging him on the spot.

As he watched Varner go into the print shop, he began thinking about Rachael. He couldn't put his finger on why at that particular moment she'd popped into his head, but he was both delighted at the pleasant thoughts she brought to mind and fearful that after his dealing with Varner, he might never see her again, especially if he was caught and hanged for murder. He shuddered at the thought.

Cotton drank the last of the coffee and strolled outside. He stretched, glancing up and down the street. He decided it was as good a time as any to get down to business with Turner Burnside. He had a lot on his mind what with Burnside, Johnny Monk, and Varner himself all knotting up his stomach, as he headed for the hotel. When he got there, the clerk was sweeping the lobby floor.

"G'mornin', Sheriff. What brings you down here? I think the restaurant has closed off the breakfast menu. Be ready for lunch in about an hour, though."

"Naw, thanks anyway. I'm needin' to have some words with Mr. Burnside. He in his room?"

"Why, uh, no sir. I saw him get on the early stage. Been gone for over two hours."

"Uh, I don't suppose you know where he was headed, do you?"

"Nope. But the stage he took was going to Silver City."

"Thanks," Cotton said, turning on his heel and breezing past the clerk. He made tracks out into the street and straight for his office. That's when he remembered the paper he'd pushed aside. He opened it, quickly scanned the contents, and slammed his fist on the desk. He dropped the paper back on the desk. Pensive for a moment, he got to thinking a trip to the telegraph office was his best move. He ran out of the jail, quickening his steps, glancing about in hopes of seeing Jack wandering the town.

When he got to the telegraph office, a tiny wooden structure squeezed between a ladies' apparel shop and the general store, he found the telegrapher busy tapping away at the key. The man didn't acknowledge the sheriff's presence until he had completed whatever message he'd been sending. When he finally looked up, pushing back in his chair, Cotton had already scribbled out the message he wanted sent. He handed it across the counter. In bold letters at the top, he'd written: SEND IMMEDIATELY. The man read it, nodded, and commenced to stroke the key once more, responding to the importance placed on the message.

It was intended for Town Marshal Bear Hollow Wilson in Silver City. It asked if he'd meet the stage and take Turner Burnside off. He requested the man be put on the first stage back to Apache Springs. It said a deputy would meet the stage on its return to ensure his safety.

Out behind a store, Johnny had scooted down behind a short fence meant to keep stray animals out of the garbage. He had seen Varner going about town as if he was just another businessman. Johnny saw him as a craven killer and nothing more. Johnny picked up with his following and surveillance. He thought it strange when Varner returned to the gunsmith shop.

What could he be doin' goin' in and out of that place? It don't make sense.

He decided to find his way to the back of the shop in order to get a better view of the goings-on inside. When he identified the back of the shop, he was pleased to see it had a small window right next to the rear door. He approached the window slowly and cautiously, stooped over so as not to be seen by anyone inside. He glanced around often, hoping no one would suddenly emerge from one of the other stores and discover him sneaking about. When he got to the window, he rose up very slowly until he had a good view of whoever was inside. He was surprised to see no one but Varner, and he was seated at a workbench. Johnny scrunched up his nose, trying to conjure up what could have happened to the gunsmith. Then it hit him.

Damn! He's the gunsmith. How'd he do that? I remember he'd worked on some firearms for folks back in Whiskey Crossing, but I don't recall him sayin' he was an actual gunsmith.

Staying low, Johnny shuffled down the alleyway toward the back of the livery. He needed to be by himself to do some thinking. And planning. And he hoped to do that before he starved to death. The memory of his last meal at the Wagner ranch caused his stomach to growl. The more he turned things over and over in his mind, the more he wished he'd just let the sheriff take care of Varner.

When Cotton walked into the jail, he found Jack reading the paper he'd dropped when he went to the telegraph office.

"Whatcha got there, Jack? A bill for Melody's services?" Cotton asked, with a smirk.

"Not quite. I just got back and this here is a note I found

lyin' on the desk. It says Turner Burnside decided *against* bein' the gunsmith. Says he's turnin' it over to Carp Varner, lock, stock, and barrel. Says he's goin' back to Mobile, where he came from."

"Yeah, I know. Already read it." Cotton walked to the window, after taking the note from Jack and wadding it up. After a few seconds, he turned back to Jack. "I reckon you know it's a fake, don't you?"

"How do you know that?"

"Burnside never lived in Mobile. And I'm pretty sure I know what caused him to leave town."

Chapter 50

———◆◆◆———

"W hat're you sayin'?"

"Someone forced him to write this note."

"How do you know?"

"Turner is spelled with an 'e', not an 'o.'"

"Why would they do that?"

"Isn't it obvious? Carp Varner must have kidnapped Burnside, forced him to leave town, and this note would appear to give him clear title to the gunsmithing business. I reckon I should have listened more carefully to that kid out at Emily's place. Now he's probably here in town just waiting for the opportunity to smoke Varner. After hearing his story, I can't say I blame him."

"Then I better get back out there and find him. You got any idea where I should start?" Jack asked.

"He's bound to be tryin' to stay outta sight. The back alleys are where I'd start."

"All right." Jack took his rifle and started out the door. "Where will you be if I should find him?"

"Bring him back here, but keep it hushed up. Don't make a ruckus. I'm goin' to have a little visit with Varner."

"What're you gonna say to him?"

"Not certain, just yet. I'll come up with somethin' that'll be sure to startle the son of a rattler, though. Oh, I sent a telegram to Marshal Wilson in Silver City to put Burnside right back on the next stage for Apache Springs. Said to tell him you'd meet the stage when it arrives. Supposed to get in here at three o'clock tomorrow afternoon."

"What'll I do with him?"

"Take him to the hotel but keep a lookout for Varner. Tell Burnside I'll be by to figure somethin' out."

"That ought to toss another pig in the bag. You gonna let Varner know what you've done?"

"Better to keep him guessin'."

As Jack left chuckling, Cotton took the note, smoothed it out on the desk, and refolded it. He jammed it in his shirt pocket and started down the street for the gunsmith's shop. On his way, he kept an eye out for Johnny, but saw neither hide nor hair of the young man. He hadn't really thought he would. But he knew one thing: if that boy was telling the truth, they were both dealing with a dangerously deranged animal without a conscience. That put things in a different perspective.

Varner was leaning back in a swivel chair with his feet on the desk, drinking from a whiskey bottle. He barely moved at the sound of the door opening when Cotton entered. His words were slurred, his mouth twisted into a self-satisfied smirk. *He must think he has me over a barrel*, thought Cotton.

"Ahh, Sh-Sheriff. I'll bet you got the note young Burns . . . Burnside left for you. Quite a surprise, eh? It was to me, too, ya know. But at least the whole things sh-s-settled and we can both move on," Varner said, slurring his words.

"Uh-huh. Yep it was a surprise. Kinda tough to take when a man gives his word then suddenly goes back on it.

Whole thing makes you wonder if there wasn't some dirty doin's."

"D-dirty doin's? Why, Sheriff, I hope you don't think I'd have anything to do with Burnside's changing his mind. After all, he's a grown man and able to make his own decisions." Varner put the bottle on the desk and sat up straight. His Schofield lay not fifteen inches from his reach. He eyed it. Cotton took notice but didn't let on.

"Yeah, I reckon you're right. Well, I sure do hope you're up to all the work that'll likely come pourin' in here once folks know for sure we got ourselves a steady gunsmith." Cotton touched a finger to his Stetson, then turned back. "Oh, I almost forgot. There's a rumor goin' around that you might be interested in runnin' for sheriff."

Varner looked startled. "Runnin' for sheriff? Ha! Not on your life. I'm not interested in always lookin' over my shoulder to spot the next crazy hombre thinkin' to plug me."

"So you aren't runnin' for office?"

"I didn't say that. I *am* puttin' my name in the hat, just not for sheriff."

"What, then?"

"Why the job that'll give me the power to influence the decision makin'."

"You mean . . . ?"

"Yep. I'm runnin' for mayor. Posters will start goin' up tomorrow." Varner leaned back with a pleased gleam in his eye. Cotton nearly burst out laughing as he walked away.

On his way back to the jail, Cotton couldn't help being amused at the thought of Carp Varner as mayor. Although, if Carp was that delusional, the sheriff didn't see any harm in encouraging him just a bit. After all the grief Mayor Plume had given Cotton over the years with his arrogance and complete lack of concern for the citizenry, he figured a little fear might do the current mayor some good. Time to let the cat out of the bag.

He altered his course and made a beeline for Mayor Plume's office. When he entered, the mayor was sound asleep with his feet on his desk, leaning back in a swivel chair that, by the looks of it, could at any moment topple over backward. The sight gave Cotton pause. The information he carried would probably be enough to send the portly mayor into a dither anyway, and he didn't want to compound the potential for a heart attack, so instead of completing a very noisy entrance, he quietly took a seat on an overstuffed chair usually delegated for honored guests. Cotton was pretty sure Plume didn't consider him to be one of those. Nevertheless, the sheriff eased into the comfortable seat, leaned on the plush arm, and let his mind wander as he awaited the arrival of the mayor back to the land of the wide awake.

Any possibility of a lengthy wait was cut short when Cotton sneezed from the lack of any sort of housekeeping in Plume's office. The noise brought the surprised mayor to an upright position and on alert.

"Oh, it's, uh, you, Sheriff. I was just resting my eyes for a moment. What can I do for you?"

"Nothing. I just dropped by to see how your campaign was progressin'," Cotton said.

"Why, er, just fine. Strange you should ask."

"Not really. I figure it's a sheriff's duty to be interested in the health and welfare of the town's elected."

"Uh, *my* health and welfare?"

"One never knows how someone will react to news of an unexpected opponent in an upcoming election."

"Opponent? For mayor? Is this a joke? What fool would do something so idiotic as to run against me?"

"Carp Varner," Cotton said with a wry smile.

It was all Cotton could do to keep a straight face at the mayor's reaction to his revelation.

Chapter 51

Carp Varner leaned back in his only chair, fingers interlaced behind his head, leaning against the wall. He'd just picked up his posters, the ones proclaiming his candidacy for mayor. He was already making plans for how he'd run his campaign. He wouldn't make the same mistake he'd made in Whiskey Crossing. There, he'd been warned not to run because most of the town was either a relative or beholden to their inept mayor. He should have seen it coming. In retrospect, if he'd gone from person to person, sticking his Schofield under their noses, maybe they'd have gotten the picture and voted him into office. Maybe.

This time, he'd be damned sure that every citizen knew who he was and what he intended to do. First off, he'd be reminding everyone that it was him that took down two of the Callahans. With the sheriff grabbing the third brother, they'd cleaned out the entire gang. He'd be certain to tell that story over and over. A story well worth repeating. Why, he could appeal to their expectations that with a team like Varner and Burke watching over the community, things would be quiet, a sure way to attract new business to the area.

When he thought back to his Whiskey Crossing days and the failed election, he also began to think about what he might do if the good citizenry of Apache Springs failed to elect him. That would be a major mistake on their part. His thoughts took a turn to the dark side as he began to conjure a plan to burn Apache Springs to the ground the same way he did Whiskey Crossing. Of course, the vast difference in size presented a circumstance he might not be able to overcome using the same technique. This would take more careful planning. And since the election wouldn't be held for another couple days, there was no point in spending his vast intellectual resources on planning retribution when he could be thinking about the many attributes he could bring to leading a community this size. Not to mention the customers who would naturally flock to his gunsmith shop. People just naturally liked doing business with important folks.

He was smiling to himself in his enjoyable reverie as to his increasing success, when another dark thought crept across his manic mind. The one thing he'd brushed off as inconsequential had slipped back into his mental meanderings, as a vivid and unsettling scene. That wavering column of smoke he'd noticed as he rode away still haunted his imagination. Could there have actually been a lone soul who escaped the inferno, the death trap he'd created with coal-oil lamps and bullets?

No! Absolutely not. I killed them all, every damned one of those fools who'd not voted for me. The mayor, bartender, liveryman, the nosy old lady and her husband at the general store, the one whore who'd been trapped in a windowless back room along with her hapless customer—all disposed of most efficiently. He could conjure up no other person who hadn't either died in the flames or been the victim of his deadly aim. Not one. That's when it hit him.

Where was that kid that swept up the saloon? I don't

remember seeing him that whole day. Damn! He must have been down the hill with his wheelbarrow dumping the manure from the livery. What if he survived and he's the only living soul who knows what I did?

That sudden speculation tied a knot in his stomach and sent his imagination soaring. *What the hell happened to that kid? Where did he go? He had no horse, and no one else's could have survived. I made certain of that. There was absolutely nothing he could have used to get away from Whiskey Crossing except his own two feet. And who the hell is going to walk three hundred miles over mountains and through desert scrub? Why hell, there's all manner of dangers out there to make a man rethink the advisability off such an adventure, and most of them lethal. And how could he ever find me anyhow? This is crazy. He'll have me looking under every rock and around every corner.*

He sat up and reached into the desk drawer for what was left of a bottle of whiskey, which, by its foul taste, had made him certain it was cut with turpentine and creek water. He pulled the cork and took a swig anyway. He needed the comfort of the euphoria he got from drinking to escape his own shadowy demons.

Cotton returned to the jail to find Henry Coyote squatting on the floor, leaning against the desk. The sheriff squinted in the dim light after coming in from a bright sun. He took off his Stetson and hung it on a peg. He stood looking down at the placid Indian with a questioning curl to his lips.

"If I had to guess why you're here, Henry, I'd say Emily sent you to find Johnny. Am I on the right trail?"

"She say more eyes needed to locate young fool. Bring back to ranch."

"She's right as usual. In fact, since you're here, I'll turn the search over to you. *But,* when you find him, I would rather you merely keep watch over him and keep him from doing something he'll regret, instead of taking him back to the ranch. Report to me when you find him, then we'll decide what to do with him. He could be helpful. Jack's out looking for him, as well. If you see him, tell him what I've told you."

Henry sprang to his feet with an agility few men half his age could demonstrate and strolled out the door, quickly disappearing alongside the building and down the back alley. Since he'd been told of Johnny's mission to make Carp Varner pay for his murderous ways, the obvious place to start his search would be the gunsmith shop. As he slipped through the alley, down past the hotel, and across the street to the empty lot behind Varner's place of business, he ducked behind a water trough when someone came out or a rear door and threw a pan of table scraps out. When the person went back inside, Henry edged closer to where he figured Johnny would have visited once he figured out what his prey did for a living.

Numerous boot prints in the dust were undeniably those of the young man bent on revenge. Smooth soles, worn nearly through by his years without a horse of his own for transportation, and low heels, scuffed and leaning from an irregular stride. He'd seen those same prints at the ranch. They would be easy to backtrack. He kept a keen lookout for any sign of the boy as he returned again and again. It took Henry mere minutes to determine the direction where the prints originated and returned to: the livery. Henry sought out a comfortable place hidden in the shadows of a rear-facing overhang behind the millinery shop, to watch and wait. He shrugged in behind a rain barrel and the whipsaw siding of the tiny building. It was nearly an hour before Johnny emerged from a side door to the livery. He looked around to make sure he wasn't seen, then, brushing off pieces of straw from his shirt and pants, he slipped into a side alley and headed for the hotel. His behavior and actions told Henry much about where the boy was planning to sleep. He'd obviously already spent time in the second-story loft where hay and straw were stored.

Henry followed, taking his own special precautions against being seen. There wasn't a person on earth who could spot the wily old Indian if he didn't want to have eyes set on him. And this was just such a case. Johnny's footsteps led once again to the back of the gunsmith shop, where he stood on his toes to peer in through the tiny rear window. Henry watched from a safe distance, close enough to come to the rescue if necessary, but far enough away to avoid discovery.

Chapter 52

As posters announcing Carp Varner's candidacy for mayor started appearing in store windows, tacked to trees, and pasted on the sides of everything from watering troughs to outhouses, interest in the upcoming election began to pick up. Carp stood out front of his little shop, thumbs stuck through his suspenders, grinning from ear to ear and beaming with pride at all those who passed by, giving each a courteous "Howdy do. Hope you'll give me your vote."

Watching the gunsmith's antics from the front window of his own office, Mayor Plume was furious, while finding it necessary to keep his dissatisfaction over the latest turn of events to himself, lest he turn those he expected to cast their votes on his behalf into ballot changers. He'd spent too many years forging a solid place in the community to shoot himself in the foot now. He'd play it very smart and act as if having an opponent was the very thing the town needed to keep things on the up-and-up. While the very thought nearly tore a gaping hole in his innards, he was smart enough to know that folks could spot a phony, and he daren't risk any behavior that might suggest he was such a man.

Perhaps it's time to go to Melody's and get chummy with some of those filthy cowpokes, as much as I hate the thought of rubbing elbows with men who only bathe when the moon is full or they're forced by circumstance to keep company with an honest-to-goodness "lady," rather than one of Melody's "shady girls," no matter how briefly. And so he wandered down the boardwalk, tipping his hat to the ladies and nodding to the gents as he passed by shop after shop. When he pushed through the double doors to the saloon, he was immediately hit with the stench of stale whiskey, cigar smoke, and spilled beer. It gagged him. He seldom ever set foot inside the place and hated it when he found it necessary to do so.

"This is a rare pleasure, Mr. Mayor," Arlo said, from behind the polished bar. "What brings you to the seedy part of town?"

"I'm, uh, looking to shake a few hands and maybe get a few opinions from folks as to what they might be expecting from my next term in office. Just a friendly visit."

Arlo looked around. and seeing only a few cowboys, each too busy trying to end up on the winning end of a hand to notice the mayor's arrival, he shook his head.

"You're sure welcome to move about and start up any conversation you'd like, but, frankly, I don't see many men in here who'll give a hoot what you do. They seem pretty satisfied with the way things are, or they live outside the town's limits and can't vote for the mayor anyway." Arlo gave Plume a weak smile. The mayor seemed somewhat disillusioned by his frankness and the low prospects of achieving his intended goal of getting folks in that place solidly behind him.

After a few minutes of scanning the faces he saw, the mayor sauntered back outside to clear his lungs of whatever poisons hung in the stale air like fog. He coughed a couple times, gave a sigh, and walked across the street to return to his office by a slightly different route, thus offering the possibility of greeting anyone he hadn't seen on his way down. Captured by the inviting smells emanating from the hotel restaurant, he darted inside for coffee and pie. He figured there might be a customer or two who wouldn't mind talking politics over lunch. At least, that was his hope.

"Know where boy stay and where he go. What you want do?" Henry asked the sheriff.

"Where is he right now?"

"Went back to livery. He sleep in loft. He wait for something."

While Cotton puzzled out his next move, Henry grabbed a cup from atop the cabinet and walked to the stove, where he poured himself some coffee. Sitting across from the sheriff, he drank and stared, awaiting some response. He knew it was futile to rush a decision from a man like Cotton Burke, an enduring, deep-thinking man of great inner strength. At least that was Henry's impression.

"If it looks like he's decided when and where he's goin' to take his revenge, stop him. Bring him here even if you have to do it at gunpoint. If there's no one here, lock him up. I can only hope he waits until after the election, so there'll be fewer people in town to catch a stray bullet if he decides to make his play. I hate to lock him up for what I think he might do, but it's the only way I know to save his life."

"Why you wait to bring him here?" Henry asked.

"Kinda wonderin' about that myself," Jack said, as he walked in on the last few words of the conversation.

"Uh, Jack, do you even know what we're talkin' about?"

"Somethin' about the election I gather. Leastways that seemed to be the gist of the conversation."

"Uh-huh. You got part of it right anyway."

"You gonna fill me in on the other part?" Jack said, plopping into the sheriff's desk chair. Cotton gave him a scowl and rolled his eyes.

"No, but I do have a job for you. It will require you gettin' the hell out of my chair. And Henry, you go ahead with your part of the plan. Oh, and go tell the lady at the hotel restaurant to get you somethin' to eat. Tell her to put it on my bill. She'll understand."

Henry left immediately at the suggestion of food.

"So, what's this job you want me to do?" Jack asked.

"I reckon I'm messin' in somethin' that isn't rightly my business, but if what Johnny claims is true about Carp Varner, I can't take any chance that he could actually win the election for mayor."

"I agree, but you can't be stickin' your nose in where it doesn't belong. Besides, you're up for re-election at the same time, and that probably makes whatever it is you're thinkin' illegal, as well." Jack raised an eyebrow to emphasize his questioning stare. "Even if you got no opponent in the race."

"You'd be right if I *was* gettin' involved, but I'm not."

"Sounds to me like you are."

"Nope, not me. You!"

"Me? What the hell can I do?"

"Spread a rumor."

Jack looked at Cotton like he'd lost his mind. "Rumor about what?"

"Not what, who. I want you to casually drop by the barbershop, livery, general store, hotel, and especially Melody's place, anywhere that people can be counted on to help spread the rumor. Start up a conversation about the election. Tell anyone who seems interested that there's a man in town who swears he personally witnessed Carp Varner setting fire to an entire town and killing every one of its inhabitants. Then drop a hint that it was likely because he lost his election for mayor. Maybe even suggest that the same circumstance might happen here."

"Whoa, pardner. Words like that could get a man shot."

"I'm countin' on it. Just be especially watchful of your back."

"You know the spot you're puttin' me in, don't you?" Jack showed no inclination to find the request amusing.

"I figure it's the best way to draw the man out, show just what sort he really is. If Johnny isn't one powerful blowhard, and what he's said is factual, it could be the best way to get Varner to jump at the bait and show himself for what he is. First, he'll probably try to find out who it is that's makin' the claim against him. Then he'll try to silence him. That's when we move in and nail the bastard. Get it?"

"Yeah, I get it. I'm just not certain I like bein' the bait, that's all. But, I'll do it."

"Good. Tell folks it's somethin' you heard and you don't have any idea who the fellow is that's made the claim. You've never even seen him. Just passin' on what's been bandied about."

Jack put on his hat, pulled it low over his eyes, and started for the door. Before he was even outside, he began muttering something about probably being taken for some nosy old biddy.

Jack's reluctance was soon replaced by acceptance that what he was doing might actually be for the good of the town when he watched one person after another eagerly take up the tale he was spreading around, embellish it a bit, then seek out the ear of another. He was so confident after watching the thing take on a life of its own that he made a wager with himself about how long it would take Carp Varner to get wind of it and explode.

He bet a bottle of rum it would take no more than a couple hours.

Chapter 53

"Is that true, Jack, that Carp Varner wiped out an entire town?" Melody asked, when she jumped on the bed while he was attempting to take a short nap. "Everyone died?"

"Appears so. Anyway Cotton is convinced the tale has the ring of truth to it."

"So who is this person who claims to have been an eyewitness? Do I know him?"

"Uh, it's not likely. Anyway, Cotton told me to keep the fellow's name a secret until the right time."

"C'mon, Jack, you can tell me. You know I can keep a secret."

Jack snorted and gave her a look that clearly suggested she'd lost her mind. And that's exactly how she took it. Lips pursed, mouth curled into a forming volcano, Melody exploded. "What the hell do you mean by that look?"

Jack shrugged as he sat up and began pulling on his boots. She started screaming as she tried grabbing him by the arm to pull him back down, but he jerked away, her long fingernails ripping the sleeve and leaving three visible scratches. But he was clearly sticking to his guns and in no mood for one of her tantrums as he began buckling on his gun belt. That's when he heard the distinctive sound of a hammer being cocked. He spun around to see Melody holding her little .41 derringer. The look in her eyes was unmistakable. Recognizing that she was dead serious, Jack made a dive for the door, almost making it before the gun went off. The bullet grazed his shoulder, plowing a thin furrow across it. He stopped, glaring at Melody with unmistakable murder in his eyes. When she saw what she'd done and the blood leaking from the tear in his shirt, her eyes grew as big as saucers.

"Oh, my god, Jack! I'm so, so sorry. I-I don't know what got into me. I—"

Those were the only words she managed to get out before he dove on her, ripping off what few clothes she had on and struggling out of his gun belt, boots, and pants. In the ensuing half hour, they made love like they were trying to kill each other, to their mutual, violent satisfaction. At the battle's climax, both lay gasping for air, perspiration pouring from their overheated bodies. Jack was the first to get a word out.

"Son of a bitch, Melody, you sure do piss me off good."

"Yeah. It used to be like that all the time. I wish—"

"Uh-huh, me too. But for now, I need to go see Doc Winters. I seem to have sprung a leak. I'm gettin' blood all over everywhere."

Still panting, he struggled into his jeans, pulled on his boots with some difficulty, and decided to forgo putting on his shirt, tossing it over his shoulder instead. He stumbled out the door and down the stairs. Melody cooed after him, "I love you, Jack. Don't forget that."

Arlo followed Jack with his eyes all the way to, and out, the batwings, with mouth agape.

* * *

When Jack tapped on Doc Winters's door, the doctor's surprise at seeing him was unmistakable.

"Jack! What the hell happened?"

"Melody and I had a few coarse words. Things got a little heated."

"Sit down. Your sleeping arrangement seems to bring a lot of tension to your life, Jack. Maybe you ought to consider finding a more amiable lady, actually marry her, and settle down. You might live longer," the doctor said, as he threaded a needle, the sight of which made Jack wince, so he lifted a bottle of brandy to his lips to ease the pain.

The first indication that Jack's attempt to spread the Whiskey Crossing conflagration rumor was having its desired effect gave Cotton Burke reason to break into a cynical smile. Word of it had apparently reached Carp Varner in a most unusual manner. He spotted several of his newly hung posters marked across the face with an "X" in red paint and the word "Murderer" beneath it.

Furious, Varner ripped down all those that he could find defaced and stomped back to his shop to get replacements. *If I find who did this, I'll blow the bastard away*, he muttered over and over. At first he thought perhaps the mayor had done it to get back at him for entering the race, but that didn't seem to be a reasonable explanation. How could the mayor have any knowledge of his past? But there was something going on, and he didn't like it one bit. His thoughts kept drifting back to that day when he'd destroyed a town, small and insignificant as it was, and his vision of looking back to see nothing standing . . . except one lone imaginary, smoky figure staring at the ruins. That figure, faceless and unidentifiable, haunted him like none other of his infamous, murderous deeds. He was unable to sleep and driven wild by an inability to keep much in his stomach that was quickly becoming a serious problem. A problem that needed solving and now!

"Where is your young friend, Henry? Is he still safely beyond the reach of Varner?" Cotton asked.

"He sleep in barn loft."

"Still at the livery, huh?"

Henry nodded.

"Go get him and bring him here. Keeping him safe will become more and more difficult if Varner's defaced posters have the effect I anticipate. Bring him in the back way."

Henry left and hurried down the alley behind the jail. When he got to the livery, he slipped inside and climbed the ladder to the loft. He could hear the liveryman out back in the corral, so he didn't think anyone knew of his arrival. His surprise at not finding Johnny curled up on a blanket behind some hay bales showed. He hurried back down the ladder and tried to pick up on the newest footprints he could find. Johnny had obviously left in a hurry, and out the front way, which was unusual. That was a careless move and gave Henry pause to consider the possible consequences of the lad allowing himself to be seen by people on the street, one of whom could easily be Carp Varner. And why the hurry?

Henry knew of the posters being scrawled across in red paint, and there could be little doubt that a man with no moral character would consider such an act sufficient provocation to use force. One more killing wouldn't make any difference to Varner. Of course, Varner couldn't possibly know who had done the deed, but Henry knew. He'd known since coming into the sheriff's office and spotting red stains on Cotton's fingers and a small can with a brush sticking out of it sitting on the top of the file cabinet. It was a devilish plan, but one that would surely bring whatever crimes the gunsmith had committed out in the open. And put an end to his aspirations to become the next mayor. That was clearly the sheriff's intention. A wry smile of approval crossed the old Indian's lips as he trotted down the street, ducking into the first alley he came to that would lead him to the rear of Varner's shop. That's where he figured to find Johnny, carrying his revolver this time. Henry had a bad feeling that the young man was coming quickly to the end of his patience with Varner being allowed to run free and even enter the race for mayor.

When Henry rounded the corner, he broke into a dead run. There, behind Varner's shop, Johnny stood on a large wooden crate, gun in hand, peering through the window.

Chapter 54

Henry dove for the skinny figure who'd already cocked his weapon and was about to fire through the window. Fortunately, the gun didn't go off as the two of them tumbled to the ground in a flurry of dust and a collective grunt. Henry scrambled to subdue the surprised boy, making certain to take control of the revolver before it went off unintentionally. He let the hammer down easily, jammed the weapon into his waistband, and grabbed the boy's shirt. As Johnny tried in vain to break free and protest, Henry clamped a bronzed hand over the surprised youth's mouth. His firm grip on Johnny's arm and tight hold on his mouth gave Henry the leverage to half-drag, half-carry the youth out of sight of the back window. That was fortunate because they had no sooner disappeared around the corner of the next building than Carp Varner, alerted by muffled noises outside, opened the rear door and stepped out, gun in hand. He scratched his stubbly face and went back inside after finding nothing amiss.

When Henry released his grip on Johnny, the boy's disappointment at losing his chance to achieve the revenge he so heartily sought was evident. He was sputtering as Henry, still keeping a firm grip on Johnny's arm, pointed him in the direction of the jail.

"Wh-where're we goin'?" Johnny groused.

"Think sheriff wants you alive. Don't know why."

"What d'ya mean, 'wants me alive'?"

"No want Varner kill you."

"Varner doesn't even know I'm still alive."

"Soon will."

"What are you talkin' about?"

"Sheriff let people know someone see old town burn up. Only one still alive. You."

"He told folks?"

"Not give name."

Johnny's shoulders sank. "So where are we goin'?"

"Take you to only safe place. Jail."

"But I didn't do anything. He can't arrest—"

"Sheriff do what best for you."

Johnny stumbled into the sheriff's office after a healthy shove from Henry Coyote. When he saw the sheriff, his ire rose. He gritted his teeth before spitting out his speech.

"What the hell, Sheriff, you can't go lockin' up folks for no reason. Don't you know that?"

"Where'd you find him, Henry?"

"Back of gun store. Him aim to shoot man."

"That right, Johnny? Were you aimin' to shoot ol' Varner?"

"Uh, well, y-yeah, I suppose. So what? He's a murderer."

"Where's your proof?"

"I'm the proof. I was an eyewitness. That's all you need."

"Only if he comes to trial. Until then, you're goin' to be the guest of the town of Apache Springs until I unravel this whole mess."

"So you're arrestin' me?"

"That I am, lad. Attempted murder is a crime. You just admitted to it."

Johnny's head drooped as he sat down on the straight-back chair across from the sheriff.

"How long do I have to be in here?"

"It won't be long. Give you a little time to get some rest, then before you know it, the whole thing will be over."

"How do you know that?"

"Because I said so."

Just then the rattle of the afternoon Butterfield Stage echoed down the street. The sheriff got up to watch as it passed. He turned to Henry.

"Jack is meeting that stage. I'm expecting a man from Silver City to be getting off. Make certain Jack brings him straight here. Maybe be best to take the back way. I'd rather Varner not see him arriving."

Henry grunted and hurried out the door, straight for the stage depot. As the stage came to a stop, he saw Jack step up to the coach and hold the door for another passenger.

Jack led a very confused Turner Burnside down the back way to the jail. When they walked in, it was immediately apparent to Cotton that Burnside was none too happy to be returning to Apache Springs.

"Hope the marshal in Silver City didn't give you too much of a start, Mr. Burnside. But it was necessary."

"Wh-why have you brought me back? I, uh, don't think it's a good idea. I have an enemy here. Nothing good can come of it."

"I assume you're referring to Carp Varner?"

"Yes, and he'd as soon shove that pig-sticker in me than lay eyes on me ever again. He made that perfectly clear."

"I figured that's why I got this letter sayin' you were givin' up your interest in the gunsmith shop. He forced you to sign that, didn't he?"

"With a forty-five to my head. I'm no coward, mind you,

but when a man like Varner makes a threat, you take it seriously." Burnside shifted nervously from one foot to the other.

"I understand. But you can put your mind at ease, because Varner isn't goin' to harm you. But in order for me to bring him down and make him accountable for his many misdeeds, I'm goin' to need your help."

"I don't understand. What can I do?"

"When the time comes, I'm going to let him know you've changed your mind and returned to town. That should shake him up plenty. Until that time, you'll be stayin' in the cell next to that young man over there."

"A jail cell? Am I, uh, under arrest?"

"Nope. We'll jus' refer to it as 'protective custody.' I heard some Pinkerton fellow call it that once."

"What do you figure to gain by all this?"

"I aim to grind a pesky cockroach under the heel of my boot, get your business back for you, and satisfy a boy's need for revenge for the murder of his friends."

"Sounds like a tall order."

"That's how I figure it, too."

Cotton looked over to see Jack rubbing his shoulder. "Jack, get some rest. When this all goes down, I'm goin' to need you at your best. Oh, and don't turn your back on Melody again."

Chapter 55

Carp Varner was seething at the insult he perceived from the defacing of his posters. He sat morosely figuring how he would go about making someone pay for the affront ever since he'd discovered the first of the red splotches slathered across his political message. Then, after replacing all he could find, he'd discovered that many more had been marked up. That was the last straw. Whoever had done it, and he suspected the mayor or one of his cronies had spent the night sneaking around town targeting him with slanderous claims, someone would pay. It was time to teach Apache Springs a lesson, and he knew just how to go about that.

He went across the street to the general store to pick up the tools he needed to accomplish his plot. He bought seven coal oil lamps and enough highly inflammable oil to fill each to the brim. He took them all back to his shop and lined them up on the counter. He unscrewed the lids to the glass bases and used a small funnel to fill each one, making sure the wicks were all saturated so he'd have sufficient flame to ignite the oil when the lamps were tossed in the air, only to come crashing down, shattering the glass and spreading flames over everything around.

He loaded his revolvers and holstered them. He opened a box of shotgun shells, shoved two into the barrels of the ten-gauge gut shredder, then stuck several more in his jacket pocket. He looked over his arsenal of death, and while his mind raced in anticipation of what he was about to do, he walked to the window to gaze for a moment on what to that point had ben a thriving, peaceful community. He was ready—ready for the results of the voting and subsequent ballot count; ready for the citizens of Apache Springs to get a taste of their own ignorance should they decide to vote against him; and fully ready to exact his awful revenge on all who would reject him. Taking comfort in his substantial arsenal, he feared no one and nothing, including the rumored quickness of Sheriff Cotton Burke. Extreme confidence, not one iota of doubt as to the outcome of his reprisal, ruled Carp Varner's thoughts. He planned to spend the night in his shop, staring out the front window. *I'm ready. Are you, Apache Springs?*

The widely anticipated day of the election finally arrived. At six o'clock in the morning, the single wooden ballot box was set up at a table near the entrance to Melody's Golden Palace of Pleasure. Voters could check off the box next to their favorite candidate, fold the paper, and stick it through a slot in the top of the box. Even if every eligible person within the town limits and surrounding countryside were to show up intending to cast a vote, the whole process should be over by noon. Although territorial law prevented an early closing of the polls.

The saloon had been forced to cease the sale of alcoholic beverages until the polls closed at five o'clock in the afternoon. Melody didn't like that one damned bit, but went along when Jack told her he'd personally witnessed a num-

ber of drunken cowboys tear a saloon apart when their candidate failed to win his respective race. Melody accepted
that Jack and the sheriff were only looking out for her
safety. Although she was struggling with the part about
Cotton giving a damn whether she lived or died.

The voting went as expected, slow and steady. And, as
anticipated, there were no more votes cast after noon. Cowboys rode in around eleven-thirty, scratched out their prefer-
ences, and dropped the papers in the box. Then they went
back outside to loaf on the front porch or occupy every one of
the benches located along the town's boardwalk. They talked,
laughed, and on occasion nearly got into a fight over something or another. None of those near confrontations erupted
into anything more significant than a puffy lip or a bruised
knuckle. Just two minutes before five o'clock, the sheriff's
deputy, Memphis Jack Stump, left the jail and wandered over
to the saloon to be prepared to secure the ballot box and start
the count. Since he wasn't on the ballot, he was the only town
official legally able to do the counting. The mayor and the
sheriff, both being up for reelection, had to remain no closer
than fifty feet from the ballot box after voting. Cotton
remained on the bench out front of his office, chatting with
Emily, who'd driven her buckboard to town to cast her vote.

"I think it went very smoothly, don't you, Cotton?"
Emily asked.

"I reckon. It isn't over yet, though."

"Are you expecting trouble?"

"I am, if what Johnny told me about the reason Carp
Varner burned a town and killed every last citizen in it carries with it the ring of truth."

"What did he say?"

"He said the reason Carp went over the cliff was because
he lost his election for mayor. I'm expecting a repeat of that
when the votes are counted. And so I'd like to suggest you
go inside as soon as five o'clock rolls around and the bal-
lots are counted." He pulled his pocket watch from his vest,
opened it, and sighed. "Which I figure to be about now."

"What'll you be doing?"

"Aimin' to throw a little kindlin' on the fire."

"What do you mean?"

"Carp Varner is—if I'm to believe what I've heard—one mean son of a bitch who'll stop at nothin' in his quest for revenge on anyone who has the audacity to reject him. He takes that kind of thing very personally. I need to be certain he understands we aren't just a bunch of hayseeds who'll stand by and be run over by a man with vengeance on his mind."

"Does that by any chance mean allowing Johnny Monk to be in danger?"

"It's important that Varner face the man who's making accusations against him."

"But he's just a boy. He could be killed. Cotton, I can't just stand by and—"

"Stop frettin', Emily, both Jack and I, as well as Henry Coyote, will be coverin' the situation nine ways from Sunday."

"By the way, where is Johnny?"

"Oh, he's locked up tighter'n a Saturday night drunk in one of the cells inside."

"You mean he's been in jail all along and you didn't send word to me?"

"Uh, yeah, I reckon you could look at it that way."

"I've been worried sick about him. I couldn't sleep at night knowing he might try something stupid and get himself shot."

"Things have been happenin' pretty fast here, and I didn't have time to ride out and tell you. Also, I couldn't send word by Henry because I needed him here. He had Johnny in his sights ever since he found where he was hidin' out here. You needn't have been frettin' so."

Emily gave Cotton a glare that could have melted butter with its intensity.

"In case you haven't noticed, Sheriff Burke, I'm a woman. That's what we do!"

Cotton didn't have an answer for that.

Chapter 56

———◆•◆———

At five-thirty, Jack emerged from the back room of the saloon with a piece of paper in one hand and a small hammer and a nail in the other. He held the paper to the siding outside the saloon and tacked it up with the nail. He stood back to allow those who might be interested take a look.

"The *official* election results are available, folks. Take your time, don't crowd around," he said, expecting all those within earshot to come rushing up. "Oh, and the saloon is now open."

Every cowboy on the porch, and all up and down the street, hurried toward the saloon, completely ignoring the sheet with the election results as they pushed by Jack in their haste to get to the bar. He was nearly trampled by their stampede to imbibe something stronger than coffee.

"Not sure why we even bother," Jack muttered, as he went inside to grab a bottle and take it over to the jail. He figured Cotton would be anxious to celebrate his win. Of course, without anyone opposing him, he couldn't lose. On his way through the batwings, Jack turned to see Mayor Plume walking briskly down the street. Not far behind him was Carp Varner taking long, purposeful strides. Varner looked like a man on a mission.

As he watched the scene before him unfold, Cotton turned to Emily and said, "Go inside, Emily. Go inside and tell the two people there to come out. Tell Johnny to come here and stand by my side."

"Isn't that Mr. Varner racing to catch up with Mayor Plume?"

"It is. Please do as I ask. We don't have much time if I'm going to pull this off without losin' our town."

Emily disappeared into the jail office, and emerged in two minutes with Johnny and Turner Burnside trailing behind her. Johnny's eyes grew wide as he caught sight of Carp Varner. His hand went instinctively to his side for his revolver; then he suddenly remembered that the Indian had taken it away from him. Instinctively understanding the boy's intentions, Cotton grabbed him by the sleeve of his shirt and yanked him to his side before he could go back to retrieve any sort of weapon.

"You won't be needin' a gun, boy. Just keep your mouth shut and follow my lead. You can speak up when I say you can. Understand?"

Johnny nodded without ever taking his eyes off Varner. The heat of the boy's anger was palpable.

When the mayor walked up to the posted results, he reached into his coat pocket to retrieve his spectacles. Rather than putting them on, he simply held them up in order to read the only number he cared about: his own. There it was— clearly he'd achieved another victory. The townsfolk felt sufficiently comfortable with the job he'd done to bring him back for a second term. Before returning his cheaters to his pocket, he noticed that Sheriff Burke, too, had been reelected, not that there was any way he could have lost. Plume felt pretty chipper about his significant number of votes over Carp Varner. In fact, Varner appeared to have received but four votes in total. Plume turned with a smug smile, only to find himself facing a red-faced Varner, his opponent. Varner took one quick glance at the totals and began berating the mayor, backing him against the wall.

"You dirty rattler! You're the one who wrote those scandalous words on my posters. You caused the folks of Apache Springs to turn against me. Admit it, you low-down snake!" Varner had hauled back to punch the mayor when a loud voice interrupted him.

"Hold on, Varner. The mayor didn't write on those posters, I did!"

"You? Why? Where'd you come up with all them lies?"

Cotton reached back and took Johnny by the arm and pulled him to his side.

"This boy claims he knows you from a Texas town called Whiskey Crossing. Seems that when you lost an election there similar to our own, you decided to make the town pay for your lack of popularity. He says you killed every living thing thereabouts—horses, mules, dogs, and the entire citizenry. Then you did the most dastardly thing imaginable, you set the town afire, and rode off like a sniveling coward. The boy says he still hears the screams in his nightmares. Any of that sound like it has the ring of truth?"

Varner thrust his left hand out and grabbed the mayor by the back of his coat, while at the same moment pulling his revolver. He shoved Plume in front of him, hooking his arm around the mayor's throat, then using him as a shield as he backed through the batwings, firing over the mayor's shoulder as he went. Varner fired three times. His bullets thudded into the front of the jail, knocking chinks out of the siding and shattering two panes of glass.

Cotton yanked Johnny back behind him, then, spinning

around, pushed Burnside and Emily ahead of him, back into the safety of the jail.

"You three stay here until you hear me tell you it's okay to come out. And Johnny, if you make one move to go after Varner, I swear I'll skin you alive myself."

He stopped momentarily, thinking back on what he'd just said. Deciding he couldn't really trust the boy to obey him, he shoved Johnny into the first cell, locked the steel door, and tossed the keys to Emily.

"Keep him in there and you'll keep him alive."

He grabbed a shotgun from the rack, made a quick check of his Colt, and rushed out the door. He knew Varner wouldn't still be in the saloon, or at least he hoped not. Odds were the man would head to his own arsenal at the gun shop, where he had plenty of ammunition to hold off whatever force the sheriff brought against him. If he was still holding the mayor hostage, things could get messy real fast.

Cotton made the best time he could, trying to make himself as small a target as possible by keeping to the shadows beneath every portico and overhang, ducking behind each water barrel, bench, and crate, even cutting through the general store to come out in the alley at the back.

Finally, he was able to situate himself in position to keep an eye on Varner's establishment. That's when he got a shock. Varner had stacked up wooden crates three high across the boardwalk in front of the shop, making it a virtual fortress. Cotton could see movement inside through the front window. Varner had apparently gone down another alley and into the rear door of his shop. At this point, Cotton had no way of tempting Varner to step outside and face him. And he sure as hell wasn't planning to bust in and come face-to-face with a fusillade from Varner's formidable cache of firearms.

He suddenly felt a shiver go up his back. He yanked his Colt and spun around to see Henry and Jack no more than three feet behind him.

"Damn! Are you two tryin' to take a couple years off my life?"

"Found the mayor out back of the saloon. Had bump on his head, but he appears to be all right. We're here to help. What do you want us to do?" Jack asked. Henry just grunted.

"I got a real bad feelin' about what Varner might conjure up in retribution for his election loss. Remember that Johnny said the thing that fueled his fury at the folks of Whiskey Crossing was his failing to get any votes for mayor. He may be thinkin' to repeat history. We better be ready for anything."

"If he starts a fire in this town full of dry timber, Apache Springs could be nothin' but embers in minutes," Jack said. "A man would have to be crazy to do somethin' like that."

"I think that's *exactly* what he is. So you and Henry start alerting every shop owner and citizen to help gathering all the buckets of sand or water you can find. We'd better be prepared for a bucket brigade from the well, too. Warn everyone who'll listen to be ready."

When Henry and Jack took off running in opposite directions, Cotton decided he'd sit tight for a while to keep an eye out for Varner's next move. He was dead certain there would be *something* happening, and soon. He also figured it to be dramatic and deadly. He had no interest in being in on the deadly part of it.

He was mulling over how he might get Varner to come out in the open and show his hand. He needed to keep the cold-blooded killer occupied while the town prepared for the eventuality of a fire spreading from business to business. He was shaken from his inner turmoil when Carp Varner burst out of the door to his shop with four glass-bowled lanterns in his hands. The glass chimneys had all been removed and each lamp was lit. Cotton ducked down to keep from being a target as Varner placed the lamps in a row along the boardwalk then spun around and returned inside, only to reappear within seconds fully armed with the same big-bore shotgun with which he'd brought down the two Callahan brothers.

He was now standing in front of the open door, shotgun aimed across the street and six-shooters shoved in holsters, gun belts, and sticking out of pockets. He was a walking army.

"Citizens of Apache Springs! You are about to learn a lesson in good manners! You should never have neglected to cast your votes for me! So now you'll feel the sting of my wrath for your own ignorance!"

Carp Varner pulled the trigger on one barrel of the shotgun, blowing the entire window out of the dress shop directly across the street.

Chapter 57

———◆———

Cotton had made it as far as the general store, shotgun in hand and pointed at Varner. His intention was to at least get the gunsmith to talk to him. That's not the way it turned out, however.

"Varner! Put that blunderbuss down and let's—"

Varner didn't even flinch as he turned the shotgun in Cotton's direction. Cotton flung himself to the ground, dropping his own scattergun, just as Varner's big gun went off, showering the earth around the sheriff with geysers of dirt. He felt the bite of some of the steel pellets as they plowed into his shoulder and leg. Before Cotton could pull his Colt, Varner had picked up one of the lanterns and launched it in the air with a high arc. The blazing missile came down on the boardwalk in front of the store in the next building. The glass lamp shattered instantly, spreading coal oil and exploding in flames. The wooden walkway, parched from the dry summer, was quickly engulfed by the fast-spreading flames. Several shopkeepers, watching from the safety of indoors, looked on in horror as the posts holding up the portico began to burn. No one dared rush outside to help, for fear of being the next victim of that awful shotgun.

As Cotton rolled over to free his Colt from its holster, a shot from Varner's Smith & Wesson dug a furrow across his thigh. He scrambled to avoid the next shot, which would undoubtedly find its mark with a fatal result. Just then, a shot from inside the door of the post office shattered the door glass behind Varner. Carp ducked back inside. Jack's smoking Remington was still in the deputy's hand when Cotton heard him call out.

"You okay, Cotton?"

"A little worse for the wear, but alive. Can you keep him inside while Henry gets some folks to douse the fire with sand?"

"I'm hopin' to do just that," Jack said, as he threw a couple more shots at where Varner was holed up.

Half-crawling, half-hopping, Cotton reached the safety of a water trough outside the town hall. He took off his neck scarf and tied it around his thigh to stop the bleeding, then stuck his head up just enough to see if he could spot Varner. He didn't have to wait long. The elusive gunman was no longer inside. He'd reappeared behind his fortress and was lighting several more lamps, just out of Jack's sight. But not Cotton's.

Cocking his Colt, Cotton crawled to the end of the trough. He stuck the barrel around the corner and fired. Varner quickly ducked back. The shot had given Varner an idea of where the sheriff was, but it had also showed Jack where Varner was. It was shaping up to be two against one, and Varner didn't like those odds. He grabbed up two more lamps and tossed them high in the air as he ran. One hit a freight wagon that had pulled up in front of the general store and parked, filled with raw lumber and bales of straw. The lamp shattered into a thousand pieces, showering the wagon and its contents with licking flames. The four-mule team that had been hitched to the wagon was instantly thrown into a wild-eyed panic. Straining at their traces and without their driver, they charged ahead down the street, out of control, weaving from one side to the other, tossing hunks of burning, newly split logs from the back, rolling every which way, and threatening to spread the fire even farther.

One of the lamps landed on a tin-roofed overhang, smashing and allowing the blazing oil to drip onto the boardwalk below. With each drop of flaming liquid, the fire walked along the dry wood like a snake seeking its prey. More of the lamps were launched. One lamp busted through the window of the dress shop, bursting into flames. The dressmaker ran from the shop trailing a burning skirt. Out of nowhere, a man came running with a bucket of water and doused her before she was badly hurt, although her hands and legs would take a while to heal from the blisters. The man helped her to a group of other women standing under the protection of a nearby portico. All around Varner's establishment, townsfolk were racing to stop the flames from eating the town like a ravenous mountain lion, as screams of terror and panic filled the air, burning embers were flung about by the rising columns of blistering heat, and white ash fluttered down like snowflakes. The town had never seen an inferno like this. It was every town's worst nightmare.

Varner raced for cover, staying low to keep from getting hit by gunfire aimed in his direction. He made his way to the back of his shop. He dove for the door and barely made it as hunks of wood were torn from the frame by Jack's .44. Jack had wisely thought to run down the alley once he saw that Varner was headed inside, returning to the safety of his shop to resupply his firepower. He'd missed his quarry, but that didn't keep him from throwing more lead through the open door and blasting the small window nearly out of its frame. He could hear cursing coming from inside.

Jack's actions had given Cotton just the break he needed to get himself situated in a better spot to confront the murderous man from Texas when he once again came through the front door. He didn't have to wait long. The flimsy door was nearly busted from its hinges when Varner crashed through, shotgun in hand, swiveling left and right to identify his target as quickly as possible. He stopped suddenly when he saw Cotton Burke standing not twenty feet away, his Colt .45 drawn and aimed in his direction.

Varner started to jerk the shotgun around to handle this threat to his freedom, in fact his very life. But whatever was going through Varner's head at that moment, it would make no difference to him or to anyone. No longer willing to give the madman an opportunity to take one more shot at him or even allow him to surrender after the devastation he'd wrought on Apache Springs, Cotton pulled the trigger. Twice in quick succession. The first bullet caught the killer in the throat, the second in the forehead, nearly taking off the back of his head. Varner stiffened, dropped his shotgun, and toppled backward like a just-felled ponderosa pine. His dead body crashed through the front window, bent backward over the frame, and remained there as life drained quickly from him.

Jack came running from around from the back as shop owners hurriedly brought out bucket after bucket of sand or water to douse the several fires caused by pieces of lumber and straw dropping from the burning wagon. At the end of the street, the liveryman had heard the commotion and, upon seeing the mule team charging toward him, raced out and grabbed their dangling reins and brought them to a halt. He quickly unhitched them from the wagon and led them inside. The fire in the wagon was brought under control by other quick-thinking citizens, and it now sat in the middle of the street, smoldering harmlessly.

As townsfolk stared in disbelief at the loss to businesses, a low murmur of voices spread angrily through the citizenry. Heads shook and tongues clucked at the potential cost of rebuilding and repairs. But while the losses were substantial, they were not insurmountable. And there had been no loss of life, save that of the villain, Carp Varner.

The town would come back stronger than ever, and everybody knew it.

Emily ran to Cotton, whose shirt and pants were splotched with blood. He swept her into his arms to let her know he would be okay, even though the pain in his leg suggested that might not be the case. As Jack leaned over the body of Carp Varner, Cotton said, "Jack, get the undertaker and then let Johnny and Turner out of their cells. I'm goin' to let Emily help me to the doc's."

Jack nodded with a look that suggested he was surprised the sheriff had been hit, then he trotted off. Henry, carrying an empty sand bucket with which he had helped put out the fire in front of the general store, swept up Cotton's shotgun from the street as well as the one Carp Varner had been wielding to do a lot of damage. As they passed the jail, Turner Burnside stood clucking his tongue at the chaos Varner had caused. Johnny had run past them to see for himself that the villain who'd murdered his friends was really dead. Cotton looked back to see the boy gazing solemnly at the corpse of the man who had brought so much misery to his life. The sheriff thought he detected a nod of relief.

Chapter 58

After Doc Winters had patched up the sheriff's painful but in the end insignificant wounds, Cotton was resting comfortably at his house with a cup of hot coffee and the smells of something cooking on the stove. Emily wouldn't hear of him fending for himself after such a traumatic day, and he had no intention of talking her out of it. She told Henry to take Johnny back to the ranch and put him to work. It was time things settled down, and she was just the one to see to it that they did.

"Before you two leave, I want to thank you, Henry, for all your help," Cotton said. "And Johnny, I know you're disappointed that Varner didn't die by your hand, but if it hadn't been for you and Rachael, he still would have showed up here with his evil intent and we'd have been caught off guard. By that reasoning, I'd say you *did* pay him back for what he'd done to you and your friends. I'm mighty glad you showed up when you did."

"Uh, thank you, sir," Johnny said, with a shy grin. He

followed Henry out the door, looking eager to see Rachael and share with her what had happened.

Jack came in as Emily came out of the kitchen with a bowl of beans and some fresh bread. He grinned and thanked her when she asked him to stay. Sipping the coffee she'd poured him, he sat and stared at Cotton.

"Those hurt?" he asked.

"What, these little holes? Naw. Sorta like bein' bee stung. Nothin' like gettin' shot in the back by a girlfriend."

Jack grimaced at the barb.

"Johnny goin' back to the Wagner place?"

"Yep," Cotton said. "Maybe he'll stick around for a while. With a little maturity, he might even make a good deputy someday. And I figure to be needin' one if you keep on hangin' around with a gun-totin' whore with no compunction about plugging you every time she gets a bee in her bonnet."

Jack blushed. He'd been had, twice. Then he suddenly seemed to remember what had really brought him by to see the sheriff. He got up and walked to the door. He picked up Varner's shotgun and a thick paper sack.

"Got a surprise. I figure this'll clear up a whole passel of questions."

"Yeah, like what?" Cotton said, with a slight groan.

"This shotgun Varner was so eager to use to blow the town apart belonged to Pick Wheeler. Recognized it the moment I saw it. Musta took it when he shot the old prospector in the back. Ten-gauge."

Cotton smiled a knowing smile. "Then I'm goin' out on a limb and guessin' that paper sack you're holdin' has Melody's money in it. Varner musta been the man sittin' on the bench outside the bank the day she started braggin' about buyin' a silver mine."

"Say, you're good. You ever thought of joinin' the Pinkertons?" Jack said, raising one eyebrow.

"What, and leave you to clean up Melody's messes all by yourself? Not on your life."

"Okay if I break the good news to Melody?"

"I reckon. Maybe that'll make your life a bit more comfortable, at least until she comes up with another dumb scheme."

After Jack left, Cotton turned to Emily.

"What do you figure will happen to Johnny and Rachael?" he asked her.

"Well, I got plenty of room, and they could both be useful at the ranch. I figure to ask them to stay, at least until they decide where their futures will take them," she said, with a slight shrug.

Cotton nodded. He leaned back in his chair with a weary and painful sigh. He couldn't help wondering what would have happened to Apache Springs if he'd not killed Carp Varner. Chances were the town would now have been nothing more than a pile of charred ruins and destroyed lives. The fear that had coursed through him at the recognition of Varner's total despotism and willingness to unleash a potential firestorm on a community—he hoped never to experience that again. Carp Varner had been dispatched in the blink of an eye to forever dwell in the Devil's own inferno.

Cotton reached over and squeezed Emily's hand.

Don't miss the best Westerns from Berkley

LYLE BRANDT
PETER BRANDVOLD
JACK BALLAS
J. LEE BUTTS
JORY SHERMAN
DUSTY RICHARDS

penguin.com

M10G0610